THE WARS OF MONSTERS

HER CURSED PROTECTORS

Shadow Shifter (prequel)
The Blood of Monsters
The Cries of Monsters
The Curse of Monsters
The Wars of Monsters

THE WARS OF MONSTERS

HER CURSED PROTECTORS BOOK 4

MIA HARTSON

ISBN: 978-0-6457298-3-2

First printing edition 2024 in United States

Cover design by Trif Cover Design

Mia Hartson

PO BOX 1052, Golden Grove Village, SA 5125

www.miahartson.com

Dear reader, thank you for continuing to the end of Raine's story. Your support means the world to me, and I hope this book gives you all the feels, laughs, and closure you're hoping for.
Mia x

Trigger warnings: This story contains death, violence, torture, war, spicy scenes, and attempted suicide. Please take care of yourself while reading.

CHAPTER 1

Outliers swarmed over the sides of the watch tower like ants crawling up a dirt mound, and I spotted Garan and the gargoyles fighting as a unit, covered in blood and surrounded by monsters. Too many gargoyles had been lost, their bodies torn apart by massive beasts with six arms and fanged, misshapen mouths. Warrick hadn't sent his outliers to persuade Garan and the gargoyles to join his cause. No, it was an execution, and I could have only guessed it was because the gargoyles didn't swear allegiance to the vampire with a god complex.

I gritted my teeth as I flew under a night sky devoid of stars, the dark clouds blocking out the moonlight. My wings tingled as they battered against the icy wind, and I swooped down toward the fray. As I neared the tower, I thought of Raine and my brothers back at the hideout.

Raine's pleading expression filled my mind, her beautiful amber eyes alight with fire. "I'm coming with you," she'd declared when I'd spoken of my intentions to respond to Garan's call. At her words, crippling fear had gone through me, and I had clenched my fists to stop from reaching for her. I couldn't handle her being taken again. Even now that she'd changed and become one of us. A monster. A beast. A shifter. *And* a fae. So, I'd left her and my brothers even though flying away from them left a coldness inside me that I couldn't banish.

"You'd better come back to us," Raine had threatened as I'd turned my back, and despite her anger, there was a wobble in her voice that was absolute torture. There were few monsters I would fight for, and even fewer that I would die for. The beautiful little female didn't know how much she'd changed me. But I owed Garan. Our childhood past was still vivid and damning in my memory, and Kade, Darian, and Asher couldn't fly. By the time they would have reached the battle, it would have been too late.

I forced the thought of them from my mind. I had all intention of returning to Raine and my brothers, and to do that, I needed clarity. Unsheathing my swords, I stretched my wings wide as I descended to the rooftop of the guard tower, cutting through an outlier before it could sink its claws into Garan's broad back. My blade sliced through the outlier's head, cutting past its glowing red eyes and down through its torso, severing the creature into two.

Garan spun toward me as the beast's body fell to the ground, his face hard and emotionless. He gave me a small nod of acknowledgment before driving his sword into the neck of another creature. Garan's stone wings flared as he blocked the claws of two more outliers, the expanse of his wings acting like shields, and then he attacked, bringing the beasts down. I fought at his back, carving through the outliers that lunged wildly at us and clearing a small space. The remaining gargoyles moved closer, filling the area I'd cleared, but more outliers streamed over the tower walls. *There are too fucking many of them.*

"We need to leave," I shouted at Garan before using my swords to sever the head of another beast. I was holding my own, but we were outnumbered, and the gargoyles were continuing to fall. "Warrick controls the towers now."

"The gargoyles have used these towers to watch the city for over a century," Garan replied with a grunt as he cleaved into another outlier. "We won't abandon them."

His arm bumped mine as he pulled the hilt of his sword toward him before driving it into a creature's chest. The outlier let out an unnatural shriek and clawed the air until Garan used his wings to silence the beast.

In my moment of distraction, an outlier raked its claws across my arm, tearing into my flesh. With a snarl, I dispatched the creature and tossed it from the roof. "And the gargoyles will die tonight if we don't take to the sky," I reasoned.

Garan made a low noise of frustration in his throat. "Then so be it," he rasped. As he said it, one of the gargoyles closest to him cried out as two outliers grabbed onto his wings and ripped them from his back. The gargoyle slumped to his knees, and another outlier tore his head from his body and let it drop with a thud.

Garan's face contorted with fury, an anguished bellow leaving his throat as he beheaded one of the offending outliers while I took care of the other. But for every creature we dispatched, more climbed over the stone walls, slipping and clambering over one another to get to us like ravenous wild dogs fighting for scraps. Their eyes glowed red like beacons of hatred as if we were their cruel owners rather than the vampire who had mutilated their forms.

"Garan!" I yelled as the inky blood of an outlier sprayed onto my face. "This is a slaughter. Your monsters are dying. If we retreat, we have a chance to fight and reclaim the towers another day. If we stay, the fight will be over."

Garan's hard gaze swept over his unit as they continued to be overwhelmed by the outliers. Another gargoyle yelled as five creatures took him down, and Garan's expression grew distant like he was struggling to come to terms with his reality.

I was certain the gargoyle general would die that night, but he blinked, and his eyes cleared as his arms shot out, his swords spearing two outliers on either side of him. "This tower is no longer ours," he growled to his team. "Gargoyles, to the sky," he commanded.

His unit snapped to attention at his order, their expressions worn and haggard as they stretched out their wings and launched upward. I yanked my swords from the body of an outlier and did the same as Garan lifted into the air beside me. Beneath us, the outliers moved into the area we'd been holding and covered the roof in a sea of crawling black. The beasts roared and leaped, trying to grab us with their clawed hands and drag us to whatever hell was waiting for us in the afterlife. An outlier grabbed the leg of a gargoyle not far from me and began clawing its way up the male, so I threw one of my swords, my blade spearing into the creature's neck. The distraction was enough that the gargoyle shook the creature off, and the outlier screamed in anger as it released its prey and fell back to its brethren.

I turned my head toward the sky, but leathery skin slapped against my ankle, an iron grip squeezing hard as a creature grabbed me. Cursing, I peered down to see an outlier attached to me, its fanged face triumphant as it hung on. Lifting my other sword, I went to slice the creature's arm, but another outlier grabbed the leg of the creature, and their combined weight pulled me lower toward the tower. I flapped my wings furiously, straining against their hold as the outliers on the tower howled and snapped in a frenzy, watching me excitedly with red eyes.

"Fuck," I snarled, cleaving through the arm of the outlier that was holding me as I continued to drop, but the creature below leaped from where it dangled, taking hold of my leg instead. Two more jumped from the roof of the tower, clawing onto me.

Cursing, I beat my wings so hard I felt the burn all the way down my back, and I lashed out at the beasts, twisting to slice through limb after limb. Garan bellowed from above, three of his knives soaring through the air and connecting with the eyes and faces of the creatures, distracting them, and then I was shooting upward, the air rushing past me as my wings carried me away from the tower.

Howling, the outliers piled on top of one another in their race to gain height and recapture their prey, but we flew into the night, leaving death behind us.

CHAPTER 2

~ Raine ~

"He should have let us go with him," I snapped as I paced, a trail of smoke leaving my nose. Lyr had ushered us into an empty training room soon after Locke left to help the gargoyles, and Kade and Asher were busy making use of the space, their muscles bunching as they tested out the various weapons lining the walls. Darian stood inspecting a rack of long spears made of gleaming metal, his inquisitive blue eyes taking in the intricate markings on the arrow tips.

I knew my monsters were as annoyed as I was at having been left behind, but their relaxed expressions weren't helping to calm my agitated inner dragon. I bit the inside of my cheek and tried to focus on the faint metallic taste in my mouth rather than the possessive need I had to shift and fly after my vampire. *Goddess, he's still an asshole.* I knew I wasn't really being fair. Locke had a history with the gargoyle, Garan, or so I'd been told. No one would tell me exactly what had happened between them in the past, but I got the feeling it was something serious. Still, it didn't stop me from cursing the vampire under my breath, and my thoughts darkened as my imagination got the better of me. *If I lose him...* I cleared my throat as my eyes started to burn. *Nope, don't think about it, Raine.*

I hadn't even seen Darian move until his long fingers pressed gently into my shoulders and his body closed in behind me. "He'll come back, lovely," my siren said softly in my ear, and I eased against him. "Locke can take care of himself."

I knew Darian was right, but I'd also seen the damage Warrick's outliers could do. I couldn't stop myself from asking the question: *What if he can't?*

The rattling of chains drew my attention to where Asher returned a mace to its rightful position before grabbing a massive ax instead. He hefted the weapon as though it was weightless, though I doubt I could have even lifted the thing if I'd still been human. Well...I mean not a monster, that is. *Because I've never truly been human...* Or not completely human, anyway. I was still trying to wrap my head around the fact that I was part fae.

Asher peered over to us, his violet eyes tracking Darian's hands on me. "Don't worry, sweetheart, I'm sure Locke is hatin' himself for leavin' without us."

"Yeah, sure he is," I replied sarcastically. "He should have let us help. He didn't even know what he was flying into! All he saw was images of outliers attacking the tower." My shoulders tensed again despite Darian's best efforts. "What if...what if the gargoyles are dead before he even gets there?"

Kade let out a long breath and stalked closer to us. "They're right," he said in that growly voice of his. "You don't need to worry."

I threw my hands up in the air in frustration. I hated this. Hated standing around waiting and doing nothing. "You've seen what those creatures can do," I replied in exasperation.

"We have, and that's exactly why Locke didn't want you goin' anywhere near 'em," Asher pointed out, his expression hard and at odds with his usually easy-going nature. "Aside from Locke, you're the only other one who can fly. Locke wasn't lettin' you near the outliers, and neither were we."

"Not until you've learned how to properly use that incredible new creature of yours," Darian added, stopping me before I could voice my protest.

I folded my arms across my chest. "Yes, I can fly, and if I had to, I could have dropped you three off, so you could have helped Locke. Then I could have flown to safety until you needed me. He didn't have to go alone."

Asher's expression was sympathetic, but his lips twitched upward. "And you would have left us there to battle against the outliers without you?" His eyes sparkled with amusement, and when I didn't answer, the demon's grin grew wider.

I narrowed my eyes at him, annoyed that he knew I was lying through my teeth. I mean, of course, I wouldn't have just left my monsters to fight the outliers without me. Even if the old me found a way to agree to that, which was unlikely, my dragon side sure as hell wasn't going to let me. These males were my mates, my treasures, and I wasn't about to simply drop them into a fight without providing some backup. Turns out that becoming a dragon made me as possessive and obsessive as my monsters. *Huh. How 'bout that.*

"Locke and Garan have a complicated history," Kade added with a stony expression, interrupting the stare-off I was having with Asher. "He wouldn't have left unless he thought the situation was dire."

I still wanted to argue, but Darian had hold of my shoulders again, and he'd redoubled his efforts to dig his fingers in and loosen my muscles. The male had serious talent when it came to working his fingers, and even though I still wanted to curse Locke, it was an effort to keep from moaning.

Not that Darian could take all the credit for the way my body was reacting. Now that I had dragon shifter abilities my sense of smell was better than it was, and the scents of my males had my mouth watering to the point there had already been one instance when I'd actually drooled. Thankfully, no one had seemed to notice before I'd swiped the spit from my chin, but it was only a matter of time.

My males smelled ridiculously delicious, and I could have sworn their scents were getting more irresistible every day. It was almost like my monsters were subconsciously taunting my dragon and making their scents more powerful because I hadn't given in and marked them yet. I tried to focus on the sensation of my siren massaging me rather than thinking about how my vampire was likely getting his ass kicked by Warrick's outliers.

Kade and Asher watched intently as I tipped my head back, resting against Darian, and my eyes were almost closed when I was yanked forward and crushed against Kade's hard chest. "Hey!" I protested, sad to be away from Darian's magical fingers, but then Kade spun me around and began digging his thumbs into my shoulders instead. The wolf shifter's fingers pressed in so hard it was almost painful, but pleasure still worked down my spine.

"I warned you about making that face while I'm around, Mahare," he growled, and I shivered, a slow grin creeping across my face. "At least I might be able to concentrate if it's my hands that are on you."

Darian shook his head at the possessive wolf, but a smile curved his lips. No doubt, Kade was as worried as I was about Locke, but for him, I was the distraction keeping him sane. Asher looked like he was considering pulling me from Kade just as the wolf had done to Darian, but he didn't. Instead, he only gave us that lop-sided grin of his, content to let Kade have me for the moment.

"What we should be considering, is how Losak and the other monsters are going to react to the news that we're here," Darian said, bringing the conversation back to our current situation. "Lyr was right to suggest we didn't join the welcome party. We have no idea whether they believe the rumors that we're traitors who sided with the fae."

I thought of Losak and his shifters. If what Nic said was true, Warrick had attacked the House of Silat because Losak had refused to ally with him. That simple fact had me liking the shifter alpha just a little bit.

"Lyr said she would speak to Losak and get clarity on their situation before she'd retrieve us," Kade growled. "She'll warn us if we should expect trouble."

"Maybe what we should really be asking is whether the shifters are seriously injured," I said softly, reflecting again on the information we'd received. "Nic said there weren't many of them, and shifters don't heal as fast as demons."

"Monsters are the most dangerous when they're wounded," Kade warned, and as if to punctuate his point, a piercing wail came from the other side of the door. Startled, I went to take a step forward, but Kade held me in place, his large hands gripping my shoulders.

My mates all stared at me for a long moment, then Darian grabbed a sword from the wall and strolled toward the door. Asher followed on his heels, brandishing his ax, but before Darian could grab the doorknob, the door swung open and Lyr appeared in the doorway. Black blood was smeared up her forearms and across her flushed face, and I straightened, my chest squeezing at the sight of her.

"We need all of you. *Now,*" the tiger shifter barked, her blue eyes flashing.

It was all I needed to know. Slipping from Kade's grip, I started for the door. Kade moved close behind me, and Asher and Darian led the way. As eager as I was to leave the confines of the training room, I wasn't prepared for what lay beyond the door. Monsters crowded the great hall, some collapsed on chairs, others bleeding on the floor while they nursed grievous wounds, and a few were motionless and covered in cloth near the far wall. The groans and cries of agony from the shifters sounded in my ears, and it was only then that I realized how effective the thick walls of the training room had been at keeping out the noise.

Lyr didn't slow her stride as she led us to where Nic was holding down Losak, his thick arms straining with the effort. Losak, the alpha of the House of Silat, lay on a low cot, naked except for his undershorts. A deep bite wound on his neck had been smeared with blue paste, but black blood still seeped out, trickling onto the cot. The snake shifter snapped his head up, his long fangs aimed at Nic's shoulder, but the wraith twisted his body, avoiding the monster's mouth. Losak snarled, his eyes flickering from black to reptilian slits and then to black again. His body convulsed violently like he was stuck in an unnatural stage of transformation, not completely in either his human or snake forms.

"What's happening to him?" Kade growled, his assessing gaze sweeping over Losak and then the wounded shifters on either side of the alpha.

To our left, Soren strained to hold down the boar shifter, Cassar. Grunting with the effort, Soren's red wings flared wide as he flapped, using his wings to help keep his balance and place all his weight on the shifter. Dean, Lyr's other mate, was bent over, holding down Losak's second-in-command, Quinn. Thick vines came from Dean, curling around Quinn's arms and legs, but the shifter kept changing form, tearing and slipping through the restraints. More vines had been extended out to Losak and Cassar, but they lay shredded at the sides of the cots.

"They weren't like this when they arrived," Lyr explained, her expression strained. "Wounded, yes, but in the past hour it's as if they've been infected by something. I can only guess they were poisoned before coming here and it's only now taking effect."

"Poisoned?" I swallowed hard as I stared in horror at the shifters and the way individual parts of their bodies kept changing before returning to human form. Asher gripped his ax tighter, and my monsters moved protectively closer to me. Like they were ready to take down any of the shifters if they managed to break free and tried to attack me.

"It's only the ones who have been bitten," Lyr continued, looking around the room to where a handful of other shifters were also being restrained. She moved closer to Dean. "I can only theorize that they were targeted by outliers with venomous fangs. That somehow, it's making them sick, though they seem physically stronger. These three are proving to be the strongest." As she said it, Quinn let out an animalistic bark, and fangs speared from between his lips. He lifted his hand as it transformed into a clawed paw, and Lyr darted forward with the intention of helping Dean to hold the shifter down. Before her hands could clasp his arm, Quinn jerked violently, lashing out and throwing both Lyr and Dean backward. Dean's hand shot out, greenery sprouting around them, and Lyr landed on a thick bed of moss that appeared on the floor. Kade and Darian moved to restrain Quinn, and Dean was on his feet in an instant, taking the position again from Darian.

Cassar grunted and thrashed, and Asher gave me a look before going to help a struggling Soren.

"Stay back, lovely," Darian told me before going to help Nic with Losak instead.

I went to help Lyr up, but she was already on her feet, her face grim as she watched the shifters.

"What about the healing paste?" I asked her, indicating to the blue smeared on the shifters' wounds. "Why isn't it working?"

Lyr swiped an arm over her sweaty brow. "It is. But it's healing their wounds slower than usual. Whatever this poison is, it's putting up a fight. We thought about confining them to individual rooms until it wears off, but they seem just as intent on hurting themselves as they are determined to attack us."

"What did Losak tell you when he arrived?" Kade growled, his muscles bunching as he pushed Quinn back down, his face narrowly avoiding the fox shifter's fanged mouth.

Lyr's feline eyes glowed as she blew out a heavy breath. "That the House of Silat was attacked by outliers hours ago. The creatures burst in through the windows while most of them were asleep, taking them by surprise."

"Damn those outlier devils," Asher cursed, and Darian's lips thinned.

"What can I do?" I asked as I stared out at the rest of the shifters. Thankfully, Lyr was right, and it only seemed that a select few of them were poisoned like Losak, Quinn, and Cassar, but the other shifters moaned and growled, most of them so badly hurt they couldn't even lift themselves from where they'd collapsed. All of the shifters who were well enough, were busy restraining the infected.

"Raine's not going anywhere near the ones that have been poisoned," Kade growled before Lyr could speak. I went to protest, but Lyr was quick to say, "I'm hopeful it will leave their systems in time as their bodies heal. But for now, Raine I need you to tend to the wounded shifters who weren't bitten." She gestured with her head to a large jar of glowing blue liquid. "Try to make it last as I don't know when I'll be able to get more. And if any of them start to show strange symptoms, yell out."

A shifter to my left groaned, his shirt dark with blood, and I said nothing as I spurred into action. Snatching up the blue jar, I began making my way to each of the wounded, removing their battered clothing so I could patch them up. Some had already been tended to, but I brought the shifters water and tried to make them more comfortable. The stench of blood made my nose twitch, my dragon senses making me keenly aware of just how badly hurt all the shifters were and setting me on edge, but I focused on the task at hand. We couldn't afford for me to lose control as well.

As Lyr hoped, with time Losak and the other shifters who'd been bitten calmed until they each fell into a fitful sleep. I checked on the deep gash slowly healing on a shifter's abdomen and took a moment to sit back on my heels beside his chair. *How long has it been?* It was hard to keep track of time without the sun shining overhead, but my feet ached, and exhaustion dragged at me. I couldn't even remember the last time I'd slept. *Was it when we were in the fae realm?* It was hard to believe that it wasn't too long ago that Warrick had been draining my blood and I'd turned. I yawned loudly, not bothering to cover my mouth with my hands that were covered in blood. When Losak, Cassar, and Quinn remained sleeping, Asher came over and lifted me into his arms.

"I can keep going," I mumbled.

My demon only tucked me tighter against his chest. "There's not much more we can do for them now. You may as well get some rest and leave them to heal."

Kade looked longingly at where Asher was cradling me to his body, but he didn't move from Quinn's side. "Darian and I will stay on watch just in case."

Darian looked like he wanted to join Asher and me, but he only nodded his head, his normally pristine silver hair streaked with blood.

"I'll stay as well," Nic added, his voice a deep rasp as his concerned gaze went to Lyr. "We can change over in a few hours. Get some rest."

Lyr reluctantly straightened before turning to Asher and me and pointing to a door on the left side of the room. "There's a guest room through there. There's only one bed, but something tells me you guys won't mind." Her lips twitched upward at that, but her humor didn't change the exhaustion clinging to her eyes. She moved her hand, pointing to another door further to the right. "And through there is a washroom. I've left you another set of clothes in case you want to get cleaned up."

I smiled at her gratefully as Asher carried me away.

I'd thought my demon was taking me straight to the guest room, but he started heading toward the washroom instead. "No, just plop me on the bed," I groaned, not caring at that moment about my current state.

Asher only chuckled and continued to the right. "Somethin' tells me Lyr will need all the linen she has. I don't think we should be soilin' the sheets straight away."

I sighed heavily. He was right, of course. Someone was going to have a fun time washing all the laundry, and I didn't want to add to the mess.

The washroom was built to be communal, with a large pool of water and various places where one could stand under the spray streaming from above. I had to wonder how Lyr was so prepared, and then I remembered she also had multiple mates, and I grinned. I mean, why not, right?

Yawning, I began peeling off my soiled clothes, and Asher did the same. The moment the warm spray rained over me, I was instantly glad my demon had insisted we bathe. *Fuck, yes.*

CHAPTER 3

~ **Raine** ~

The water turned gray as it mixed with the blood washing from my body, and my chest tightened. Whatever relief I'd found instantly vanished as I thought of the wounded shifters beyond the door. My mind then went to Locke, and my heart rate picked up as my thoughts began to spiral. *What if the attack with the gargoyles was a trap for my vampire?* It was possible Warrick was still salty that Locke didn't want to join him. He'd already tried to murder his son once.

Sensing my distress, Asher came up behind me and began using his fingers to rinse the blood from my hair. I leaned against my demon and forced myself to take deep breaths as I focused on the light tugging against my scalp. Panicking wasn't going to help Locke. And it certainly wasn't helping to keep my inner dragon calm.

"I can wash myself, you know," I said half-heartedly, glad Asher was able to distract me from the messed-up situation we were in.

"Now where would be the fun in that?" Asher chuckled as he teased out the knots and ran his fingers through my strands.

A soft smile lifted my lips, but I didn't say anything more as he pulled gently on my hair, working it until it was clean. When he was done, he brushed his hands over my shoulders and kissed my collarbone. Something hard prodded my back, and I became all too aware of how Asher was naked just like I was. Completely and gloriously, naked. I swallowed hard, remembering how incredible his piercings felt as they rubbed inside me. *Stop it, Raine. Now is not the time,* I internally chastised myself, but Asher's scent of musk and leather grew stronger, and my inner dragon rumbled to life, urging me to mark him and claim him as mine already.

The tip of Asher's nose slid up my neck, making me shiver as he inhaled. "You know, you smell different now that you've changed, Sharachi," he murmured against my skin.

I scrunched my face, surprised by his comment. "Good different or bad different?"

He paused, silent for a moment before answering. "You've always smelled like coconut and steel, but now..." He hummed in approval, and I rolled my eyes as I grinned.

"And now?" I prompted.

"Now you smell like *toasted* coconut and steel."

I spun to face him. "Oh great, so I smell like my insides have been roasted," I mean, it made sense, part of me was a dragon after all.

He chuckled, pressing his forehead to mine. "Let's go with—"

"If you say 'charred' I might have to hit you."

"How about...sweetened?" he suggested.

I winced. "Yeah, that isn't any better. Now you're making me sound like a dessert."

His answering laughter made my heart warm. "Sweetheart, you've always been more than dessert. I'd say you're all seven courses." He became thoughtful before adding, "Minus the slimy toadstools." His lips twisted to the side, and he gave me that lopsided smile that always made me melt.

My breathing became shallow, and heat ignited in his eyes. He pressed closer to me, and I ran my hands up his wide chest, enjoying the way his muscles twitched at my touch. Water beaded on his horns and dripped from his hair, and my breath caught as his violet gaze dropped to my lips and then lowered to where the water trailed between my breasts. He dipped his head, a predatory glint in his eyes, but something moved in my peripheral, jerking my attention to the side. We turned in unison, and my brows shot high as I gasped.

My vampire stood a few steps away, fully clothed and covered in blood. Strands of sodden black hair shaded his eyes, and bloody footprints trailed behind him. His weapons were gone, but otherwise, he looked as if he'd stepped into the washroom straight from the battlefield.

Asher's brows slammed down. "Garan?"

Locke tilted his head toward the door, though his black eyes remained fixed on me. "He made it. The remaining gargoyles are in the hall."

Asher blew out a long breath and nodded. "Good to see you're in one piece, brother."

"Wait, the *remaining* gargoyles?" I asked, my heart beginning to race, partially because of the shock and relief of seeing my vampire, and partially because my head couldn't wrap around the idea of more casualties unless I heard him say it.

"Many were lost," Locke replied, his face devoid of emotion though I knew the vampire well enough now to see through his mask.

My shoulders fell as I absorbed the bleak news, letting the knowledge settle on top of everything else that had already happened with the shifters.

Asher scrubbed a wet hand over his face. "Fuck."

I stared at Locke, wondering what he'd just seen. He stood silent for a moment, but then as if something snapped inside of him, he moved briskly forward, stepping into the spray and grabbing me like I was the only one who could pull him from the darkness. The water streamed down his face, clinging to his eyelashes, and dribbling down his chin, and he pulled me hard against him, his touch demanding, wild, and desperate as his hands slid over my body.

"You're an asshole, you know that?" I said, a wobble in my voice. I told myself I'd be angry with him when he returned, but now all I felt was relief.

"I know," he rasped, and it was the way he said it. The way his voice cracked, the deep sound filled with regret as if he hated himself, that had me reaching up and digging my fingers into his black hair.

His arms tightened around me, the wet leather of his coat brushing against my skin as he pressed his forehead against mine and closed his eyes.

"But I couldn't handle the thought of you being taken from me again," he whispered.

My lips trembled. I knew he was talking about Warrick capturing me, and a coldness seeped through me, goosebumps pricking on my skin as I remembered waking as the ancient vampire's prisoner. I had no intention of letting that monster get his hands on me again. I nodded. "I understand, but next time you still have to let us help."

Locke's throat bobbed as he swallowed, and I slowly began pulling off his coat. Asher helped slide the leather from the vampire's shoulders, and he tossed it to the side.

When I removed Locke's shirt, he grimaced, and my face paled at the deep scratch marks raked into his arm.

"You're hurt," I choked out.

"It's nothing," Locke growled quickly, and my gaze flicked from the wound to his eyes. *Nothing?* A puff of smoke escaped my mouth as I gaped at him in frustration. The males insisted on being hyper-protective toward me but had no regard for their own safety.

"Easy, my beautiful mate," Locke said smoothly, the corners of his lips curving upward, and hunger shining in his onyx eyes. It was as if seeing the fire in me helped to bring back the Locke I knew. The arrogant but savagely protective male with a cold exterior. *My beautiful mate.* My possessive inner dragon preened in satisfaction at hearing those words on his lips. *Mine.* Desire pooled between my thighs, and I licked my lips. "You've never called me your mate before," I pointed out, and Locke's grin grew wider like he knew just how much hearing those words had affected me.

Asher gave the vampire a shit-eating grin. "'Bout time you admitted it out loud, brother."

I half expected Locke to have some witty retort to that, but his only response was to finish undressing and slam his lips onto mine, pulling me tighter against him.

Ho-ly fuck.

My lips parted as his tongue plunged into my mouth, and I kissed him back just as fiercely, my eyes stinging at the relief that he was back with me. With *us*. By the time he finally broke the kiss, I gasped, only just remembering to breathe.

"Locke," I whispered as his hard length pressed against my belly. "But your arm?"

"It will heal soon, but right now I need you," he replied, surprising me with the vulnerability in his tone. He lifted me effortlessly, his hands gripping under my ass as my legs went to either side of him. "When I was out there, all I thought about was you," he rasped as he rocked his hips, sliding the length of his cock along my center. "And your expression when I left."

I tried not to think about the lump growing in my throat as Asher came up behind me, pressing in close. "Told you he'd torture himself for it," my demon murmured in my ear, his hot breath making me shiver.

Locke's gaze hardened at the comment. "Even after the tower, I couldn't come straight back here. There were more gargoyles trapped around the city, and we had to save them. But it didn't matter how many lives were spared, all I thought about was you." He thrust inside me, and I whimpered as his cock buried deep and his clawed fingers pricked against my ass while he was careful not to pierce my skin.

Asher reached around from behind, his hands squeezing my breasts, and his chest acting like a wall for me to press my back against. As if he had been waiting for Asher to position himself, Locke gripped me tighter then, and his slow thrusts picked up speed until he was fucking me so hard I could hardly breathe. Asher's firm hands helped to keep me steady, and I cried out, my inner muscles clenching at the relentless pace. The world seemed to still around us, and my body heated, the water turning to steam as it connected with my skin.

"Asher," I gasped in alarm, worried that I would hurt them both, but my demon only kissed my hair.

"You won't hurt us, sweetheart," he said reassuringly. "Your creature won't let you."

My dragon relished the attention, and I felt the sensation of her claws raking along the walls of my mind as if she was warning me that if I didn't take Locke's cock like a good girl, she'd come out and play.

"Then he'd better fuck me harder," I breathed, and Locke gave me a vicious smile as he began moving so fast I'd hardly registered the thrust before he was thrusting again, hitting a spot so deep inside me I reached my hands back and grabbed onto Asher's shoulders for support.

"I might understand why you left us," I told Locke through a moan, "but force me to stay behind again, and my dragon will eat you." I'd meant the comment as a joke, but as the words left my mouth and my dragon roared internally, I suddenly wondered whether it was true. *Fuck. Dragons don't actually eat their males, do they?* I knew of insects that did that, and truthfully, I knew nothing about the beast I'd become. The thought made my body tense as I panicked, but Asher reached around, his thumb rolling my nipple and sending an extra line of pleasure straight to my clit and distracting me.

"She could try," my demon chuckled. "But you're not the only monster here, Sharachi."

I grinned, my worry easing. *Right. Because they're monsters, too.*

Locke grunted as he thrust, and my skin sizzled, the steam around us so thick now that I could hardly see him. "You won't hurt us," Locke snarled. "Because you're ours, and your dragon knows that."

At those words, I cried out as I shattered, my toes curling as stars burst behind my eyes. Locke roared his own release, jerking as he spilled inside of me. When his muscles relaxed again, he lifted me off him, and Asher helped lower me to the floor. Neither of them released me, and considering the fact my legs were shaking, I was glad.

"Ash is right, by the way," Locke said, running his fangs lightly along my shoulder. "Now that you're a monster your blood smells even more enticing than it did before." I shivered at his touch.

"Told ya," Asher said.

I grinned. "That goes both ways. You monsters really do smell good enough to eat." As if to prove my point, my stomach grumbled loudly. "See."

Asher's expression softened. "You need rest. I'll hunt for some food. Locke, you bring her to the room. The others will point it out."

At that, Asher stepped from the spray of the water and grabbed a towel from the rack against the far wall. Wrapping it around him, he snatched up a clean pair of clothes Lyr had left on a low bench and strode straight into the hall without putting them on first, closing the door behind him.

The moment my demon was gone, I turned my attention back to Locke, my mood changing as reality came crashing around me and I thought of the wounded shifters and gargoyles beyond the door. "None of this is going to end well, is it?" I said quietly.

Locke's gaze darkened, his black eyes searching my face. "I'll never let Warrick touch you again."

I took a shuddering breath, feeling the intensity of Locke's stare. "It's not me I'm worried about."

CHAPTER 4

~ Raine ~

I awoke sandwiched between Darian and Kade instead of nestled between Asher and Locke. At some point, my monsters must have switched places while I'd slept without me noticing. I would have been annoyed if I didn't feel so good. My dragon loved sleep it seemed, and I burrowed back into my monsters' arms, feeling like a dragon retreating to her lair as the tantalizing scents of sandalwood, coffee, sea salt, and patchouli made me feel at home. The bed in the guest bedroom was large and easily fit the three of us, but my siren and wolf shifter had their limbs sprawled on top of me like they were determined to trap me there. Which suited me just fine.

Grinning, I contemplated giving them both a rather pleasant awakening, but my thoughts sobered when my mind went to the wounded monsters beyond the room. We were so fucked. Sighing, I closed my eyes. It had been chaos from the moment we stepped through the portal and returned to Katakin, and this was the first time I'd had a moment to really think.

If I could unearth the secrets Prince Azaren had embedded in my mind when we were in the fae realm, I could figure out how to break the curse over the monsters. Then we might have a fighting chance. Warrick would lose his outliers and his power over the monsters of Katakin. Sure, we'd still have to deal with the fae, but unless we found a way to stop the outliers, we were all as good as dead.

Concentrating hard, I searched my mind, trying to find anything that I remembered about the curse. I thought of the light winding through me as the fae prince worked his memory magic on me, and I tried to capture that feeling as I dug deep into my memories.

I frowned, thinking about what Prince Azaren had said about my bonds with my monsters. That I wasn't cursed, but rather, they were bound to me so they'd be compelled to protect me. The five of us hadn't had a chance to discuss the discovery, but the knowledge drew me even closer to them. The fact that our bond wasn't something Warrick had created with ill-intent, but a spell someone had placed on me out of love, filled me with warmth. I had no idea who could have placed the magic on me, but that was a mystery I'd have to contemplate another time.

I pushed past the thought, and the image of a page from one of Sharou Zanae's books appeared in my mind. A beautiful illustration of a winged beast was depicted in gold. I remembered seeing the drawing when the prince entered my mind in the fae realm. *If I can just figure out what it means...*

More images appeared in my mind like I was mentally flipping through the book, but none of it made any sense. The fae text was also there, but the words hadn't been translated, and I couldn't read anything it said. *Prince Azaren must have left more information than this.* The current image I could see was an illustration of a scaly demon with horns bathed in light. *What does it mean?*

I wrinkled my brow in frustration as I mentally flicked through the images, trying to connect the pieces Prince Azaren had left for me. Clearly, the fae prince thought I was more intelligent than I actually was because the only thing I was getting was a headache. I was so lost in my mind that I didn't break focus even when I felt Darian and Kade untangle from me and shift on the bed.

It wasn't until long fingers gently parted my thighs and a hot, wet tongue slid up my center that my eyes snapped open. All thoughts of the curse evaporated as pleasure made me writhe on the mattress.

Kade was sitting up, stroking himself as he watched Darian's head bob, my siren's silky silver hair tied behind his head. *Goddess, yes.*

Darian's hands slid under my ass, and he pulled me closer to him, dragging my back against the sheet and lifting me into the air a little so he had better access as he continued to eat me out.

Oh fuck, the sheets! "We're not meant to make the bed dirty," I mumbled, my breathy warning turning into a moan as Kade laughed darkly.

I was lower now, in line with Kade's hips, and as Darian teased my sensitive clit, I turned my head and reached for Kade's cock. My wolf shifter sucked in a sharp breath as he angled his hips, helping to guide himself into my mouth.

Darian began fucking his tongue into me as Kade's cock hit the back of my throat, and I groaned against the mouthful. Kade's hands wound into my hair, and he pulled hard enough that a delicious sting of pain rushed over my scalp. *Fuck, yes.*

I sucked Kade harder, gripping the base of his cock and swallowing him until he was growling my name. *More.* I wanted *more.*

"Darling, why is it that I get to work, and yet all your attention is on our wolf," Darian said, lifting his head to pout, though amusement shone in his eyes.

I smiled around Kade's cock, but I didn't stop. I was enjoying the way Kade's body was tightening, his hands pulling even harder on my hair. Pain didn't have the same meaning now that I was a dragon, and I shifted my head, trying to show him that I could handle more.

"Our little dragon is always so eager," Darian murmured in approval and let out a dry chuckle. "But let's see if we can shift some of that focus, shall we?" At that, he sat up, his arms winding around my thighs as he lifted my ass into the air and pushed his massive length inside of me. I cried out around Kade's cock, my gaze shooting to Darian as he pulled back and slid inside me again, making me feel so deliciously full.

His lips pulled into a sensual smile, his face flush and eyes bright. "Now, that's...better," he said as he drove me crazy, moving in and out of me so slowly it was torture of the best kind. It wasn't until I was gripping the sheet hard with my free hand, and begging with Kade's cock in my mouth that he finally picked up speed, giving me the pace I wanted.

With the first hard thrust, my teeth accidentally scraped Kade's cock, and my wolf shifter grunted at the sudden pain. Darian grinned as I mumbled an apology. I licked and sucked Kade again while struggling to focus as my siren fucked me.

Reaching across, Kade's fingers found my slick clit, and it was all too much. I exploded as Kade spilled into my throat, his cock pulsing in my mouth and his warmth dribbling down my chin. Darian watched his cock slide in and out of me, and then he let out a low sound of appreciation in his throat as he tensed and found his own release, his fingers digging into my ass.

My chest heaved as Kade removed himself from my mouth, and I swallowed, loving the taste of him on my tongue. Darian took his time, admiring me as he pulled back and lowered my ass to the bed. Then he leaned over me and grinned as he pressed a kiss to my sweaty forehead.

"Morning, lovely," he murmured against my skin.

CHAPTER 5

~ Asher ~

Gripping my axes tighter, I eyed Garan from across the training hall. Overnight, many of the shifters and gargoyles had healed from their ordeals with the outliers, and they were all startin' to talk about how they wished for Warrick's blood. Somehow the vampire had gained information on which houses had joined the rebellion, and it seemed he wasn't interested in letting them live. It had been Lyr's idea for us to start sparring to give the gargoyles and shifters a distraction. The monsters that were well enough stood in a circle against the walls, their attention hyper-focused on us.

Garan always was an unreadable bastard, and I lifted my axes as I sprinted toward him. The gargoyle hadn't slept since Locke had brought him and his team underground, and I was hoping this would help the fucker unwind.

In hindsight, it wasn't my wisest move considering the gargoyle's reputation.

Garan's expression hardened as I attacked, and he turned his body, flapping his stony wings and using the wind he created to slow my advance. Of course, it wasn't enough to stop me. I cried out as I brought my axes down, and the clang of steel rang out as he blocked me with his swords.

And then we were moving across the floor, the gargoyle always managing to block my attacks before my weapons could connect with his stony flesh. Step, lunge, parry, spin. His steps were slow, his heart not in the fight, and it wasn't long before one of my axes scraped against his back. It wasn't enough to penetrate his stony exterior, but it was right over the spot where I knew he'd been wounded by an outlier. He frowned, his muscles tensing as he turned to face me again and finally began attacking. *There we go.* His sword moved like a blur as his expression darkened, and I dodged to the side, his blade narrowly missing my shoulder. The shifters growled and roared their approval on the sidelines, but the other gargoyles watched in stony silence, their gazes trained on their general.

I recovered quickly, my tail flicking out as I readjusted my stance, but then I scented her. Toasted coconut and steel wafted to me from across the room, the powerful scent mixed with... I grinned as I realized what she'd just been up to with Kade and Darian. *Where the fuck was my invite?* In my moment of distraction, Garan's sword slipped through, slicing a deep line across my bare torso and making me curse. I peered down at the rapidly healing wound across my chest and smirked at the gargoyle who gave me an emotionless stare. "Let's call that a win, shall we?" I conceded, much to the dismay of the monsters around us.

Hefting my axes onto my shoulders, I shouted, "All right you bastards! Now that you've had a show, get busy."

Some of the monsters grumbled, but many were now staring at Raine and my brothers, having noticed their arrival. Cassar and Quinn leered at Raine like she was a piece of meat, and Locke, who had been watching my fight with Garan, now looked like he was imagining creative ways he could torture them just for daring to look at her. I could understand the feelin'.

When none of the monsters moved to go spar amongst themselves, I sighed internally, not altogether sure whether they were simply too interested in my dragon, or if their lack of action was because of my reputation and connection to my crazed mother. Before I could make one of them bleed to get their attention off Raine, Lyr seemed to materialize out of nowhere and barked, "You heard him! We need to prepare ourselves."

This time, the monsters finally broke up around me and began sparring with one another, probably because they knew Lyr owned this joint, and they didn't want to be on her bad side. *Fuckers.*

Lowering my axes, I joined Locke and strode to where Raine stood watching alongside Kade and Darian.

"Enjoy the show, Sharachi?" I asked with a grin.

"You mean, did she enjoy seeing you get your ass handed to you?" Darian teased lightheartedly, his eyes glowing brighter than the last time I'd seen him.

Raine didn't answer, her distracted gaze watching the gargoyles as they formed up, sparring with lethal precision as Garan criticized their stances and lunges. "There's only thirty of them," she murmured. "When I'd seen them in the sky, there'd been so many."

"Gargoyles don't retreat easily," Locke said coldly as a way of explanation.

Sadness tinged Raine's eyes as she understood his meaning, and she nodded as if in acceptance before turning to me and smiling like she'd only just realized I was there. "I always enjoy seeing you in action, Ash," she said, finally responding to my question, and my grin stretched wider as her hungry gaze lingered on my defined abs. The female was even more insatiable now that she'd found her dragon, and I fuckin' loved it.

"We need to clear the air," Kade growled low, disintegrating my fantasy image of Raine licking my abs. "Losak and many of the shifters are staring at us like we're the enemy. We need to be on the same side if we're going to survive Warrick and the fae."

"I agree," Lyr said from behind me, nearly making me jump around and swing an ax into her throat. Now that *would* have been a fuck up. The tiger shifter needed a bell or somethin' to announce her arrival.

"We're of no use to each other if there's no trust." Lyr went on. "We've received word that more of the rebels from the other houses will be joining us. Once they've arrived, we'll hold a council, and you can explain yourselves. I'd thought the fact that you helped the wounded would have softened whatever rumors have been circulating about you, but it appears I was wrong. Until the meeting, you five had better keep a low profile."

I cracked my neck, all too aware of the monsters that were still glaring at us even while they sparred.

"That's probably wise," Darian commented, and he held out his arm for Raine. "Come, let's leave before these monsters begin to lose their eyes and become useless for the war."

She frowned as she took his arm. "Their eyes?"

"Yes, lovely," he replied, patting her hand. "It was one thing when we had to tolerate their stares during the Week of Orash, but we're beyond that now. You might not yet bear our mark, but if they keep staring at you like that, especially while my scent is on you, it's possible I might not be able to stop with just their eyes."

She gaped at him, and I grinned. Darian was usually the calmest and most diplomatic of us four, and to hear him admit that he might lose control was fuckin' refreshing.

Lyr raised a brow and planted a hand on her hip. "As romantic as that is, I need everyone in one piece."

"We'll keep to ourselves for now," Kade growled before Darian got the chance to respond. Gesturing to the doorway, my wolf brother began leading us from the room.

All the while, I couldn't wipe the smile from my face. *I always knew she'd be fun.* In the beginning, I just hadn't realized that she'd become so much more than that.

CHAPTER 6

~ Raine ~

Over the nights that followed, monsters streamed into the underground hideout, crowding the space. Thankfully, Lyr had created her bunker near an existing network of caves, and monsters were starting to camp in the tunnels.

We mostly kept to the confines of our room, though there were times we had to venture out. Word spread that Locke had fought alongside the gargoyles, and that the rest of us had helped tend to the wounded shifters of the House of Silat, but it didn't stop the rumors about us from circulating. There were still some who believed we had tried to ally with the fae, and that we were simply biding our time until we could rejoin the enemy again. Lyr might have thought the monsters would be glad to have me, the first dragon shifter, on their side, but so far, it sounded like they didn't believe that at all. Everyone was on edge, and with Warrick attacking rebels in the city, no one knew who they could trust.

Sighing, I sat on the bed between Asher's legs with my back pressed to his chest. His broad arm draped over my naked torso, his index finger lazily drawing circles on my belly. Kade dozed beside us, his thick arms folded behind his head. With not much else to do, we'd been taking advantage of the alone time, and the edges of our sheets were now singed from a time when I'd climaxed and accidentally let out a stream of fire instead of a cry of ecstasy. We'd been quick to put out the flames, but I still scented the charred fabric.

Asher's finger was starting to trail lower when the door to our room opened.

"Take it up with the tiger shifter!" Darian called back to someone as he laughed and entered the room. He held a large jug filled with brown liquid with one hand, and four goblets with the other. Locke strolled into the room next, his black coat flapping behind him, and he closed the door in a monster's face, though I couldn't see who it was.

Dropping onto the bed with an impressive show of grace, Darian beamed at Asher and me, and Kade stretched before sitting up.

"Trust you to find the good stuff," Asher commented with a grin.

"It wasn't easy, either," Darian replied, suddenly serious. "It seems Lyr and her mates prepared for every situation, however, they didn't consider that some of us prefer our drinks to burn on the way down." He shook the goblets in his hand. "Luckily for us, Kenric had the good sense to bring some liquor with him, and I can be rather persuasive."

Kenric? It took me a moment to recognize the name of the Orc alpha. "The monsters of the House of Axeran are here?"

"They arrived hours ago," Darian explained as he passed goblets to Asher, Kade, and me while keeping one for himself. Locke had his own goblet, and Darian proceeded to fill them all with wine.

When half the jug had been emptied, Darian drank from his goblet and let out a satisfied sigh. "Thank you, Kenric."

I swallowed down some of the liquid from my own goblet, surprised to find that the alcohol didn't burn at all. I guess when you have literal fire inside of you, an alcoholic drink just doesn't quite cut it anymore. *Well, damn.*

"How many other houses have arrived?" Kade asked after draining his goblet in one go.

Darian tilted his head. "Along with the House of Axeran, we now also have Borren and the demons from the House of Thorem, and a number of the lower houses. It seems that Cordelia and the sirens of the House of Saceris have sided with Warrick, as have the vampires of the House of Nesarin."

Cordelia? I clenched my jaw at the name of the siren who'd betrayed Darian to become alpha of the House of Saceris. Darian had loved her deeply, and she'd rewarded that love by conspiring against him.

"It's no surprise Cordelia would side with Warrick," Asher said. "Warrick probably offered her riches and power if she allied with him. We all know that female has no loyalty."

Darian didn't react to Asher's comment, but I knew how much Cordelia had hurt him, and I moved my leg, sliding it on top of Darian's. He ran his fingers along my calf, but when he stared at me there wasn't a trace of pain in his crystal blue gaze.

Locke folded his arms across his chest. "The vampires won't turn from Warrick either. I'm sure they believe in Warrick's cause, even if they're uncomfortable with the idea of him having power over all of them."

"What about the wolves?" Kade asked, his nostrils flaring.

"Nic just announced that the House of Worzel will be here shortly," Locke confirmed. "Some of the packs from the lower houses are already here."

My heart began to race at the news. Darian and the others had filled me in on everything that had happened when I'd been taken by Zacal and his wolves. Apparently, because Kade had killed Zacal in his wolf form, he was now the rightful alpha of the House of Worzel again. While I was happy for him, the thought made my insides twist. *Will he leave us for them?* Kade had stayed away from the House of Worzel because he'd thought he was the reason many of the wolves were murdered years ago, but now that the truth was out that it was Zacal and Warrick who'd been behind it, I couldn't help but think just maybe he'd want to return to his pack.

Sensing my distress, Kade grabbed my hand closest to him, and his golden eyes bored into mine. "Nothing could change the fact you're my mate, Mahare. I won't leave you."

I smiled weakly. I wanted to believe him, but I knew the rules in Katakin. When it came to the houses, especially a high house, monsters mated with those who were the same kind and who belonged to their house. I wasn't a wolf, and his pack would never accept me. My monsters talked about wanting to place their mating marks on me, but it was easier to entertain that fantasy when there wasn't a house of wolves expecting Kade to lead them.

"What 'bout the House of Faren?" Asher asked, referring to the high house of Shadows. I remembered the house alpha, Mabel, with her unnerving milky, white eyes.

Darian tipped back the rest of his drink and poured more liquid into his goblet before shaking his head. "As far as I've heard, the consensus is that the wraith has allied with Warrick, but no one is particularly certain."

"Does that mean she might still join us?" I asked hopefully.

Darian shrugged. "Mabel always acts in her best interests, and she's let it be known more than once that she believes becoming a monster was one of the best things to happen to her. I guess it comes down to what Warrick is offering her."

I ticked off the high houses in my head. "So, out of the high houses, four have sided with the rebels along with many of the low houses..." I trailed off as I remembered what Lyr had said nights ago. That the monsters who had joined the rebellion were the ones who wished to be human again. "So all of these monsters really want to be human?" I questioned, still finding it hard to believe.

Locke was the one to answer me. "The rebellion started that way. Now there are also many who have joined because they know removing the curse may be the only way to defeat Warrick and his outliers. But yes, there are many monsters who want to be human again. They've simply never been able to talk about it until now."

I wrinkled my brow, deep in thought. "Well, whatever the reason, having four out of seven high houses joining the rebellion is great, right?"

"The lower houses follow the lead of the higher houses," Kade replied. "With the three high houses still allied with Warrick, he still has a sizeable portion of the Katakin monsters on his side. And that's not including his entire army of outliers."

"And we have no idea when the fae army will get here," I added grimly.

"Don't sound so bleak. Four houses is still promisin'," Asher said casually, though his arm tightened around me like he was imagining taking me away somewhere safe, far from the war. How I'd ever thought the demon was terrifying was beyond me.

"You do know I'm a dragon shifter now, right?" I said with a smile and a puff of smoke left my nose. It was as if my monsters had become even more protective since I'd changed, and my dragon wasn't a fan of being coddled.

Darian arched a brow at me.

"My dragon is getting antsy at being kept inside," I said with a shrug. "I'm finding it hard to keep from shifting." My gaze went to the singed sheets, and I smiled sheepishly.

"You're not the only one who's restless," Locke commented.

I went to ask more about the situation in the hideout, but before I could speak someone pounded on the door. Darian downed the rest of his wine as Locke opened the door a crack, careful to block anyone from seeing into the room. I'm not really sure why he bothered. I mean, sure, Asher, Kade, and I were butt naked, but I was a shifter now. Everyone was going to see my bits eventually.

"What is it?" Locke asked icily.

"The House of Worzel has arrived," Nic's gravelly voice replied. "The council is convening." I shared a look with my monsters and started lifting from my position against Asher. *Here we go.*

CHAPTER 7

~ Raine ~

After dressing, we followed Nic to where the alphas and seconds of the houses, and a few other influential monsters had gathered in a large sitting room. Garan stood at the back, along with his second-in-command, Chaol. Kasey and her mate, Tristan, stood on the other side of the room.

I didn't peer at the she-wolf who'd kidnapped me. From what Kade had told me, Kasey had turned on Zacal after hearing the truth about the attack that happened with the wolves all those years ago. While I could forgive that she'd handed me over to Warrick, I still couldn't forgive the fact that she'd been one of the wolves who'd tortured Kade for years. I was pretty sure if I set eyes on her my dragon instincts would take over, and the last thing we needed right now was me attacking the wolf. Especially as she was currently the acting-alpha of the House of Worzel, seeing as Kade still hadn't officially taken his place.

At some point, we were going to have to talk about what Kade planned to do, and I dreaded when that moment would come. Forcing myself to focus on our current situation, I followed my monsters toward the only unoccupied armchairs. Darian sat down before pulling me onto his lap. Kade took the chair beside us, and Asher and Locke stood at our backs.

At the opposite end of the room, Lyr stood in front of a roaring fire, the flickering blue flames casting her shadow across the carpeted floor. Her long white braid over her shoulder was weaved with tiny black roses, and her mates, Dean, Nic, and Soren stood at her sides.

"Now that you're all here, I'll get right to it," she said, one hand planted on her hip. "You all know why you joined this rebellion. Katakin City has fallen to one of our own. Beneath our noses, Warrick created monsters that are unlike anything we've ever seen—unnatural creatures that only obey his command. If we allow him to control our city, we're all going to end up dead."

There were grumbles of agreement around the room, and Lyr sucked in a breath and continued, "But what you don't know, is that the fae have declared war and intend to march upon us."

At that, the room erupted into a cacophony of outcries and protests.

"How could you know that? The fae haven't launched an attack with their full army since the years after the curse," Losak shouted above the noise, that distinct hiss hanging on his every word, and the monsters quieted as they waited to hear the answer.

Lyr's expression was hard. "The source doesn't matter. The fact is, we've received word confirming the fae *will* attack, and we need to prepare ourselves."

"If that's true, then we're all fucked," Kenric commented, his booming voice filling the room and his large body shaking with laughter.

Quinn turned his pink gaze our way. "Let's not be cryptic, shall we? This is because they went to the fae realm, isn't it? Why else would the fae be declaring war only now? They did something, and now we're the ones who must pay the price." He narrowed his eyes at us. "Let me guess, the fae king didn't want your traitorous alliance?"

My monsters all stiffened, and I glared back at the shifter. *And to think we helped that asshole when he was suffering from the outliers' poison. So much for gratitude.*

"We didn't leave to ally with the fae," Darian drawled, sounding way too relaxed for the situation. "We went to try and prevent a war. We found a fae prince had been captured and tortured by Warrick in the mountain. We left to try and gain the prince's good favor and return him before the fae themselves discovered what had happened."

"They would have burned down our world looking for him," Kade growled.

"And yet, now we receive word that war is on the horizon," Quinn retorted. "So, you either failed spectacularly or this was your plan all along."

Darian shrugged. "We knew our actions might not be enough to stop what was coming. Warrick tortured their prince. We can't be surprised that they'd retaliate, especially given the history between our kind."

Quinn still glared at us, and I had to stop myself from shooting fire across the room to make him quit looking at my males like that. *I wonder if I could singe his perfect eyebrows without burning him to a crisp.* Clearly, explaining why we went to the fae realm wasn't stopping the shifters from hating us. At that thought, I held my breath, waiting for Darian to mention that the other reason we'd gone to Zalei was to find a way to break the curse over Katakin, but he didn't.

Locke folded his arms across his chest and lifted his chin. "And let's not forget Raine saved all of us when we faced the outliers nights ago in that ballroom. If it weren't for her, you'd be dead now."

"Oh, that's right," Cassar piped up beside Quinn, looking at the faces around the room. "It was the newblood who hadn't turned who ended up savin' us all with her magic. I know some of you are inclined to think she's some kind of savior, but I'm willin' to bet she's a fae spy. You claim you went to the fae realm to try and stop this war, but only the fae can control the elements like that.

For all we know, she went to the fae realm to report to her king. And now we're also expected to believe she's a dragon shifter?" He sneered, and a cruel glint shone in his eyes. "No, our first act should be to remove the rat from the rebellion."

No one saw Locke move. One moment he was standing behind me, and the next he was across the room with his blade to Cassar's bobbing throat. Darian's grip tightened around me, and Asher and Kade shot to their feet, their bodies tense as their hands hovered over their weapons. *Well, fuck.*

Quinn snarled, and Losak hissed, his eyes changing to black slits and scales starting to sprout over his skin, but they didn't try to attack Locke. Everyone in the room stilled, their focus on my vampire.

Locke pressed his blade harder against Cassar's throat, and the boar shifter glowered at my vampire. "Raine is no spy. You threaten her again and I won't give you the chance to utter another word," Locke said, his icy voice so eerily calm that it had a chill racing down even my spine.

Cassar let out an animalistic grunt. "Do that and see what happens," he goaded.

For a moment, I thought Locke might take out the shifter, but Losak hissed, "That's enough. Cassar will keep his mouth shut."

The boar shifter looked like he wanted to argue, but Locke gave him a hard look and Cassar kept his lips pressed together, following the order of his alpha. Locke stared Cassar down for another moment, his sword close to breaking the shifter's skin, but then he lowered his blade and returned to my side.

Asher blew out a breath. "Well, that could have been messy." From the way he said it, I honestly wasn't sure if he was relieved or disappointed.

Lyr gave Locke a pointed look as if she was telling him to behave before she began addressing the monsters again, "Raine is not a spy, and why the fae are attacking doesn't matter. What matters is how we react to the situation. We believe if we offer King Adrien up as an offering to the fae king along with Warrick, we might stand a chance at creating a truce. Especially after we explain that Warrick was the one who captured and tortured the fae prince."

Kenric barked out a laugh. "King Adrien is long dead."

Lyr looked hard at the orc alpha, and he stopped laughing.

Losak's brows slammed down. "You mean to tell us that the stone king is still alive somewhere in Katakin after all these years?"

This time it was Dean who responded, the flickering shadows on his green face making him appear more imposing. "It's not like he's been walking around the city. He's entombed."

At that, a few monsters gasped, while others shouted curses and protests. Lyr lifted her hands to stop the rising noise. "In his current state, he's unable to cause harm. We'll keep him entombed when we hand him over to the fae. Soren and I will leave at daybreak to retrieve him. We could use a few more volunteers."

There were murmurs around the room, but before anyone had offered to help, I blurted, "I'll join." All eyes turned my way, and I blanched under the attention. Still, I didn't regret putting my hand up. Being cooped up in the room hadn't been too bad because Asher and the others were with me, but I needed to get out. This was the perfect excuse. Not to mention, I was hoping that by volunteering it would help to ease some of the suspicions about me.

"We'll go too," Kade growled in agreement quickly, and I smiled at my wolf shifter.

Kasey watched Kade from across the room, but he ignored her stare.

"Even if we have the king, there's no way we'd be able to imprison Warrick," Kenric said. "His outliers will eat us alive."

"It's the only option we can see that might appease the fae," Soren replied, tucking his wings in tighter and moving closer to Lyr's side. "If their entire army attacks while the monsters are divided, we won't be able to match them."

Kasey commented from across the room. "Why not leave Warrick's outliers to wipe out the fae? Then once they're gone and Warrick's forces are weakened, we can overpower him."

I ground my teeth together. I wouldn't tell them I was part fae. That would only make them suspect I was a fae spy even more, but I had to bite my tongue to stop myself from disagreeing with Kasey's statement. *They can't want all those fae to die at the claws of the outliers, can they?* From the nods coming from the monsters around the room, it was clear they could.

"None of us know how many outliers Warrick has, nor do we know how he is creating them," Lyr replied. "If we can negotiate a peace treaty with the fae, they may be open to finally breaking the curse over Katakin. We need them to understand that it may be the only way to rid ourselves of Warrick and his outlier army. The fae have never been our enemies. King Adrien was the one who broke the treaty between our kind, but before that, there was peace between our kingdoms. Blood has been shed on both sides, and it all started with King Adrien. Many of you are here because you're tired of being monsters. You remember what it was like before the curse, during a time when the streets were filled with laughing children and the city was full of life. We need to stop acting like the monsters the fae think we are, or we'll never break the cycle. Queen Izla didn't intend to condemn all of us, only King Adrien. I was there when she unleashed the curse.

The fae are the only ones who can help to reverse this out-of-control magic."

Kasey still looked like she wanted to argue, but the expressions had changed around the room as the monsters started to realize this discussion wasn't only about surviving. I understood then that many of the monsters truly believed the fae could make them human again, and I squirmed against Darian, my shoulders feeling heavy. They didn't know I was the one carrying the secrets that could free them.

"While we're getting King Adrien, the rest of you must prepare yourselves for what's to come. Hopefully, we can come up with a way to capture Warrick."

"How do we know Warrick and his outliers aren't already on their way here?" asked a male goblin I'd never seen before. I could only guess he was from one of the lower houses that had joined us. "If someone is giving Warrick information on which houses have joined the rebellion, isn't it possible he might know our location?"

Lyr shook her head. "There is no way to know for sure, but I believe our hideout is still secure. We received word that the vampires captured and tortured one of the demons from the House of Thorem, and that's how Warrick got his hands on the information. Thankfully, Borren has assured me that the demon didn't know of this place. Either way, we must all take turns keeping watch over the camp."

Whispers and chatter sounded around the room, and Kasey spoke up. "What about the other high houses in the city? We need them on our side."

Lyr stared at her with an unreadable expression. "Warrick has too much influence with the House of Nesarin for them to join us, but Nic is going to discreetly visit Mabel and try to get the House of Faren to come to our side."

"And what of the House of Saceris?" asked another monster I didn't recognize. "Could Cordelia not be persuaded to do the same?"

Lyr's uncertain gaze found Darian, and my siren showed no emotion as he said, "The sirens will not listen to me."

"That may be true, but you're our best chance at getting through to them," Dean countered.

There was a beat of silence before Darian nodded. "Perhaps, but I do believe they are a lost cause."

Lyr gave him a reassuring smile. "Well, we will have to hope you can find a way to convince them."

"And what about the Taratun council," Kenric questioned. "How much of a threat do they pose?"

"Like the House of Nesarin, the Taratun will not be swayed. We should assume they will remain allied with Warrick, especially seeing as Warrick and Perene are members of the council. In any case, there is nothing to be done," Lyr answered.

The gargoyles had been silent for the entire council, but Chaol finally spoke up. "Do we know how the outliers will act without Warrick there to command them?"

Lyr turned her attention to the gargoyle. "We hope that without Warrick, the outliers won't have the mental capability to form coordinated attacks. We should be able to slowly eradicate them if we work together." She let out a resigned sigh. "It's the best plan we've got."

There were grumbles around the room, but when there were no more questions Lyr called the meeting to an end and the monsters began to disperse.

When it was only us and Lyr and her mates still present, Asher clapped his hands together and grinned. "Well, all right then. Who's ready to bring in a king?"

CHAPTER 8

Ten years ago

I was in Zalei, realm of the fae. Or at least, that's what the male named, Xander, had told me. If I believed him that meant I was absolutely *not* on my island anymore, though, I'd figured that out the moment a bear with horns had attacked me, and I'd been saved by three men. Well, *men* wasn't exactly the right word. They were fae as Xander had also pointed out, not human. Two of them looked only a little older than I was, and the youngest appeared to be around my age.

I fidgeted nervously with the skirt of my ragged nightgown as I followed my new companions further into the depths of the strange forest I found myself in. We trekked past pale white trees, and I tried not to think about the fact that I had no idea where the fae were taking me.

It was obvious these fae weren't the same beings as the Katakin monsters who visited my island. The village elders had always spoken about the monsters being hideous and cruel, and so far, these fae had proved to be the opposite. They'd saved me without knowing who I was and until I could find a way to return home, they seemed my best bet at staying alive. Also, as much as I tried to mentally prepare myself for the idea that they could be leading me toward something terrible, I couldn't shake the feeling that I was safe. Which was crazy, because more than once I saw eyes blinking back at me from the darkness of the trees, and from the strange clicking and scratching noises I could only guess what creatures they belonged to.

I shivered at the thought and almost yelped when something warm landed across my shoulders.

"Sorry, I thought you were cold," Xander said hurriedly, seeming almost as startled as I was as he stared at me. "But if you'd rather I take it off..."

It took me a moment to understand that the soft warmth across my back wasn't the body of a monstrous creature about to pin me down, but Xander's silken cloak.

A small smile crept over my face as my fingers lifted to trace the smooth fabric. "No." I swallowed. "I mean, thank you. I just thought—"

"That it was another Choram bear?" the youngest fae teased, and my cheeks heated though I knew I had no reason to feel embarrassed for running from that wild beast. The idea might have been laughable in this place, but I knew that's what any islander would have done.

"That's enough, Ellis," Xander said, waving him off before turning back to me. "You don't have to worry," he said reassuringly. "Nothing will harm you while we're around." His voice was warm and kind, but I focused on what he'd said. *While they're around. Does that mean I'll die in this forest without them?*

When he continued to stare at me, I nodded slowly, surprised when the small action made his shoulders visibly relax. I was no one to him but some poor girl they happened across. "Why did you save me?" I blurted, unable to stop myself.

Xander frowned. "That bear wasn't playing around. If we hadn't acted, you wouldn't be here."

"But you could have been killed," I pressed, his reply not giving me the information I wanted.

Ellis snorted and gave me a toothy grin. "If you think that was impressive, you wait until you see how we fight against the king's soldiers."

"Quiet," Xander reprimanded, whirling on the fae.

I slowed my steps. "The king's soldiers?"

Xander's gaze settled back on me. "Forgive my brother. Sometimes he doesn't know when he should hold his tongue."

Ellis made a vulgar face, and Xander pinched the bridge of his nose. I smiled softly, momentarily distracted from the small piece of information Ellis had given away because Xander's reaction reminded me so much of how I sometimes felt with Raine. Seeing my smile, Xander's lips curled upward as his gaze connected with mine.

For a moment, I couldn't do anything but stare back, his glittering-blue eyes holding me in place. The girls on my island wouldn't believe me if I ever made it back there and described him to them. The male had an ethereal beauty that was too sculpted to be real, pointed ears and all. Now that he didn't have his cloak, I could see more of his lean, muscular body, and his short dark hair that contrasted against his pale skin and blue eyes almost made it seem like he was glowing in the moonlight.

"We're close," Nathaniel, the fae on my left side said to Xander, and I blinked as if I'd been woken up from a dream. "Are you sure this is a good idea?"

Ellis tapped his chin. "What he means to say is that you don't intend on bringing her in like this do you? Bernan will croak if he sees her ears and realizes what she is. In fact, I think I can hear him now, starting to rattle off some long speech about the war with the monsters."

War with the monsters? I opened my mouth to ask what he was talking about, but Xander replied, "Of course, not." He turned to Nathaniel. "Can you bring Samson to us?"

Ellis laughed. "Samson? What's he going to do? Bore her to death with one of his lessons about plants?"

Ignoring Ellis, Xander asked Nathaniel, "Unless you have a better idea?"

Nathaniel still looked concerned, but he didn't answer and simply started through the trees again without us.

I stood awkwardly as we waited, leaning against the trunk of a large tree and ignoring the way the wood bit into my back. The more time that passed, the more my heart raced. Xander had asked me where I was from when we'd first begun trekking through the forest, but I hadn't said much other than confirming I was from a human village. As much as I wanted to go back, there were already monsters tormenting my people, so I didn't want to give too much away. And in any case, there wasn't much more information I could give them other than to describe the island and explain the full situation of what had happened with the monsters. But for now, I kept my mouth shut.

Xander stood close to me, but Ellis paced in front of us and stared into the trees every so often like he was contemplating following Nathaniel.

I was about to pluck up the courage and ask about the war with the monsters when rustling came from the bushes close by. Ellis jerked toward the sound, and Xander straightened a moment before Nathaniel appeared from between the trees. He was followed by a male who looked at least a decade older, with golden hair tied in a short ponytail, and a scholarly look about him.

The newcomer's thick brows lifted when he spotted me, and his face only paled further when he noticed the shape of my ears. My stomach dropped. If humans were rare in this forest, it was possible they knew nothing about my island.

"You shouldn't have brought her here," the newcomer, who I assumed was Samson, said in a hushed whisper to Xander and the others as he ushered them over to him and turned his back to me. "Have you forgotten our history?"

"She's not one of them," Xander replied. "We all know the humans in Katakin were turned into monsters. She must be from somewhere else."

"Even if she's innocent and has nothing to do with them, it doesn't explain why she's here," Samson countered. "Nathaniel has already told me about the portal. If she came through while you had it open, you must send her back."

"To where? She can't tell me where she's from. That portal was for us to get here. There's no way to explain how a human used it to cross worlds."

Cross worlds? I nearly choked, but I cleared my throat when all four of them peered my way.

"She's obviously not a threat," Xander said, pulling their attention back to him. "If we leave her out here alone, she'll die."

"He's right," Ellis said, nodding enthusiastically. "We found her running from a Choram bear. She'd be dead in minutes." He stretched his neck, looking Samson up and down. "Say, you didn't bring any food, did you?"

My mouth dropped open at how casually they were talking about my death, and Xander gave me a sympathetic look.

"She needs our help," he said to Samson. "When we find out where she's from, we can send her back." Samson still didn't look convinced, but Xander added, "Just imagine the stories she has about a world beyond our own. She could have useful information for...uh, educational purposes."

As Xander said the last part, curiosity sparked in Samson's eyes, the reluctance finally leaving his expression. His gaze swept over me like he now saw me as a treasure trove of information. Unfortunately for him, I still had no intention of telling them all about my island.

"Hmm fine," Samson muttered, still staring at me. "But she can't go into the camp looking like that."

"And that's why you're here," Xander replied, his demeanor brightening now that the older male had agreed to let me join them. "We need you to glamor her ears so we can pretend she's a runaway from the city."

I pushed off from the tree. "Glamor?"

Samson's eyes brightened even more, like the fact I didn't know what the word meant only further fueled his curiosity.

"Can you do it?" Ellis prompted, ignoring me.

Samson rubbed his chin. "It's been some time since I've had to glamor anyone, and it's never been to disguise ears, but I don't see why it wouldn't work."

"Good," Xander replied. "Make sure it's convincing."

Samson nodded and took a step toward me, but I jerked away, self-preservation kicking in. He halted his approach and turned his head to Xander, who smiled at me in that way that made my heart pound.

"It won't hurt," Xander assured me calmly as he stepped forward and took my hand in his. "It's been a long time since our kind have seen a human. Samson will only use a little magic to disguise your ears."

"Magic?" Even though I'd seen Nathaniel charm that bear, it was still hard to come to terms with the word being used so casually. The closest thing we had to magic back home was when our physician would use natural poultices of herbs to heal people.

"Yes, magic," Xander replied, and I was all too aware of how his hand was still clutching mine. "We'll remove the glamor when we can return you to your kind, but for now, this will have to do."

"And I'd better do it with haste," Samson added, looking pointedly at Xander. "They were expecting you to return hours ago. The celebration has already started, and I fear my absence will also be noticed."

"Not to mention, I'm *starving*," Ellis added, making a show of rubbing his belly. His mood had improved considerably at the mention of the celebration. Xander gave Ellis an unimpressed look, and I didn't move away as Samson approached me again, my hand still held firmly by the fae with the dazzling blue eyes.

Samson's face scrunched with concentration and my ears and face began to tingle and heat. Just when the sensation was bordering on pain, the tingling abruptly stopped, and the older male stepped back. All four fae stared at me, and I trembled as I let go of Xander's hand and reached up, my eyes flaring wide as I felt the elongated curves of my ears leading to pointed tips.

"I-I can feel that they're different," I stammered.

"They're not the only things that have changed," Ellis commented, and my heart hammered as I moved my hands to my face. My nose was sharper, and my cheeks more defined. Even my eyebrows felt like they were a different shape. "What did you do to me?"

Samson rocked back on his heels, looking very proud of himself. "Yes, well I did say it had been a long time since I'd had to glamor someone. Does it matter if my magic changed more than her ears? At least she looks more like a fae, and we can always remove the glamor when needed." He beamed at Xander. "I dare say no one would question that she belongs in Zalei now."

"I still don't think this is a good idea, Xander," Nathaniel commented, his expression serious.

Xander ignored him and said to me, "Come. Let's get you introduced."

CHAPTER 9

~ **Cara** ~

Xander led me further into the forest, and I tried not to think about my changed appearance as our scenery changed. Strands of my long hair rested on my shoulders, no longer a mousy brown but a lilac color, just like the shade of the purple flowers we had back at home. I reminded myself that the fae Samson said the glamor could be reversed. Until then, I would have to accept that this was the best way for me to blend in.

Slowly, the boulders scattered between the trees became larger until they reached the height of my waist. I frowned at the evenly placed silver rocks that gleamed in the moonlight. *Weird... It's almost like they form some kind of wall.*

Our group stopped before a boulder directly in out path, and I stared at the surface of the rock which was so smooth it showed our reflection.

"Let us in Ode, it's been a long night," Xander said to the rock like he thought it would answer him. There was a long pause, and I was starting to question the fae's sanity when a feminine voice came from seemingly nowhere.

I'm not sure why I was so surprised considering I'd literally just been kidnapped by monsters, sent to a strange world, and had my appearance altered by fae magic. But then again, I'd never had the wild imagination my sister, Raine, did.

"It's about time! Tori and Euren have been looking for Samson, and it wouldn't have been long until they came to me to ask if he went out," the feminine voice squeaked, speaking fast. "Not to mention you three should have been back hours ago. Where have you been!"

Xander shifted slightly and peered at me. "Just let us through. We'll fill you in once we're inside."

The feminine voice let out a barely audible huff, but she must have done something because Ellis called out a moment later, "You're the best, Ode!"

There was bell-like laughter and then the reply, "And don't you forget it."

I smiled at their exchange, already wondering if this Ode was their sister considering the casual familiarity. My smile fell when the silver boulder began glowing vibrantly, and Xander turned to me. "Ready?"

The answer to that question was a big fat 'No', but I said, "Would it matter if I wasn't?"

He appeared troubled by my answer, but I took a step toward him, and he led me forward all the same. As we passed between the two boulders closest to us, the air changed, and a tingling sensation rushed over me, making the hairs on my arms stand on end. As fast as it had come, the feeling faded, and I gasped as the forest ahead of us changed. Instead of thick trees and boulders, I was now staring at a large clearing with green grass and a moss-covered path lined with small rocks that led to a row of colorfully painted huts.

"Is that—?" I began.

"Our camp," Xander finished for me with a smile.

My brows rose. "But just a moment ago this was all trees."

Samson came to stand closer to us. "Yes, the illusion is a powerful one. And a good thing, too."

"You are all unbelievable," a feminine voice came from above, making me lift my gaze as I instantly recognized the feminine voice we'd heard earlier. I expected to find someone scaling down the nearby tree, but my mouth fell open when I spotted a girl with long, pink hair, a plump figure, and large translucent wings fluttering down toward us. That's right, she was *flying. Where did she come from?*

"One of the watch platforms is up there," Xander whispered as if he'd heard my internal question.

I was still staring when the female noticed me tucked behind Xander. Her turquoise eyes became round as she caught sight of me and took in my matted hair and torn nightgown. "Who is this?" she squeaked, and I promptly snapped my mouth shut.

"Xander's new pet," Ellis replied with a grin, moving forward to crowd into the female's space. "Miss me?"

Her cheeks heated at his question, but she waved him off, her confused expression going from me to Samson and Nathaniel, and then to Xander. "Is this true? Is she from the northern camp? I didn't think we were taking in any newcomers right now."

I waited, expecting Xander to give the excuse he'd told me to use while I was there. That I was a runaway from the city, and that they'd rescued me in the forest. But instead, he replied bluntly, "We found her on our way back. She's a human, and we needed Samson to disguise her ears."

What in the name of the goddess? I said nothing as Ode's jaw dropped, her brows lifting. "A human?" she squeaked, fluttering her wings.

Ellis grinned as he curled his arm around her shoulders. "Yep. And you'd better not let anyone in on the secret or things might actually get really interestin' around here,"

Ode blinked a few times, still gaping at me as she processed the news. "So is she...?" she trailed off.

"No, not one of them," Xander answered. "The humans in Katakin were all turned into monsters. My best guess is something strange happened with the portal we created, and she ended up here by mistake. I promised her we'll give her a place to stay until we can figure out how to get her home."

Ode swallowed, her gaze still glued to me.

"Ode," Xander said, finally pulling her attention to him. "You can't breathe a word of this to anyone. Can you show her around and help her blend in? Can I trust you with this?"

At his last question, Ode blinked rapidly a few more times and straightened. "Yes. Yes, of course. But, uh, what's her name?"

Five pairs of eyes turned my way, and I shifted uncomfortably. Xander had asked me the question after they'd saved me from the bear, but I hadn't told him then. Now I realized there was no point in keeping it a secret.

"Cara," I replied softly.

Ode smiled. "Cara. Well, that's nice. I'm Odelia, or Ode for short as I'm sure you've gathered. My shift on watch duty just ended, so uh, how do you feel about parties?"

I gave Xander a questioning glance. "Parties?"

"Oh, it's amazing," Ode said, waving her hand and fluttering her wings. "We don't get to relax much around here, but we always celebrate the first night of summer. There's food and wine, and music..." She stared off dreamily.

I glanced reluctantly at Xander again, but he was already talking to Samson and the others and striding away from us. A part of me wanted to follow them, but Ode took my arm, drawing my attention back to her. I forced a smile to my face. "Sounds...fun."

She beamed, any reservations she had about me completely melting away as she led me along the mossy path. "So, I have to say, Samson's glamor is very well done because I wouldn't have realized what you were otherwise."

"What I am?" I asked.

"You know," she said, then leaned closer and whispered, "A human."

"Yeah, I get the feeling there aren't many of us around here," I replied.

Ode's brow furrowed. "Actually, I think you're the first we've encountered for nearly two centuries."

Centuries? I wobbled on my feet, but Ode held me firmly, keeping me upright. "Everyone always talks about how dangerous your kind is, but you seem really fragile. It's probably a good thing Xander and the others found you on their way back."

I cleared my throat. "And where *were* they coming back from?"

Ode chewed her lip, silent for a moment, but then her face brightened, and she released me to gesture dramatically with her arms. "Ah, here we are! Welcome to my humble abode."

I turned to the building in front of us and this time I was the one gaping. The structure was twice the size of my cottage back home and made from oddly shaped colored sheets of glass that fitted together like pieces of a puzzle.

"What do you think?" Ode prompted when I didn't say anything.

"It's incredible," I whispered, admiring the patterns of the glass. I'd never seen anything like it.

"Come on," she said, grabbing my arm again and dragging me toward the diamond-shaped door. Despite the glass exterior, inside the building it was all soft silks, crystal furniture, and fluffy cushions.

"You live here?" I asked, feeling overwhelmed as glowing white orbs around the room filled the space with light.

"Yep. All by my lonesome," Ode responded, and though she was smiling, there was a hint of sadness in her eyes.

I frowned. "Oh, I thought you and Ellis might be—"

"Together?" Ode cackled. "No Xander and Ellis are the sons of Corak, the leader who runs this place."

"Wait, so they're like the chief's sons?"

"Well, I'm not sure what a 'chief' is, but Xander's next in line to take over from Corak when she dies if that's what you mean."

When I remained in stunned silence at the idea that I'd been saved not only by fae but by the sons of their leader, Ode went on. "Xander is like a brother to me. He saved me a few years ago, much like he saved you I guess, though there was more screaming and well... fire." Her voice became quieter as she trailed off, staring out through one of the glass windows like she was picturing a scene from her past. Abruptly, she realized what she was doing and spun her head back to me, a wide smile on her face. "But I make it a point not to dwell on the past. I have my place here, and I honestly couldn't be more grateful."

I didn't fully grasp what Ode was sharing with me, but from that brief glimpse of sadness, I knew enough. She was lost just as I was, though I couldn't imagine exactly what she'd lived through.

"Anyway, it's a good thing I live alone as it sounds like you'll be staying here for a while," Ode continued to babble. "Can't say I've ever had a human as a guest, but I'm sure we'll find a way to make it work."

"Just until Xander finds a way to send me home," I added, unsettled by how enthusiastic she was getting.

"Exactly!" she agreed and began tapping her chin with her finger. "Now, let's see what we have for you to wear. We don't get newcomers at the camp often, so we'll want to put you in something that makes a good first impression." She tilted her head, scrutinizing me, and wrinkled her nose. "And something with a little less...dirt."

• • • • ● • ● • ● • • •

Ode let me bathe and then fussed over me for a good while, adding color to my face and taming my hair. Apparently, the only dresses she owned were a vibrant pink that matched her hair, so I wore one with a simple neckline and velvet pink leaves that wrapped around my chest. It wasn't what I'd usually wear back on the island, but the garment was surprisingly comfortable, and I was glad to be out of the nightgown.

When she deemed us ready, Ode led me through the eerily quiet camp, past the glass homes of numerous other fae and toward a deep valley. When we reached another line of large boulders, much like the ones we'd encountered to get into the camp, she paused and leaned close to my ear. "Remember not to let anyone know you are, well, you know," she whispered, "But I'm sure Xander and the others have already been telling everyone that they found you. So take a deep breath and smile. Everyone is super friendly." She then paused before adding, "Well, mostly. There are a few fae you'll want to steer clear of, but they should be pretty obvious."

Not waiting to see if I had any questions, she stepped closer to the boulder in front of us, pulling me with her. The rock's surface was smooth and silver like the boulder Xander had spoken to when we'd approached the camp, and I waited to see what would happen.

Ode cleared her throat. "It's me, Ode of Ferlay, and uh, Xander's guest, Cara."

There was silence for a moment, but then the air shimmered in front of us, and Ode grinned as she yanked me forward between the boulders. The same tingling sensation I'd felt earlier rushed over my body, but like before, it disappeared a moment later.

"Holy Goddess," I breathed as I took in the sight in front of me. Like the camp, the party must have been hidden by some kind of illusion until we passed the boulders, and I wasn't prepared for it.

Hundreds of fae were spread around the valley, laughing and chatting as they drank wine and ate from a massive banquet spread out on a long oak table. A band with five winged fae played the strangest music I'd ever heard, the notes of the wooden instruments jarring and yet seeming in complete harmony, and the fae were in groups lounging on what appeared to be huge white mushrooms, sitting on carpets of moss, and lazing in rock pools that steamed and bubbled.

"They look like you," I gasped, pointing to a whole group of winged fae who were giggling and flying high above us.

Ode tipped her head back to see where I was indicating. "You mean, Ferlay pixies? Yes," she said with a smile. "But we're not the only ones with wings." Lifting her hand, she pointed to the smaller winged creatures whizzing and darting between the fae I'd spoken about. "Those are Tudora pixies."

"I'd thought they were fireflies," I commented, squinting as I tried to make out their small bodies."

"Shhhhh," Ode warned, bringing her finger to her lips. "They're tiny but fierce, and you do *not* want to call them any kind of insect. What they lack in size, they make up for in attitude. They also control chaos magic and have a nasty habit of making others think they attract bad luck. They're probably some of the fae you should try to stay away from."

"Right, steer clear of the Tudora pixies," I agreed.

Looking back at the other groups of fae, Ode gestured with her hand to a group of female fae wearing moss-green dresses. "Over there, we have the nymphs. They can turn into trees when they want to and have different abilities, though it's always something to do with nature. Like the power to make trees grow fruit even in winter, or make impressive wooden weapons." The nymphs were talking to some blue fae lounging in the rock pools, and Ode went on. "And those fae are water nymphs."

"Let me guess, they control water in some way?"

Ode's eyes sparkled. "Something like that. Most of the fae here are able to control the different elements is some way, but some fae have completely different powers depending on their heritage."

"You mean, like how Nathaniel can speak to animals?"

Ode didn't look surprised that I knew Nathaniel's power. "Exactly like that."

To our left, a group of fae lounged on giant white mushrooms as if they were armchairs, and I had to ask,

"And what about them? What are they doing?" They all had the widest grins, and they laughed and chatted louder than all the other groups of fae. In the middle of the group, Ellis leaned his back on a mushroom and sucked what looked to be a giant yellow bubble into his mouth.

"...First we make them still, still, still, then we're going to kill, kill, kill!!" the group of fae cheered before guffawing and spluttering, some of them almost falling off their mushrooms. A small pile of the strange yellow bubbles rested on the ground, and the moment Ellis's bubble was gone, he reached his hand down, scooping up another bubble. As he lifted it to his lips, his gaze found us, and he grinned stupidly.

Ode pursed her lips as she stared at him. "Those would be our camp idiots. Stay away from that stuff. Every year a group of them go out to collect the gas that the Piti toadstools give off when they're planning to digest someone. Knox and Yanee are wind and water fae, and together they can catch the yellow gas in those bubbles before the toadstools get them. The gas is mostly harmless and makes you deliriously happy, but it takes a while before you can see straight again."

I stared at her in horror. "Did you just say when the toadstools are going to *digest* someone? As in... *eat them?*"

Ode waved her hand like I was overreacting. "They won't hurt you unless you disturb their family, and they only need to feed like once in a decade. But I swear these guys are going to turn their brains to mush."

Her gaze lingered on Ellis when she said the last part, and I didn't miss the way he watched her, almost like he was daring her to join him. Her cheeks reddened, and she turned back to me. "But you must be starving! Let's find you something to eat."

At that, she turned her back on him and led me over to the huge banquet table, collected two silver plates, and handed one to me. My stomach grumbled at the sight of the luscious fruits, vegetables, and assortment of meats, but I didn't reach for anything, not even when Ode started piling what looked to be small honey cakes onto hers.

"Is it all, uh, safe?" I asked her quietly, and she whipped her head to me.

To my left, a short fae with a neat brown dress who was busy refilling one of the platters let out a harumph and glared in my direction. *Oops.*

"Yes, it's all *incredibly* delicious," Ode said loudly, making a show of looking around at all the platters as if she couldn't decide what to choose next, and I got the feeling her answer was more for the fae in the brown dress than it was for me.

The short fae sniffed and then finished refilling the platter before walking off and quite literally disappearing into a tree. I tried not to gape, which was easier to do because the moment she was gone, Ode whirled toward me. "Don't ever say anything bad about the food!" She hissed and then sighed. "I should have warned you. Brownies are temperamental, especially when you're talking about their cleaning or cooking. Trust me, you do not want one of them on your bad side, otherwise, we'll be left eating oatmeal or mushrooms for months."

I nodded seriously and tried not to think about how she'd used the word *months*. I wouldn't be in this place for that long…would I?

"But yes, it's all safe to eat," Ode went on, more casually now that there weren't any brownies around. "And by that, I mean it won't kill you, though try to stay away from those purple ones over there." She pointed to the platter the brownie had just refilled. "Those are sour fruits, and they'll leave your tongue swollen for most of the night."

"What? Then why are they on the table?" I spluttered.

Ode shrugged. "Not everyone has that reaction. To the water nymphs, they taste sweeter than a honey cake. Or so I've heard."

I stared back down at my plate.

"Look, Xander is a great guy," Ode said softly, "And I'm sure he'll do everything he can to get you home, but until you came along we hadn't seen a human for a very long time, so I think you'd best get used to eating our food, because the reality is…"

"I could be stuck here," I finished quietly.

She darted her gaze around, double-checking that no one was close enough to hear us, and her expression was sympathetic. "Just for now. My point is, eat up or Xander will think I'm doing a crappy job at getting you settled."

Deciding that I had no choice but to trust the pixie, I piled a honey cake and two of the more familiar-looking fruits onto my plate. Ode smiled approvingly and led me to a small unoccupied wooden table with two chairs.

Fae stared at me as I passed, but no one approached us, and I took that as a good sign. Trying to act like I belonged, I bit into the blue fruit that was shaped almost like a peach.

"Yeah, you might want to be careful with that one, it can be a bit...messy," Ode commented with a laugh as sugary syrup dribbled down my chin. I rushed to swipe it away and had only finished swallowing my mouthful when Ellis strode toward us, a yellow orb in his hand.

Ode followed my gaze to the male fae, and she lowered the honey cake she'd been about to pop into her mouth. "We don't want any of that here, Ellis," she said tightly.

"Well that's good, cause this one's mine," he replied with a grin. As he walked, he lifted the ball to his face, his lips parting as he prepared to suck the gas into his lungs, but he stepped on a pebble, upsetting his balance.

"Watch it!" Ode cried out, but it was too late. The orb fell from his hands, landing right on my head. An audible *pop!* sounded in my ears, and then all I could see was a haze of yellow as a rancid, sour smell filled my senses. I coughed and spluttered, waving my hand in front of me, but the gas disappeared quickly.

"Shit, sorry," Ellis said before bursting into hysterical laughter.

That's not good.

"Cara, are you all right?" Ode squeaked, coming closer to me.

"I, uh...yeah?" I replied uncertainly as her face began to stretch, her cheeks growing so wide she looked like a chipmunk. "Did you eat something fun-ny?" I asked, my words beginning to slur.

She shook her head in alarm. "It wasn't me. You inhaled the gas of the Piti toadstools. How do you feel?"

I thought hard, though it was difficult to focus when the colors of my surroundings began blurring together into a swirly, strange pattern. *So...pretty.* I smiled wide, feeling my head spin.

"Great. This is just great!" Ode paced beside me, her wings looking like streaming pink clouds.

"She's fine," I heard Ellis say. "It was only a small dose. I'm sure she'll be back to normal soon."

"Fine?" Ode squeaked, then lowered her voice to whisper in a hushed tone. "We have no idea was that stuff does to humans. And oh. Oh crap! Xander's coming this way with *Corak!*"

Ellis laughed again, but this was followed by an "Oof!" as Ode jabbed her elbow into his side.

"This is serious!" she hissed.

Ellis shook his head and blinked a few times. "Calm down. It'll be fine."

Grabbing one of my arms, he lifted me to my feet and grinned. "We really need you to pull it together for a moment. Just nod and smile, all right?"

I swayed, and Ode grabbed my other arm.

"Uh, can we help you with something?" Ode said smoothly as Xander approached with an older female by his side.

I stared at Xander. The colors had mostly returned to normal around us, but I had to bite my lip to stop myself from laughing at his abnormally elongated chin.

Xander eyed Ellis and Ode, and his gaze lingered on me. "Corak would like to speak with Cara."

"Are you sure it has to be now?" Ellis asked sheepishly, and I blinked, happiness swirling inside me and making me want to flop onto one of those cushy mushrooms I'd seen earlier.

"Time is not something that should be squandered," replied a crisp, feminine voice, and I peered at the female beside Xander. She was a foot shorter than him, with her silky black hair pulled into a high bun, and inquisitive blue eyes rimmed with thick black lashes. I remembered what Ode had said about their leader, Corak, being Xander's and Ellis's mother, but this female only appeared to be a decade older than Xander. *Maybe Ode meant to say she was their older sister?*

"So, this is the fae you've been telling me about," the female mused, emphasizing the word 'fae' as she looked me over. Amusement glinted in her eyes as she looked at how Ode and Ellis were holding me. "I'm not sure your brother was the right one to task with helping her settle in."

Ode opened her mouth to speak, but Xander was quick to say, "You're right as always, mother."

Corak went on, not acknowledging his response. "And you already know I don't approve of this situation. Tonight, you can all have your fun, but come dawn, we must resume the fight. If we're to ever hope to make a difference, we can't have distractions such as this."

When we all remained silent, she let out a sigh and went on. "But I suppose it's too late now. If she's to stay here, you Xander, are to take full responsibility for her. If she reveals herself or proves herself to be a nuisance, it will be up to you to correct the situation."

Even in my happy state, I understood the threat in those words. I didn't let myself think about how exactly Xander would correct the fact that I was there. Thankfully, I was hoping I'd be back on my island and away from these fae sooner rather than later.

"Of course," Xander replied, his gaze fixed on me. "Nothing will deter us from our mission."

"Good," Corak said. "I'll leave you now to enjoy the night as promised, but I expect you and Ellis to both be present during the morning briefing." She paused and scrutinized me for a moment longer, then added, "*Without* the new fae." At that, she turned on her heel and marched away.

Ode sagged against me now that Corak's back was to us, and Xander shot Ellis a glare.

"What? It was an accident," Ellis defended.

Xander still looked unimpressed with his brother as he held his hand out to me. "Will you walk with me for a while?" he asked, his intense gaze piercing through the strange light haze fogging my brain.

Neither Ode nor Ellis commented as I stepped away from them, and my stomach flipped as I took Xander's hand, his fingers curling around mine.

Xander led me slowly across the grass, careful to help me keep my balance. "How are you feeling?" he asked with concern.

I angled my head, looking up at his striking face. A rainbow of color shone around his black hair, almost like a halo, and for a moment, I couldn't speak.

"Cara?" Xander prompted, his gaze tracking over my face.

My foot clipped a clump of grass, and I nearly toppled, but he held me steady.

"I'm fine," I replied, feeling like an idiot.

"The effects of the gas will wear off soon," he reassured me. "Or at least, it would for a fae. Let me know if you start seeing anything unusual."

Unusual? I laughed at his absurd comment, and he smiled at me.

"Then again, I guess this all must be strange for you," he corrected.

I nodded, feeling as if he didn't quite understand just how different his world was from mine. I remembered then Corak's words about the briefing and the small bits of information I'd heard that had hinted about a war. Even while I was intoxicated and overwhelmed with my surroundings, I knew there was something darker about the camp I was in. Truthfully, I wasn't sure if I wanted to know all of the fae's secrets.

I stepped over a small branch and nearly yelped when I thought I saw eyes staring back at me. Swallowing, I said, "When do you think you'll be able to send me back?"

Xander was quiet for a moment, and when I peered at him his expression was unreadable. "Someone will come to question you tomorrow. Try to give them all the information you know. We'll find a way to get you home."

Unease went through me, and I wasn't entirely sure if it was because I was going to be questioned or the way my heart squeezed at the idea of never seeing Xander again if I was sent home. I chastised myself internally and forced a smile to my face. "Thanks."

CHAPTER 10

~ **Raine** ~

The grass squished under my boots as Lyr and Soren led us through an ancient graveyard that lay on the outskirts of the forest, not too far from Katakin city. Moss covered the cracked tombstones, and trees had sprouted between the crypts like the forest had decided to reclaim the gravesite. Dean had stayed behind at the hideout to keep the peace between the houses, and Nic had already left before us to try and convince Mabel and the House of Faren to join our cause.

"Well this isn't creepy at all," I commented as we stepped past a tombstone that had been carved into a statue, presumably of the person who'd been buried. The man stared sightlessly across the graveyard, his nose and one arm missing as if someone had purposely defiled the monument. He reminded me of the nymphs we'd encountered in the fae realm, but this time, I was sure the male was only stone and wouldn't render us unconscious. Pretty sure, anyway. I squinted at the small inscription at the foot of the statue. "He died over two-hundred years ago," I murmured under my breath.

"They all did," Kade said, coming up beside me and staring grimly at the statue.

Asher shrugged a shoulder. "We're immortal now, remember?"

"We didn't need the graveyard after the curse changed us all, lovely," Darian added, twisting his head toward us as he glided between the tombstones.

I didn't hide my confusion. "But there are still ways monsters can be killed."

"We no longer mourn the dead," Locke added coldly, though his expression softened as he stared at me intently.

I locked eyes with the vampire, and there was something in his gaze that told me he wasn't sure if he believed that anymore.

"You guys coming?" Soren called out, and I turned my head to see he and Lyr had stopped before the door of a large marble-stone crypt.

We hurried over, passing rows of tombstones to get there.

"Is this the place?" Kade growled when we'd reached them.

Lyr shared a look with Soren before turning back to us. "It is. But before we enter, there's something you should know."

Asher folded his arms across his chest and widened his stance. "Let me guess, the king isn't alone down there?"

Lyr shifted on her feet. "When we entombed King Adrien here in the years after the curse, we didn't do it alone. Vasken, one of the queen's personal guards, helped us to seal him in."

Soren ruffled his wings before pulling them in tighter. "We trapped the king in a tomb and sealed the stone with magic."

"But the king isn't the issue," Lyr went on. "Vasken was very close to the queen, and he didn't do so well when we couldn't find her. Vasken helped Queen Izla escape that day when she created the curse, and King Adrien captured him and tortured him mercilessly for it. After we rescued Vasken and entombed the king, Vasken became obsessed with the idea that he had to stay in the crypt and make sure King Adrien never escaped. He insisted it was his duty."

"Wait, so you're telling us that this guard, Vasken, has been down there all this time?" I asked in surprise.

Lyr's expression was filled with regret. "I visited often and tried to convince him that he didn't need to remain there, but as the years passed, he always refused to leave."

"We haven't entered this crypt in decades," Soren added grimly. "Not after the last time."

"What happened?" Kade asked.

Sadness filled Lyr's eyes. "Vasken lost himself completely,"

Soren lifted his hand as if he was tracing an invisible scar on his jaw. "We were taken off guard when he attacked us in his shifted form. We nearly didn't make it out of there in one piece."

"In the years before that, Vasken had begun rambling and yelling at us to not let the king out," Lyr replied. "I think he came to believe that anyone who goes down there is going to free the king, and he's willing to do whatever he can to make sure that doesn't happen."

Darian eyed the crypt like he could see the creature within. "What type of shifter is he?"

Lyr looked uneasy when she replied, "He's a chimera. One of the strongest we've seen."

I wasn't exactly sure what that was, but Asher let out a low whistle, and Kade cracked his neck like he was getting ready to shift.

"Good thing we're not here to remove the king, then," I said sarcastically, pretending to be chipper.

Locke stared intently at me, and I almost thought he was going to ask me to wait outside or something stupid, but he only held my gaze as he pulled out his swords.

My hand went to the hilt of my blade, but Kade drew my attention to him. "We need to know that you won't do anything reckless, Mahare," he said, his golden eyes flashing. "Just because you're a dragon shifter, doesn't mean you're invincible."

I freed my sword, glad to have the weapon in my hands. "And to think when you met me, you couldn't wait to put me in dangerous situations," I joked light-heartedly. "What happened?"

Kade stepped closer until his chest was pressed against mine. "You know what happened," he growled, his hungry gaze fixing on my face as he lifted his hand to run his thumb across my lower lip.

Well, damn. Trust the wolf shifter to find a way to get me all hot and bothered right before a fight.

Lyr cleared her throat, and Kade stared at me for a moment longer before stepping back.

"Not that I want to break this up, but we're burning daylight," the tiger shifter said. "We need to get this done and transport King Adrien back to the camp. Everyone ready?"

When no one protested, she turned to the crypt door and forced it open.

• • • • • • • • • • •

~ Kade ~

Darian and Asher entered the crypt after Lyr and Soren, and I stepped through after Raine, my eyes quickly adjusting to the dim light as the torches along one wall flared to life. Locke came in behind us, closing the door after him, and we began making our way down the stone steps.

A faint rasping sounded from somewhere in the darkness, and I cocked my head, my ears morphing and becoming pointed as I listened with my wolf hearing.

"What is it?" Locke asked from behind me.

I listened for a moment longer, before answering in a low growl, "Breathing."

"Maybe Vasken's asleep?" Raine whispered optimistically, though her heart was pounding faster than normal.

I breathed in her scent to calm my inner wolf. The fact that she'd turned into a monster hadn't changed the bond that was between us, and the need to protect her made me want to shift and tear out the chimera's throat before he could get to her.

We reached the landing of the crypt without incident and entered a wide circular space. In the middle of the stone floor, a large tomb rested silently, the stone devoid of any markings or etchings to identify who lay within. Around the crypt, tall stone pillars stood like looming guardians, and darkness led into a series of tunnels. A musky, feline scent lingered in the air, and at the base of the tomb, the bones of animals had been piled up.

Lyr touched what appeared to be the skull of a rabbit lightly with her boot.

"He left the crypt to hunt," Soren commented as he went to stand beside her. "At least he didn't starve."

Lifting her chin, Lyr turned her attention to the tomb, and her eyes filled with hatred. "King Adrien's in there," she said coldly, and I continued to scan the area, watching for any sign of movement around us.

Raine walked around the tomb, inspecting the stone structure. "You're sure?"

"Yes," Locke confirmed before Lyr could speak. Undoubtedly, my vampire brother could hear the king's faint heartbeat through the stone, just as I could. To know for certain that the king was still alive filled me with rage. He didn't deserve to live. I reminded myself that we would be delivering him to the fae, and hopefully, they would bestow upon him the punishment that he deserved.

Asher sheathed his axes and moved closer to the tomb. Running his finger along the lid, he lifted his hand to peer at the layer of dirt before wiping the dust onto his pants. "All right, well how about we get this asshole out of here before the beast wakes up, shall we?"

I voiced my agreement. I could still hear steady breathing coming from somewhere down one of the tunnels to our left, meaning the chimera was likely still asleep and hadn't awoken the moment we'd entered the crypt. If we were lucky, as the years passed it was possible the creature had entered some kind of hibernation slumber, and we might be able to remove King Adrien without being detected. For his sake, I fucking hoped so.

Asher widened his stance and gripped the tomb, and Soren, Locke, Darian, and I did the same.

Raine went to join us, but Lyr stopped her. "Well, now, let's not deprive them of their chance to show off," she said sweetly to my Mahare, and Raine stifled a laugh as Asher winked at her and flexed his muscles. Darian's lips twitched upward at the demon, and Locke seemed too preoccupied to give a shit.

"It'll take some effort detaching it from the base, but after that we should be all good to go," Soren instructed as he adjusted his grip on the stone. "On the count of three. One... Two... Three."

Grunting, I lifted the stone, my fingers slipping slightly as I tried to keep hold of the fucking thing. The stone held fast at the base, but then a crack sounded as the stone crumbled, and the tomb came free. Carefully, we lowered the tomb to a spot on the floor a few feet to the left.

"That wasn' so hard," Asher said with a grin, rubbing his hands together to get rid of the dust.

Lyr rolled her eyes, but she gave us an appreciative smile. "Well, that's the hard bit done. Now let's get it back to camp."

"Is he..." Raine began and trailed off thoughtfully. "I mean, is the king awake in there?"

"No clue," Lyr answered casually. "He was when we shoved him in there."

Raine made a horrified face that the fucker definitely did not deserve, and Darian gave her a reassuring smile. "I would suspect that after so many years trapped in there, he would have entered a weakened state where he is no longer completely conscious."

Raine still looked way too sympathetic for the king who was responsible for destroying our world. "He doesn't need your kindness," I growled, pulling her attention to me. "If you knew all he did, you'd see this was mercy compared to what he deserved."

She swallowed, her eyes filling with understanding. If I'd had my way, I would have ended him myself. "Why didn't you take his life?" I asked Lyr and Soren seriously. "When you had him in a vulnerable position."

"Unlike the gargoyles whose skin and wings only have a thin layer of stone," Soren began, "King Adrien is completely made of nearly impenetrable stone. We tried to kill him multiple times before we came up with this plan. If there was any other way—"

Soren was cut off as a roar shook the crypt, the sound echoing off the walls and stinging my sensitive ears.

"Fuckin' devil's awake," Asher cursed, grabbing his axes and moving closer to Raine.

Claws sprung from Locke's fingers as his eyes turned onyx black, and Darian pulled three stars from the belt across his chest. Soren flapped his wings before folding them again and pulling the sword from the scabbard at his side. The five of us circled Raine and Lyr, who pulled out their own weapons and stared down each of the tunnels.

"Remember Vasken is a friend," Lyr said as she gripped her knives tighter. "Subdue him, but don't kill him."

Asher stepped to his right as he peered down a tunnel, and a rib bone crunched under his boot. The answering roar was louder than the previous one, and Asher cursed under his breath. "Don't you dare fuckin' say it," Asher shot at Darian before the smirking siren could comment.

"If I have to choose between your friend and us, I won't hesitate to end his life," I told Lyr, but the tiger shifter didn't have time to respond.

A beast prowled into sight from one of the tunnels to the left, and its angry orange gaze fixed on the displaced tomb. Opening its jaws, it roared again, the sound making the stone walls rattle, and then the creature attacked.

CHAPTER II

~ Raine ~

I wasn't prepared for the monster that stepped from the shadows. The beast had the head of a mountain lion but with tall horns, a sleek scaled body with four clawed paws, and a long tail that ended with a snake's head. Its glowing eyes fixed on Kade, and I cried out as the creature leaped into the air, its front paws outstretched.

Kade shifted to his wolf form in an instant, and the pair of them became a heap of fur and claws, growling and snapping at one another. In a swift movement, the chimera's large teeth gripped the back of Kade's neck, and the beast threw the wolf to the side. By the time Kade was on his feet again, the monster was bounding toward Asher.

Asher tightened his grip on his axes as he eyed the creature and prepared to go for its throat, but Lyr shouted in alarm, "Don't hurt him!"

Cursing, Asher dropped his axes at the last moment and lifted his hands, straining to hold the chimera back as its powerful jaws snapped at his face. The beast's tail curved around, the snake's fangs coming dangerously close to Asher's legs. "If you don't want me to kill it, a little help would be nice!" Asher grunted right before two of Darian's stars glanced off the beast's hind legs, and Kade barrelled into the creature's side, sending it sprawling with him.

My dragon strained to be let out, patches of my skin rippling and thickening, but Lyr's hand landed on my arm. "You can't shift," she warned. "If you do, your dragon might kill him."

I placed my hand over hers as emotion clouded her eyes. "Then you'd better get that thing under control," I told her seriously as smoke trailed from my mouth. Because my dragon wasn't happy that there was a little kitty hurting her monsters, and all it would take was the scent of their blood, and I was pretty sure I'd be roasting that thing.

Lyr shifted, her clothes tearing off her as thick black and white fur sprouted over her skin, and she changed into an impressive snow tiger. She wasn't as large as the chimera or Kade, but she darted forward with incredible speed, quickly moving to distract the chimera from Soren who had joined the fight, and then skirting away before the creature could swipe at her with his paws.

"We need to knock him out," Soren yelled as Lyr continued to distract the chimera and the rest circled the beast. The chimera's tail snapped out, nearly clamping onto Darian's arm as he dodged out of the way.

I thumbed the pommel of my sword as I watched in agitation. Fire burned in my belly, and I shook my head, mentally trying to keep my dragon at bay as my skin grew uncomfortably warm. *My treasures. My mates.* The thoughts echoed in my mind, and as Asher was thrown backward, my teeth started to elongate into fangs. I was sure I was about to give in and shift when Locke stepped up beside me and turned my head, so I was staring at him and not the beast attacking my mates.

His eyes were pure onyx black, his fangs protruding from his lips, but otherwise, he was calm as he stared at me. "Give them time," he said as he held my gaze.

"Why aren't you helping them?" I hissed back, but I already knew the answer. He was there for *me*. To protect me even though I was now a monster just like them.

"I'm here for the same reason you are," he said. "Because I'd much rather kill the feral monster than watch it harm those I care about. I'm not sure if I'd be able to control myself. But if you think I should risk it..."

"No," I replied quickly, remembering the worry in Lyr's gaze when the fight began. Whoever Vasken was, he was important to her and her mates, and I didn't want to be the one responsible for his death.

The chimera's roar was deafening, but the cry abruptly changed to a whimper and then there was silence. I pulled my gaze from Locke's and peered over to where the others were around the chimera. The monster was at Asher's feet, its chest barely moving as it breathed, and it transformed before our eyes, its massive form shrinking until a naked male was lying on the stone instead of a beast. I could only guess Asher had been the one to render the monster unconscious because he pumped his fist into the air and turned to grin at me like he thought he'd won some kind of competition. I rolled my eyes, but all I really felt was relief.

Kade and Lyr shifted back to their human forms, the pair of them appearing battered and bruised, but otherwise unharmed, and Darian and Soren stared on with grim expressions.

"Next time, I suggest we contain the beast *before* we try to take away its toy," Darian suggested as he began retrieving his stars from around the room. Yanking out a star from where it was lodged in a stone pillar, he wiped the weapon on his pants and slid it into his belt. Locke and I moved closer to the disarmed male on the ground, my inner dragon finally settling now that the threat was unconscious.

"What do you plan to do with him?" Kade asked Lyr and Soren as he grabbed his weapons belt from where it had fallen to the ground when he'd shifted.

Lyr sighed, staring at the bony male at her feet. "For now, we'll have to leave him here, but I'll return with Dean, Nic, and Soren when I can. It'll take time, but I'm hoping we can bring him back to his usual self. If we're lucky and we can convince the fae to remove the curse, that'll help."

"Even if the curse is removed, the mind can be hard to heal," Darian said quietly, and I didn't miss the way my siren watched Asher subtly for his reaction to the comment. But Asher wasn't paying attention as he strode over to me and lifted me into his arms, making me cry out in surprise.

"What are you doing?" I squeaked as he propped me on his shoulder like he was placing me on an imaginary pedestal.

"I figure I deserve a reward seein' as I didn't fuck up for once, and I managed not to kill that thing. It just so happens I choose you to fulfill that role," Asher replied.

I scoffed in disbelief. "That wasn't a game, Ash. We were helping out Lyr and Soren, and there's still a tomb that needs to be transported."

Asher grinned as he dropped me from his shoulder and caught me with both arms. "Could have fooled me," he said, then he smashed his lips to mine. I melted into him, all too glad to have some attention after I just had to sit by and watch them fight. When our lips parted, Locke, Darian, and Kade were around us as well, staring at me like they all expected a turn.

"I think you're all forgetting about our cargo over there," I said with a grin, indicating to the stone tomb.

"He's only sleeping, lovely, and we haven't forgotten," Darian said with a devilish smile. "But if you don't kiss me like you just kissed Ash here, I'm going to start thinking your dragon has a favorite."

My smile split wider. They were all equally my treasures, but I wasn't about to tell him that. Sliding from Asher's arms, I grinned as I strode over to Darian and let him take me in his arms.

· · · ● · ● · · ·

~ Locke ~

It took two hours of carrying the tomb in the wretched daylight for us to return to Lyr's hideout. The entire time I could hear the ancient king's rapid heartbeat thudding faintly from inside his coffin of stone. It was beating faster than when we'd first found the tomb in the crypt, and I was starting to wonder whether our actions had woken the devil. Not that I gave a fuck. If what Lyr said about the tomb being magically sealed was true, whether he was awake or in slumber was of no consequence to us. The bastard could suffer in there for eternity for all I cared.

At one point when the king's heart had sped up to the point it was erratic, Kade's gaze had slid to mine, and I'd wondered if he was thinking the same damn thing as I was. That it was a punishment worse than the curse itself, and it would be better if the other monsters in Katakin didn't know how to pull off such a feat.

When we arrived at the camp, Soren took us through a back entrance that led directly into a private area that the other monsters didn't have access to. We left the tomb in a cell where it could be guarded until it was time for us to transport the king to the fae. The plan was to leave for the House of Saceris the next day during daylight hours when it was more likely that the outliers in the city would be sleeping. We could only hope that Darian would be able to reason with the siren bitch, Cordelia, but she was as untrustworthy as they came, and I knew Darian was dreading his return to his former house.

"I'm goin' to hunt for some food," Asher told us as he broke away from our group, and Darian went with him mumbling about needing to find more wine before his encounter with the sirens.

Kade placed his hand on the small of Raine's back and guided her into our room, and I followed after them, closing the door behind us. By the time I'd turned back around, Kade was lounging naked on the bed, soiling our sheets with the dust and grime he'd collected at the crypt, and Raine was staring at me intently, her concerned gaze flicking over my face.

"I look worse than I am," I reassured her.

"Well, that's a relief because you look like death," she said with a small smile that didn't reach her eyes. "Is it because we were out in the daylight?"

I shrugged, moving further into the room, but she only followed me.

"Come to think of it, I haven't seen you drink from any of those black vials since we've been back in Katakin. Don't you need the blood to survive?" she questioned.

I spun toward her only to find her inches away from me, and I stared into her fiery amber eyes. For a moment, I wasn't sure what to say. How could I tell her that since tasting her blood, the synthetic stuff tasted like ash in my mouth? How could I tell her that her blood had sustained me for nights, far longer than synthetic blood ever had and that when she was around me, the urge to sink my fangs into her neck had me wanting to give into every primal need I had? I'd nearly given in when I'd taken her in the washroom only nights ago. The memories of her blood filling my mouth when we were in the fae realm were almost torturous.

"Locke," Raine repeated, breaking me from my thoughts, and I lunged for her. She gasped against my lips as I kissed her, and then I was lifting her to the bed and placing her onto her back beside Kade.

My thigh moved between her legs, pressing against her core, and she moaned deliciously into my mouth. Her lips warmed to the point they sizzled against mine, and smoke filled my mouth. Realizing what she'd done, she pulled back quickly. "Sorry," she rushed out.

I blew the smoke into the air and gave her a wicked smile. "You don't ever have to apologize for who you are, Raine."

She swallowed thickly and writhed as I pressed my thigh against her again. "Neither do you," she gasped, and my attention was so focused on her lips that it took me a moment to realize what she meant. That *I* didn't have to apologize for who I was. I would have laughed if I had it in me.

"Oh, my beautiful Raine, if only you knew how wrong you are," I breathed. Leaning down, I grazed my fangs along her neck and enjoyed the way she squirmed and panted. Kade chuckled from beside us, and I turned to see my wolf brother fisting his cock. I smirked, thinking of the times when we'd bedded females in the past. How long had it been? I'd wager over a century, at least.

Kade, Asher, and Darian had been with Raine many times over the past nights, but I'd held back, knowing my thirst might get the better of me. I'd hoped I'd find a way to stomach synthetic blood again, but no matter how many vials I choked down, her blood was still all I could think about. I was at the point that if I didn't do something about it, I was going to become a real danger to her.

"Locke's never been the best with words," Kade growled, his eyes sparkling mischievously, "and he's even worse at admitting his faults out loud, but someone needs to explain that since drinking from you in the fae realm, the synthetic blood isn't sustaining him. It's why he's been so moody these past nights."

Raine frowned in confusion, and I glared at my wolf brother.

"Is that true?" she asked softly, and I steeled myself for her judgment. When I didn't answer, she prompted, "Locke."

I unclenched my jaw and let out a long breath. "If you'll let me," I finally said with reluctance. "I won't take more than is necessary. But your blood..." I trailed off unable to say the words out loud. Even now I was still ashamed of what I was. Ashamed of being a monster who needed to feed on the blood of others to survive like a damned parasite.

But as I peered at Raine's accepting face, she smiled widely at me, desire shining in her eyes, and I could swear there was the flickering of actual flames in her gaze. "Why didn't you ask earlier?" she said quietly like she was struggling to contain her own excitement. Before I could answer, her finger transformed, showing the tip of a dragon talon. "Wow, I did not think that was going to work," she said with a grin, staring at the claw. Then she slashed a shallow cut on her neck. Her blood welled at the wound, and the scent of her filled the room, igniting my hunger like nothing else ever had. *Fucking seven devils.*

"Mahare," Kade growled in warning as my eyes changed to pure black and my claws extended. "What are you doing?" he asked, his body tensing like he was preparing to protect her from me.

"Oh, fuck. I was trying to make it easier for him. Did that not help? I mean, I have blood. He needs and wants my blood. So, um, maybe he should just drink already?" she said it like it was the obvious solution, and when she worded it like that, I could believe that it was.

I stared down at her, all too aware of the blood pumping through her veins, and her beautiful body still beneath me. "You're too fearless for your own good," I growled.

She smiled and bared her neck more, her words coming out soft and breathy. "I'm not afraid of you Locke, and if this is what you need, take it. I trust you."

Fuck. "I don't deserve your trust," I rasped, but she waited patiently for me. Closing my eyes, I made a tortured sound and fought to control myself as I let the scent of her blood draw me closer. A snarl ripped from me as my lips neared her throat, but she didn't flinch or shy away. She remained still, and when I opened my eyes, her gaze burned bright with anticipation as if she was as eager for me to drink as I was. This female was made for me. I felt it deep in every part of me, and I would protect her like the queen she was.

My lips brushed against her cut, the blood smearing around my mouth, and she gasped as my fangs sank in.

My venom spilled into her bloodstream, making her moan as the taste of sweet, toasted coconut overwhelmed me, her fiery blood burning deliciously as it slid down my throat. *So fucking delicious.* Power crackled through me, every part of me seemingly coming alive as energy flooded my system.

More. I sucked in deep, and Raine whimpered. Growling started from close by, but before Kade could intervene, I released her neck, hissing as I licked her blood from my fangs. Kade watched me carefully, observing my every move as if he was still ready to tear me from her if needed, but when Raine blinked up at me, her wide eyes still cloudy as she felt the bliss my venom was giving her, my mind was clear. I would never hurt my mate. *My beautiful Raine.*

The whites returned to my eyes, and Kade relaxed as I began peeling off my clothes. When I was naked, I moved to undress Raine.

"You remember our rules?" I asked Kade as I moved to a position lower on the bed.

His lips twitched upward. "You just drank from her brother, and you didn't get anywhere close to killing her. I don't think those rules apply with her."

Raine lifted her head off the pillow. "What rules?"

I smirked, knowing Kade was right.

Raine wiggled like she was growing impatient, and Kade pulled her on top of him so her back was pressed to his chest. His cock teased her entrance, and I kissed up her thighs, my tongue sliding over her slick clit as I licked and sucked, enjoying how she tasted on my lips. Kade pushed the tip of his cock inside her, not giving her more than the head, and she writhed for us, gasping as her body demanded more.

"Oh goddess, please," she whispered, and I loved hearing her beg for more.

"You want Kade's cock thrusting inside you?" I chuckled against her pussy. "Stretching you until you scream?"

"Yes," she gasped, and Kade growled possessively as he reached around and squeezed her breasts.

I sucked harder on her clit, my teeth grazing the sensitive nub, and Raine moaned. I would never tire of this. Would never stop craving the way her body made me want to lose control and sink inside her.

"Locke, please," she rasped, her body squirming against my wolf brother. "Kade. I need—"

My teeth sunk into her thigh at the same moment that Kade pushed fully inside her. She cried out as my venom entered her system, pushing her closer to the edge in that one instant.

Claws peeked from Raine's nails as she grabbed the sheets, and Kade nipped at her neck as he thrust inside her over and over.

The rush of blood sent another surge of energy through me, and my cock grew painfully hard. Releasing her thigh, I breathed heavily as I took in Raine's flushed face, and I shared a look with Kade.

"Turn over," I instructed Raine as Kade pulled out, and she let us spin her, so she was facing Kade. The next time he entered her, I sucked my finger and slid it into her ass, careful to go slow.

"Oh goddess," she cursed.

I chuckled darkly. "Too much?"

She moaned in response, baring her ass more, and I began pumping my finger in time to Kade's thrusts as I palmed myself with my other hand, wishing I was inside her. When Raine shattered, Kade and I erupted as well. Smoke filled the air, huffing from Raine's mouth as she gasped and shuddered. It wasn't until we'd all calmed and relaxed beside each other on the bed that I realized Raine was grinning at me. Even Kade looked smug as shit.

"What?" I asked, certain I probably still had blood smeared over my face, and for once I was in no hurry to wipe it away.

"You're smiling," Raine said, "And I just, I like seeing you like this."

I frowned, noticing the full curve of my lips.

At that moment, the door opened, and Asher came into the room carrying a tray of sliced meats and cheeses. Darian held a jug of wine.

The pair of them stopped just inside the room, and Asher gave us an impish grin. "So, who's hungry?"

CHAPTER 12

~ **Cara** ~

Six years ago

"I thought I'd find you here," Ode chirped, her wings fluttering as she flew to where I was perched high in a tree. She settled onto the branch beside me and held out her hand. "Here."

I turned my gaze from where the sun was setting over the forest, bathing everything in yellow and orange, and eyed the small bundle of cloth on her palm. "What is it?" I asked suspiciously.

Her grin split wide, her pink lips twisting into a smile. "You didn't think I'd forget, did you?"

Raising a brow, I returned her smile with my own. "You don't need to be here worrying about me, Ode."

She waved her free hand. "Pish. I've finished my shift. Go ahead. Open it."

I stared back at the bundle she held and took it, unfolding the fabric to reveal...*a black stone?* Flecks of glittering blue shone on the surface, making the stone sparkle in the golden light.

When I stared at her quizzically, she explained, "Some say the pebbles at the very bottom of the lake are supposed to bring good luck, and others say they grant wishes." She shrugged. "I had Reno find one for me. It's pretty, right?"

I struggled to keep a smile on my face, even though I was so grateful she was thinking of me. I wondered what she'd traded Reno, the young water fae, for it. "Wishes?" I asked quietly.

Her expression softened, and her smile fell as she studied my face. "Oh, Cara, I hadn't thought it would make you sad. I wanted to give you something special. If I'd realized—"

"It doesn't make me sad," I said hastily, cutting her off and sniffling as my hands wrapped tighter around the stone. "Thank you, Ode. Really."

She still looked concerned, but I reached over with my free hand and squeezed hers. "It's not that I don't want to stay here, it's just, it's been four years and I thought..."

"That Xander would have found a way to send you home by now," she finished, her shoulders drooping.

I nodded, blinking a few times to stop my eyes from tearing. "I need to get back to my sister. It's not that I don't like it here. I do. But she needs me." I thought of all that had happened since my time in Zalei. At first, I'd been reluctant to share details about my island, but as the days turned to weeks, I'd eventually begun to tell them everything I could in the hopes it would help. But nothing I said ever did. Xander, Nathaniel, and Ellis had made countless portals for me, but none of them had ended up leading to my home. Talking about my island, which could be located literally anywhere, wasn't enough for them to go by.

Sighing, I traced my finger along the curved tip of my right ear. The glamor Samson had placed on me was still in place, and according to him, it would last indefinitely unless it was altered. For four years, I'd kept the fact that I was human a secret, and no one knew besides Xander, Ellis, Nathaniel, Samson, Corak, and Ode. The fae accepted me as their own, and I knew I should have been grateful. Being in Zalei had to be better than wherever the monsters had been planning to take me, but it was now only six years until the next choosing, and Raine would be of selection age by then. I had to get back there before the Night of the Offering.

"Xander will find a way," Ode said solemnly. "He always does. It might not be tomorrow, but he will."

It was the same thing she'd been telling me for years, and as much as I believed Xander was trying his best, I was starting to wonder whether I'd ever see Raine, my father, or my island again. I tried to remind myself that the odds were good that Raine wouldn't be selected during the next offering to the monsters. There would be dozens of girls on the island of selection age, and only twelve were chosen every decade. But today was the anniversary of when I arrived in Zalei, and every worry rose in me, my fears squeezing my chest and making me feel as though I was choking.

I was back to staring at the sunset when Ode whipped her head to the side. "Xander?"

"What is it?" I asked, my heart leaping to my throat at the concern in her voice.

Ode tilted her head, listening carefully, and then her round eyes shot to mine. "They've returned. We need to get down there."

• • • ●•●•● • • •

As we walked into the camp, I knew something was wrong. Usually, when Xander went with the fae warriors to run missions in Zalei the casualties were minimal. When they'd return, we'd honor the fallen before celebrating the return of the party. But as we moved between the glass houses fae were rushing about in a panic. Some were shouting orders, and others were slumping to the ground, crying and consoling one another. Ode chewed her bottom lip, and I tried to calm my racing heart. *What has happened?*

"I thought they'd gone on a peaceful mission?" Ode murmured to me.

"Th-they did," I stuttered. "Xander told me they were going to aid a community in the mountains that has been terrorized by three Sares lions. He said they were just going to help set up some barriers to protect the village. Even Corak insisted on going as she was the most experienced with the beasts."

But as I took in the commotion around me, I knew that somehow the fae king had to be involved in whatever had transpired. Xander had explained to me why the Forgotten Fae fought against the fae monarch, King Chalir. He'd told me of the human king who had murdered the late King Jazrec, and how the former fae princess, Izla, had cursed the humans and turned them into monsters. It had been King Chalir who'd forced the fae army to mobilize and go to Katakin to fight the monsters, even though there had been an outcry from the fae that many wished not to fight the unknown threat and for the portals to Katakin to be closed instead. Corak and the members of the Forgotten fae fought for those who had been forgotten by the kingdom, which now included many of the smaller communities around Zalei who received no help from the royals when they were in need.

A fire fae went to pass us, his armor splattered with grime and blood, and Ode grabbed his arm. "Horax? What's going on?" she squeaked.

The male fae's eyes were vacant when he answered. "We never made it to the village. He was waiting for us."

"He?" Ode pressed. "Are you talking about the king?"

The male's gaze kept shifting like he wasn't sure where to focus, but he nodded. "There was an ambush waiting for us the moment we exited the forest. Seems the king's getting tired of our influence in the kingdom. And Corak." He paused, his face scrunching as he fought against the emotion that was gripping him.

"What about Corak?" I asked.

Horror widened the male's eyes like he was replaying a memory in his head. "They showed no mercy. Sucked her soul away before we could react. Sh-she's gone."

"Gone?" Ode squeaked.

No. I swallowed hard, my heart pounding in my ears. "What about Xander?" When the fae didn't answer right away, I grabbed his shoulders and shook him lightly. "Where are Xander, Ellis, and Nathaniel?"

"The healer," he managed, and it was all we needed to hear. Ode and I released him, and I started running toward the heart of the camp. Rushing to the only house with white panels of glass.

Ellis and Nathaniel were waiting outside, looking as beaten up as the fire fae had. Ode rushed to Ellis, and he grabbed her around the waist, burying his head into her pink hair. The two of them had finally admitted their feelings for one another a year ago, and Ellis held Ode now like he'd been afraid he'd never see her again.

"Xander?" I breathed.

Nathaniel's gaze met mine, and my heart shattered at the pain I saw there. At the defeat. *No. No!*

"Cara," Ode called out as she tried to reach for me, but I pushed past Nathaniel into the building only to find the space occupied with wounded fae and at least a half dozen healers tending to them. *Oh, Mother Falia.*

"Where's Xander?" I blurted to the closest healer, and she pointed with her head to a door down the hall on the opposite side of the room.

"Thank you." I rushed between the cots in the direction she'd indicated. When I reached the door I was after, I paused, taking a moment to steel myself. Was he dead? My throat burned, but I went inside.

Three healers stood bent over a mangled form, and they peered up as I entered.

"You shouldn't be here," one of them chastised, but then I heard the rasping words come from the form on the cot.

"Cara?"

A sob escaped me. *Xander.* "It's me," I said softly.

There was a pause and then Xander rasped, "Everyone out."

"But Xander—" one of the other fae healers began.

"As the new leader of the Eastern camp of the Forgotten Fae, I command you to leave me," Xander ordered.

I sucked in a breath. *The new leader.* The confirmation that Corak had to be dead made my knees weak.

Without another word, the healers filed out of the room and closed the door behind them. I went to Xander's side and kneeled beside his cot. The male was nearly unrecognizable with deep wounds all over his body and scorch marks across his usually handsome face.

"Xan," I whispered, my voice wobbling as I used the nickname he'd told me to call him. Clear blue eyes stared at me, and a tear streamed down my cheek. "You shouldn't have sent the healers away. You need them to fix you up."

His cracked lips bled when he tried to smile. "Fae can heal from many things, but not from this. I've lost too much blood."

"But you're immortal," I protested. "I've seen fae recover from broken legs, and all number of injuries."

He let out a low rattling breath, and I couldn't stop staring at how pale he was. I pressed my fingers to his bloody cheek, jerking my hand back when I found he was ice cold. "Not this," he repeated. "I'm sorry, Cara."

"Sorry?" I sniffed.

"I promised to send you home. If I could have..." Regret shone in his eyes.

I shook my head. "It's not your fault."

He let out another pained breath. "Ode will take care of you. I'm sure she will. And when I'm gone, Ellis will take over as leader."

"Don't worry about me. Not now," I told him, swallowing hard.

"But I do worry," he said quietly. "Ever since we saved you from that bear..."

I smiled softly, remembering how he'd rescued me even when he'd had no idea who I was. "I'm not that same girl," I replied. "It'll take more than a Choram bear to take me down now."

"I know," he said, and his eyes crinkled with pain as he reached up, his hand cupping the side of my face. "Say hello to your sister for me when you find her. If anyone can find a way, it would be you."

At those words, I couldn't stop the tears. Ode had become a dear friend, helping me adapt to everyday life with the fae, but it had been Xander who'd shown me the true beauty of Zalei. Who'd trained me so I could survive in the forest and who'd given me a deep understanding of their ways. It was Xander who'd checked on me every night when he wasn't away, and who'd shielded me from the curiosity of the fae when I'd first arrived. It was Xander who made me shiver every time he touched me, and who made my heart feel like it would burst every time he smiled. I wasn't prepared to lose him. I'd lost my home, my younger sister, my father, and my entire life.

Xander's eyes closed, his chest barely lifting as he struggled to breathe. "Goodbye, Cara."

"No. Xander, no," I whispered, my throat raw. He couldn't die like this. The Forgotten Fae needed him. *I* needed him.

"Tell me what I can do to help you!" I begged, my voice cracking, but he didn't reply. Tears streamed down my face, and I dropped my head as I sobbed, placing my hands on his chest. But as my fingers touched his bare skin, my palms pressed against his chest, power erupted from me. The rush of energy exploded, shooting out and moving through my body until it was flowing into Xander. I gasped at the jolt of power, and then I could feel everything he could. Every wound, the pain, the weakness, the agony. I whimpered as I took it all and gave him a piece of myself in return. I wasn't sure how much time passed, but suddenly strong hands were shaking me, and the pain had subsided. I sagged, feeling as though I'd run half the forest, but then I was staring into Xander's vivid blue eyes.

"What did you do?" he said, his voice no longer weak, but strong and deep, and full of concern.

My gaze tracked over the smooth skin of his face and over his muscled chest that was still marred with blood but without a gash or burn mark to be seen. "How?" I asked.

He smiled, and his lips were no longer cracked and bloody but full and luscious, and *healed*. "You saved me," he replied in astonishment as he stared at his healed hands and arms. "No other healer in Zalei would have been able to do that. No other *fae* can do that."

"I-it can't have been me," I said shaking my head. "I'm only human." I was a nobody, but even as I said the words, I could feel my power slowly building again, strengthening me. Something bright caught my eye, and I peered down to where a gem the size of my fingertip and in the shape of a diamond had formed on my wrist. The sparkling blue was the same distinct color as Xander's eyes, and I ran my fingers over the smooth stone, surprised to find it was incredibly warm.

Xander gazed at the gem, and then his eyes met mine. He stared at me like I was the most precious thing he'd seen, and he'd ruin worlds to keep me safe. When his lips met mine, it was like stars colliding and new worlds being born. It was warmth, and life, and hope, and as more tears streamed down my cheeks, I gave myself to him. I gifted him my heart, and he promised that we'd find my sister together.

CHAPTER 13

~ **Darian** ~

We traveled through the night and made it to the House of Saceris without encountering any trouble. Lyr's scouts had been watching the movements of the outliers in the city, and by following her strict directions and moving between a series of safehouses, we managed to stay out of sight and avoid the monsters that crossed our path.

Asher nudged me with his arm. "Let us come with you, brother."

We stood beneath a bridge that crossed over the river closest to the House of Saceris, and I'd been lost in thought as I stared at the glowing water. Patterns of blue reflected on Asher's concerned face, and I forced my lips upward into a smile.

"Not this time," I replied simply, unable to push the thought of Cordelia from my mind. When I'd caught my siren lover conspiring against me all those decades ago, I could have bent her to my will or killed her, but instead, I'd let the conniving female have what she desired. To become alpha of the high house. After the sudden death of our last alpha, I had been the strongest candidate to succeed him. But I had finally seen the house for what it was, and I no longer wanted a part in it. Still, even then when I'd discovered Cordelia was bedding my so-called friend, Hersondal, and planning against me, even when my heart had been torn out leaving a chasm inside me, Cordelia had been surprised and disappointed when I'd announced I was leaving the house. Oh, another monster might not have noticed, but I'd seen that flitting expression of shock and the way her lips had thinned before she'd regained her composure. It was probably the only time I'd ever truly seen her. Possibly, she'd hoped that she'd have both Hersondal and me at her beck and call. I didn't dare believe that it was because she had any genuine feelings for me.

But whether she did or not, I was the best equipped to appeal to the sirens of the House of Saceris. If Asher or any of my other brothers went in there, the sirens would likely entrance them to be their little puppets before they could even plead a case for the rebels. And Raine... Oh, I'd kill them all if they tried to hurt her.

"I don't want you to have to face them alone," my lovely dragon said, her fierce gaze watching me.

I took her hands in mine and pressed a kiss to her fingers. She hadn't said much as we'd made our way through the city, but from the way she kept fidgeting with the hilts of her blades, I knew she was worried for me.

"If you were to join me, I fear the outcome would be less than desirable for the sirens. No, I'll be back before you even realize I'm gone," I reassured her.

She looked like she wanted to protest, but Kade spoke first. "I hate this as much as you do, Mahare, but the sirens don't play well with outsiders. If Darian's to have any hope of getting through to them, he needs to do this alone."

Raine clamped her lips together and let out a puff of smoke from her nose.

"If I had my way, we wouldn't be here at all," I said quietly as I pulled her against me and rested my chin on the top of her head. "But we need the sirens to join the fight."

"You said yourself, the sirens would have simply allied with the more powerful side," she replied. "What makes you think you can trust them, even if they do agree?"

"Trust them?" I laughed. "Well now, no one said anything about that, lovely, but if they're going to listen to anyone, unfortunately, it's probably me. If I can sow enough seeds of doubt about the alliance with Warrick, it might be enough to force Cordelia's hand."

"And if they try to capture Darian and hand him over to Warrick, that's when we come in," Asher added with a grin, rolling his shoulders and bouncing on the spot like he was excited at the thought of having to bust into the sirens' house.

Kade grunted his agreement, his tense muscles bunched as he scanned the water flowing beside us.

"I wouldn't put it past Cordelia to try and imprison you," Locke added, his hood pulled low over his face. "That bitch is still bitter you left her. It might not even be to hand you over to Warrick but for her own purposes."

Raine frowned, a possessive growl rumbling deep within her. "If she tries to keep him, I'm going to roast her ass," she said seriously, pulling back to stare up at my face.

I very much enjoyed the thought of her doing just that to Cordelia. The siren alpha may have prided herself on her ability to weave her webs behind closed doors, but I had no doubt Raine would burn through it all if she wanted.

"As much as I would love to see that," I said with a sensual smile, "I don't think Cordelia would be stupid enough to try and imprison me. There's a reason I was going to become the alpha of the high house."

Raine grinned at that, but her smile soon fell as sunlight began streaming through the surrounding buildings, announcing the dawn of a new day. The sound of dozens of sirens beginning to sing in harmony carried on the air, and I turned my head to the rushing water of the river. "But now, it looks like it's my time to shine," I said reluctantly as I pulled away from my sweet Raine. Taking off my weapons, I stripped until I was standing completely naked.

Raine openly admired me, biting her bottom lip as she grinned, and I had to fight hard not to damn the sirens and drag her against me. After Cordelia's betrayal, I never thought my heart would heal, but what I felt for Raine was beyond what I had with the siren. I took a deep breath, trying to calm myself. The last thing I wanted was for Cordelia to think my desire was for her.

"If I'm not back in an hour, you'll know what that means," I said to my brothers.

Asher flexed his muscles. "We know."

"Try not to be late," Locke warned, his eyes turning black.

With that, I startled Raine with a kiss that left her breathless and dived into the river.

· · · ● · ● ● · · ·

The moment I was submerged, my body shifted taking on my siren form, and I moved powerfully through the water, my long fishtail making the swim nearly effortless. I smiled, enjoying the way the cool water glided along my scales. Sweet Toros, it had been too long since I'd been in the water. But there hadn't been time, and now wasn't the opportune moment either.

Leaving my arms by my sides, I shot through the river until I was beneath the House of Saceris. In the center of the house was a great garden and an opening to the river, and I peered up at where light shone on the surface of the water. The song of the sirens vibrated down to me making my heart yearn, and I took a moment to compose myself. Then with a flick of my tail, I swam toward the female who'd tried to destroy me.

When my head broke the surface, I let instinct take over and began singing. It had been too long since I'd sung the song of the sirens. My first notes were clumsy, the lyrics fuzzy in my memory, but soon my voice was perfectly blending in with the others, lifting the melody and adding a depth to the song that had been missing since I'd left the house. More than one voice weakened and wavered as I appeared in the middle of the House of Saceris, but despite their obvious surprise, none of the sirens dared ruin this. They kept singing, their voices strengthening as they became accustomed again to my sound, my rich tenor now leading the song. Power rippled in the air as the blue water glowed bright around us, and every siren in the house trained their attention on me as they sang, spurred to sing louder by the energy humming in the air. By *my* energy that compelled them to take notice. It would have been so easy. Too easy to unleash my power and bend them to my will, but I wasn't there for that.

I eyed the sirens sitting with their tails draped over stones and touching the water around the great garden, the sunlight shining through the glass panels above us making the plants glisten. I'd imagined being back in the garden countless times over the years. Despite all that happened there, deep in my heart I longed for the days when I'd sing surrounded by the members of my house, being fawned over by females and males alike, and leading them in song. My little garden in the mountain had been my own personal paradise, but it was nothing compared to the grand beauty of the garden in the House of Saceris. With the river flowing beneath, and the expanse of greenery throughout the space, it was an oasis in the city. No one else dared to enter the house from the water beneath, so it was not an entrance they defended strongly. And it was supposed to be *my* oasis. That is, until Cordelia had taken it from me.

As the song reached the final chorus, I finally allowed myself to set eyes upon the female who had betrayed me all those years ago. Cordelia sat on the grass beneath the shade of a large palm tree, her long golden hair covering her naked breasts and her coral-colored fishtail only just touching the surface of the water. She narrowed her eyes a fraction as she stared at me, the only indication that she was irritated by my unexpected presence. Undoubtedly, she'd spin the situation to make it seem as if she had invited me. The alternative was that she'd try to imprison me like my brothers had suggested, but of all the sirens present, she was the one who truly understood the strength of my power. No, I didn't think the female would dare.

Three males sang beside her, each of them touching Cordelia in some way, but it was the largest male with the moss-green tail who tightened his possessive grip on her as he openly glared in my direction. I smiled at the male who'd conspired with my lover against me. The male who I had once thought was a close friend. *Hersondal.*

Cordelia smirked and slid her hand lower on his chest, all while watching me as if she'd decided my presence could be advantageous to her, and she was excited to see how I'd react. I'd thought it would hurt more to see them together like this in the position I had once dreamed of for myself. The brief times when I'd seen Cordelia over the years had usually resulted in me drinking myself to oblivion and finding a monster to fuck while Asher kept me sane.

But this time I felt nothing but contempt as I stared at Cordelia and her mate. Instead, my heart thought only of my lovely little dragon who waited for me beyond these walls, and my brothers who had seen me through my darker times. No, the longer I stared at the sirens, the more I realized I wasn't the same Darian who had walked the halls of this house, laughing and enjoying the pleasures that it withheld.

As the song came to an end, I curled my lips into a smile, showing no concern as Cordelia gestured to the sirens around the pool, and a group of them formed a half circle behind me, claws extending from their fingers. I believe their intent was to intimidate me, but I simply waited patiently as if I were part of an audience content to see the performance finish.

"Darian," Cordelia said, her hypnotic voice filling the silence, "what a pleasant surprise it is to have you join us. Especially during these times of," she waved her hand in the air before finishing with, "uncertainty."

"I'm glad you welcome my presence," I replied, giving the crowd my most charming smile.

"Of course," Cordelia crooned. "We sirens pride ourselves on our hospitality."

She was baiting me, I knew, but my smile didn't waver. "That's good to hear because I come bearing a message. One which you would do well not to ignore."

Her eyes tightened. "And what message would that be?"

The sirens all watched me, enraptured by the conversation.

I took a deep breath. "I ask you to join the Katakin rebels. To lend your power to those who are fighting against Warrick and his tyranny."

"What?" Cordelia looked aghast. "You can't be serious?"

"I wouldn't be here, otherwise," I replied, finally letting my smile fall.

Cordelia stared at me for a long moment, and then she let out peals of laughter. Many of the sirens laughed with her, but others remained silent as they watched intently.

"Oh, my dear Darian," Cordelia said when her laughter tapered off, "you of all monsters should know better than to come here with such a ridiculous request. You can't honestly expect us to leave the comforts of our house to join the monsters who are currently being hunted by Warrick's beasts."

"You know of the attacks?" I asked, my composure evaporating as I clenched my jaw.

Cordelia's eyes flashed like she was enjoying herself. "Of course, I do. It's not exactly a secret that Losak and his shifters were driven from their house."

"Then you know the threat Warrick poses to us all," I replied. "There's no life for the sirens, or for any of the monsters while Warrick controls this city."

"So far, the only ones without a life are the monsters who have chosen the losing side," Cordelia countered.

I shook my head in disbelief at her ignorance. "We need to unite and rid ourselves of Warrick and his outliers, so we can have balance again between us."

"Balance?" Cordelia laughed bitterly. "Says the male who left our house in the face of defeat and found a way to ignore the council's rules and remain free from ties."

I saw it then. The hurt in her coral eyes, but I couldn't feel sympathy for the female who took everything from me, including her own love.

"Defeat?" I chuckled darkly. "You may have these sirens fooled into believing you wield the power to lead them, but what happens when you can no longer serve Warrick and he sends the outliers your way? You are no alpha."

"You dare show such blatant disrespect," Hersondal spat, starting to slide further into the water as if he was intent on fighting for his mate's honor, but Cordelia tightened her grip on his muscled arm. Hersondal stilled, his surprised gaze going to her, but Cordelia didn't take her attention off me.

She gritted her teeth. "Come now, my love," she told Hersondal. "I presume he said that in jest. I think we can excuse our guest this one time. He's clearly forgotten our ways, and my strength." As she said the last part, the half-ring of sirens behind me shifted closer. Lifting her chin higher she said, "As the rightful alpha to the House of Saceris, the sirens know I have their best interests at heart."

I almost coughed when she said the words "rightful alpha," but I swallowed down the urge. "Is that so?" I countered. "Because I remember when the sirens were both feared and revered in Katakin, and the House of Saceris was one of the most powerful high houses in the city. I never thought it would weaken and ally with an enemy of our kind."

Anger flashed in Cordelia's eyes, and she pursed her lips, but she didn't release Hersondal's arm. "You speak of allying with the rebels as if it is the answer to all our problems. You are not the alpha of this house, and I cannot expect you to understand my actions. I have no desire to place us on the losing side. It is not my fault if the other houses in Katakin aren't able to see sense as I can."

"Hmm..." I hummed thoughtfully. "Or could it be that the other houses aren't solely focused on self-preservation as you are? They know Warrick won't settle on destroying the fae. He'll use this city as his own personal laboratory and you're the animals willingly walking into his cells. I have seen what he's capable of, and if you remain oblivious in this house, delusional in your thinking that you're safe as long as you abide by his rules, you'll see what happens when he decides you're no longer helping to fulfill his purpose. This house is no more a haven than a building made of paper would be. It'll burn just as easily as the rest of the city."

"Tell that to Losak and his shifters who sided with the rebels," she hissed.

I sighed, knowing nothing I said was going to get through to her. "That's the thing about this house," I mused with a sad smile. "All anyone cares about is themselves, and all you speak is lies and deceit, and yet, you expect harmony." I stared at the faces around the garden. "When Warrick turns on the House of Saceris, they'll see you for the pitiful siren that you are. All whispered secrets and empty promises. They'll understand the truth when they're bleeding beside you."

Cordelia's face paled, her grip loosening on Hersondal's arm, and her mate roared. "That's enough! Take him."

Instantly, the half circle of sirens closed around me, and two burly males grabbed hold of my arms, pulling them tight behind my back.

"If you won't see sense about Warrick, think of the fae. Is this truly who you want leading you when you're facing the fae's army?" I called out. "A siren who needs her mate to speak up for her?"

The sirens held me tight, but I didn't miss the uncertainty in the gazes around the room. Gasps and murmured whispers erupted, and I smirked.

"The fae haven't attacked with their full force since those early days," Cordelia said indignantly, though her face remained a shade paler than usual. "Warrick has assured us that his outliers will be going to the fae realm to neutralize them."

"No," I said shaking my head, strands of my silver hair flicking around my eyes. "War *is* coming, Warrick has ensured that, and he has no idea just what the fae will bring. All the vampire is doing is weakening us before the real threat gets here."

"Shut him up," Hersondal ordered, and one of the sirens to my right smashed his fist into my jaw. I licked the blood that bloomed on my lip, and Cordelia tracked the movement, her hungry gaze trained on me despite the trace of fear my words had brought to her eyes.

Hersondal glowered as he puffed out his chest and glided through the water toward me. "Giving you to Warrick will be almost as satisfying as it has been to watch you drink yourself to the bottom of the social ladder," he sneered.

I eyed the sirens around me, no longer interested in conversing with the male who clearly couldn't even satisfy his own mate. Many of those who were once my friends were unable to meet my eye. "Whether you believe me or not, have a hard think about what side you are on," I said, projecting my voice so everyone could hear. "Whether it be the fae or Warrick's outliers, neither care for your politics and lies. Right now, you have a choice, and the rebels need the sirens on their side. With the sirens, we stand a chance at surviving what's to come. But if you choose to stay on this path, when you're staring down the Devil of Death, just remember that you're the ones who made the choice."

Hersondal growled as he lunged for me, but before he could attack, my song began filling the air, entrancing the entire house. A shudder went through me as power rippled in the air, and I thought of the only other time I'd done this. It had been in the nights after I'd discovered Cordelia and Hersondal. I'd entranced them all to prove to myself and them that I was right to be outraged. That not one of them could match me. Even Hersondal who'd boasted that his power surpassed mine had been entranced by my song, but as I'd stared into their faces, I'd understood that they'd never truly be loyal. So I'd released them and left the house. Now, I did it to remind them that in a world of monsters and at a time of war, it was only magical and physical power that mattered.

Hersondal was the last to fall silent, his hands lifting into the air as if he was about to try and cover his ears like one of the human newbloods, but before he could his eyes glazed over, and all of the sirens turned their mindless attention to me. My notes didn't falter as I moved away from the males who'd loosened their grips on me in their confusion, and I dived into the water.

The sirens swam after me, clambering to follow in my wake, but they were too slow. By the time I was deep in the river and had lost sight of them, I stopped singing and allowed myself to glide through the water at a leisurely pace.

The last time I had left the House of Saceris I'd been a shell of the siren I once was, ruined by the actions of Cordelia and the other sirens, and the realization that my perfect world and my house was nothing but lies.

But this time as the water slid over my scales and I left the place I'd called home so long ago, I felt peace. I'd tried to get the sirens to do the right thing, but now it was up to them.

When my head burst above the water, my silver strands sticking to my neck, four intense gazes fixed on my face. I lifted myself from the river and padded onto the stony platform beneath the bridge.

"Thank the devils, Dar, we were about to march over there and let Raine incinerate that siren bitch and her friends for tryin' to imprison you," Asher said, grinning broadly at me. The demon was holding his axes, and he looked as if he was more intent on getting his weapons bloody than letting our lovely dragon have all the fun.

My lips curved into a smile, and I turned my attention to the others. Locke and Kade watched me calmly, waiting for me to divulge what had happened during my encounter with the sirens, but Raine looked agitated like she really had been close to breaking into my old house.

I raised a brow, amusement making my lips twitch. "I'm guessing Ash wasn't entirely joking when he spoke about unleashing your beast on the sirens?" I surmised.

She gave me a weak smile, and within two strides she was before me, her arms winding around my neck as she pulled me closer to her and planted her lips on mine. Instinctively, my hands slid behind her back, pressing her hard against my chest as I surrendered to the demand of her touch. No, I had no regrets as I left the House of Saceris behind me. All I needed were my brothers, and my delectable Raine in my arms.

When she finally pulled away, her face flush, and my need making me want to drag her into the water, her words came out breathy. "I needed that," she panted. "If you monsters keep running off, I might not be able to stop myself next time."

As the image of Raine's dragon crashing through the House of Saceris to save me from the sirens appeared in my mind, my cock hardened even more. Oh, I wouldn't have minded if the little female had remained human, but now that she was a dragon shifter, it was a relief knowing I didn't have to worry as much about her. And I'd be lying if I said I didn't enjoy her new possessive nature. Perhaps I should have stayed long enough with the sirens that the dragon did come after me. Raine had already shown she could break free from my power, so resisting those of my brethren should have been no issue. Seeing that we had her on our side may have helped to persuade them to join the rebels.

Kade tossed my clothes at me unexpectedly, launching the ball of cloth into my chest, and I caught my garments before they could fall to the ground.

"Get that look off your face," the wolf shifter growled as if he'd understood where my thoughts had just gone, and he wholeheartedly disapproved of the idea of Raine being anywhere near the sirens.

I smiled innocently as I began to dress.

"Did Cordelia see reason?" Locke asked, his arms folded across his chest. "Will the sirens join us?"

I hated having to be the one to deliver the news, though not one of them looked hopeful. I pulled on my shirt and replied, "I warned you that the sirens wouldn't change sides easily. I tried to point out how allying with the rebels would leave them in a more desirable position, but it's hard to know whether my words had any effect. I fear Cordelia is more likely to divulge my efforts to Warrick than she is to take my warning to heart."

"You did what you could," Asher said, finally sliding his axes into his belt. "If the sirens choose to sell their souls to the devil, there's nothing we can do about it."

He was right, of course, but despite feeling joyful that I was free of the house and all it held, there was still a part of me that felt responsible for them. A part that wished I could have made them see reason.

CHAPTER 14

~ Raine ~

Darian's hair dried as we made our way through the city, his sheet of silver strands gleaming like silk under the warm sun. No one had spoken as we made our way down the streets, picking our way between the buildings, and avoiding the few outliers that were prowling the streets in the daylight. Every now and then we'd pass a space where a house had been raised to the ground or a wall had been destroyed leaving the building leaning toward rubble, and I didn't need to ask the others to know what had happened. Warrick's outliers were making a mess of the city.

It wasn't until we'd made it past the last outskirts of the city and entered the forest that I felt as though I could breathe easily again. Darian and Asher walked on either side of me while Kade scouted ahead, and Locke walked behind, his cloak pulled low and his dark gaze alert and watchful. I turned my attention to the side, observing Darian's face. He'd seemed relaxed when he'd returned from the House of Saceris, but I knew it couldn't have been easy for him. Dealing with Cordelia, his ex-lover, had to be hard enough, but I still remembered what he'd told me that day when he'd taken me to his private garden in the mountain. There was a part of him that longed to be with his own kind. With the sirens. I tried not to think about how that thought made my gut twist.

Waiting while my siren had visited his old house alone had been hard, and my inner dragon had damn near forced me to shift and hunt after him. It wasn't until he was before me again, and I was sure he was unharmed, that I managed to calm myself. It was a good thing too because if Cordelia had hurt him, my dragon instincts would have forced me to visit the House of Saceris after all.

"What will happen if Cordelia and the sirens don't decide to join the rebels?" I asked quietly.

"The sirens won't fight us," Darian answered, turning his head my way. "Not unless Warrick forces them to."

I wasn't surprised by his answer. From what I'd learned about the sirens, they cared about perfection and beauty. Violence, however, wasn't high on their list.

"And what are the chances that Nic has convinced Mabel and the high house of Shadows to join?" I asked hopefully.

"Low," Asher answered bluntly. "But don't worry sweetheart, we'll get you through this."

I gave him a sly look. "You mean, my dragon will protect you."

He grinned. "As long as you're incineratin' the fae or the outliers, I'll happily watch."

I frowned then as I pictured myself in my dragon form tearing apart the fae. No one had spoken about the fact I was part fae, and I wasn't sure how they felt about it. So far, they'd acted the same toward me, but how was I to know that they wouldn't wake one day and detest me as well? My heart squeezed.

Asher stopped and spun me toward him. "Hey. I didn't mean it like that."

"You did," I replied sadly. "But I don't blame you for it. You've been enemies with the fae since the curse was created."

He lifted my chin and ran his thumb along my jaw. "But we were friends with the fae once. King Adrien's the one who ruined that, and we have him back at the camp. This doesn't change who you are. And it doesn't change that you're ours."

Theirs. A puff of smoke left my mouth and went into Asher's face as my chest eased again, and Asher coughed.

"Fuck, sorry," I said, fanning the air to try and make the smoke disappear as Darian laughed. *Damn dragon.*

In Asher's moment of distraction, Darian pulled me toward him instead. "Don't apologize, lovely. We happen to adore your dragon. And contrary to what you might think, after our recent visit to the fae realm I don't hate the fae either."

"They tried to kill us," I pointed out, while my inner dragon preened at the praise.

"They did," Darian agreed, but Prince Azaren also showed us how this all truly is King Adrien's fault. If it weren't for him, we might still be living harmoniously, and all this talk of war would be nonexistent."

Asher crowded my other side and draped his arm over my shoulders. "Dar's right, Sharachi."

I cleared my throat, trying not to become overwhelmed by what they were saying. It wasn't until that moment that I realized how worried I must have been about the fact I had fae blood in me. As I went to ask more about our intentions with the fae, Kade stopped abruptly, his furry ears twitching as he turned his attention to the left. The rest of us did the same, Asher's hands flying to the axes at his sides, and Darian reaching for the stars across his chest. I strained my hearing, trying to pick up what Kade had identified. The steady thud of a heartbeat and the soft pad of feet sounded in my ears.

"I hear it," Locke muttered, his wings flaring behind him like he was preparing to launch into the air.

"Stay here and keep Raine safe," Kade growled to Asher and Darian. "We'll check it out."

Oh, hell the fuck no. I'd had to deal with Locke leaving to help the gargoyles, and just now Darian facing Cordelia and her pod of venomous sirens alone. I wasn't going to be staying behind this time.

Before anyone could stop me, I'd moved away from Darian and Asher, and I was shifting. My clothes tore and fell to the ground as my body grew, scales bursting from my skin as my dragon took over, my chest expanding and my large claws digging into the dirt. My dragon shook its head, enjoying the sense of freedom after being caged for so long. For a moment, all I could do was stare like a prisoner in my own mind, controlled by my animalistic instincts as my dragon roared, but then I remembered what Kade had taught me. That I needed to accept my dragon was a part of me now. Taking a mental breath, I calmed my mind and tried to see the situation for what it was. I was still me, just a larger, much scalier, extremely frustrated version of me. It took a few long moments, but slowly I cooled my fury, and before long, I was in control as I blinked large eyes, staring at the world around me that was now colored in shades of green.

And then I was charging forward. The flapping of wings sounded to my right, but I didn't need to turn my head to know my vampire was flying beside me as I trampled bushes and pushed past trees. To my right, Kade ran in his wolf form, his shaggy body faster than my dragon on the ground, and Asher and Darian were somewhere behind us.

I already knew I was going to hear about this later, but I didn't care. The wind was magic as it brushed against my scales, and power rippled through my muscles making another satisfied roar burst from me.

Blue flames shot from my mouth incinerating a decayed tree that had fallen long ago, and I enjoyed the taste of smoke on my tongue.

The individual that we'd detected moved further away from us, the pitiful creature likely startled by my roars, but they were within sight in a matter of seconds.

The fae scout stared with wide eyes as the five of us burst from the trees, entering the clearing, but he didn't stop what he was doing. His hands moved through the air as he whispered something to himself, and a ring of blue fire appeared before him.

All right, Raine, you can do this. Don't burn the innocent fae. We just want to talk to him.

I opened my massive maw as I ran, intent on snatching him away from the portal rather than devouring him, but he slipped through before we could reach him, the ring of fire disappearing a moment later.

Fuck. I dug my talons into the dirt, tearing up the grass as I came to an abrupt halt right where the portal had been. Kade circled us, sniffing the air as if he was trying to detect if there were any other fae around, and Locke's onyx eyes fixed on me as he folded his wings.

Kade shifted back, naked as he stalked toward me, and Asher and Darian sheathed their weapons.

"Guessin' Raine didn't like your idea to keep her behind again," Asher commented, giving Kade a lop-sided grin.

I wasn't surprised he was all cheery about it. Like me, Asher had hated waiting while Darian had gone to talk to the sirens without us.

Kade's golden eyes remained on me, and I got the distinct feeling he was trying to anticipate my next move. Luckily for him, now that I had more control, and my creature had identified them as my mates, I'd do anything to protect them, even while in this form. But I still wasn't entirely sure what would happen next.

"We need to get back to Lyr and the camp. If the fae are sending scouts, things are moving much faster than we anticipated," Locke said, though he was watching me as carefully as the others.

It didn't escape my notice that they'd circled me now, almost as if they thought I was a threat. Not that I blamed them.

I flicked my tail playfully, and Asher moved back just enough that it avoided smacking into his chest. My demon grinned, his lips twisting as he eyed me like he was about to grab hold. *Oh, just you try...*

"Are you ready to go, lovely?" Darian asked me with an amused smile.

I snorted out smoke. I was definitely *not* ready to shift back again just yet. If I couldn't capture the fae, and I couldn't mark my mates, I needed to do something else.

"In the early days when I was getting used to my wolf form, I'd get times like these," Kade growled, his deep voice making my dragon want to grab him and haul his ass back to that cave we'd been in not too long ago. "My creature demanded release, so I'd have to either fight, fuck or..." Kade said.

"I'll stop you right there," Darian said holding up a finger. "I don't know if you've noticed this, but none of us happen to have a dragon form."

"Or run," Kade finished, ignoring the siren. "In her case, I'd say flying would work best, but we can't afford to draw more attention than we already have. Run with me, Mahare. Run until the trees thicken and your beast is soothed by the burn in her limbs."

I blinked, still hung up on his second suggestion, but as Kade shifted back to his animal form, his majestic brown wolf sprinting into the trees, I didn't hesitate to follow him. And as my paws pounded on the ground, my muscles stretching and contracting with my movements, I knew Kade had been right. I longed to stretch out my wings, to feel the frigid air above the clouds, but for now, this would have to do.

This time, Kade didn't keep pace with me. He ran ahead just enough that I could always glimpse his furry tail and his back paws as if he were goading me to move faster. I relished the challenge, careful not to knock down the trees at my sides and create more of a disturbance in the forest. My head was just shorter than the tallest branches, and with any luck, the monsters that were sleeping the day away hadn't been awoken by my antics.

We ran for a good while, Locke, Asher, and Darian following behind us until my legs began to burn. Flying, I suspected, I would be able to do for a significant time without tiring, but my large body was heavy, and eventually, I slowed, smoke puffing from my mouth as I panted. Kade noticed I'd fallen back, and he curved around, coming to stop by my side as he stared at me again with those golden eyes. I knew what he was waiting for, and this time, my dragon side didn't fight it.

The change happened quickly, my body shrinking and shifting until I was in my human form, covered in sweat and dirt, and completely butt-naked. Kade followed my lead, changing back as quickly as I had, and I beamed up at him.

"Thanks," I gasped, my chest still heaving. "I needed that."

He nodded. "Like I said: fight, fuck, or run."

Right. I sure hoped next time we'd get to go with the second option.

CHAPTER 15

~ **Raine** ~

Back at Lyr's underground hideout, the mood was bleak. After our arrival, we'd only had time to dress before Lyr had announced an urgent meeting. Surrounded by the alphas and higher members from the different houses, Nic had explained that he hadn't been able to convince Mabel, alpha of the high house of shadows to join us. Darian couldn't confirm whether Cordelia and the sirens had been swayed, but he made it clear there was a strong possibility they'd remain allied to Warrick, and Locke sharing news of a fae scout being present in the forest wasn't well received.

As soon as the meeting ended and the monsters disbanded, I went with my mates to one of the massive training rooms. Honestly, I would have preferred to head toward the washroom, but the tension during the council had been high, and it seemed wrong to be bathing after talking about the impending war.

I grunted as my fist landed in Kade's open palm. I was starting to learn how to use some of my monster abilities while still in my human form, and Kade let out a grunt of his own, fur rippling over his hand and disappearing again as he absorbed the strong hit.

"Good," my wolf growled, and I grinned. "But you need to stop holding back," he added.

My brows lowered as I readjusted my stance. "If I do that, you won't have a hand left for me to punch," I said matter-of-factly, though Kade didn't so much as smile at the comment.

His shoulders remained tense as he faced me, and I knew he wasn't just on edge because of the meeting we'd come from. All around the room, the monsters were watching us as they trained, some being more subtle about it than others. The fact that we'd been the ones to see the fae scout hadn't worked in our favor given the rumors that had circled about us siding with the fae, and there had been more than one snide comment suggesting we'd purposely let the fae go. When I'd gone to point out that it was my fault as I went after the fae in my dragon form without really understanding the situation, Locke had been quick to cut me off.

Now as Kade and I trained, Asher, Darian, and Locke were busy sharpening their blades close by, but it was clear they were also keeping guard.

I was still lost in thought when Kade's chest pressed against mine, his intoxicating scent filling my nose as he leaned toward my face. "Don't worry about me. My wolf can take it."

I bit my lip, remembering what Lyr had said about me being the only dragon shifter to have existed. "But what if you can't?" I asked, genuinely concerned. I didn't even know what I could do, so how were they supposed to know?

A low possessive growl rumbled from his chest, and his breath puffed on my face. Speaking so quietly only I could hear him, he growled, "I don't care what the fae prince said about the protection curse binding us to you, you're my mate and my feelings haven't changed now that you're a shifter as well. My wolf wouldn't still be intent on claiming you if I couldn't handle you. Now," he said, his voice becoming louder again. "Show me what damage you can do, because when we go to war, I need to know that you're going to be able to tear through those outliers and face off the fae. I need to know you won't hesitate."

I swallowed, my thoughts again going to my sister and my fae heritage.

"Kade's right," Asher agreed, striding toward us. "When you're on the battlefield, we need to know you'll be able to hold your own, no matter who you're facin'. It won't be like fightin' the newbloods."

I hated all the talk of war, but I knew they were right. If the fae didn't accept our offer of peace, we'd have to fight, and I wasn't going to stay behind while my monsters walked into battle. I appreciated that they never once asked me to either. As much as I still liked the idea of grabbing my monsters and hoarding them away in some hidden cave, we couldn't run from this, and I needed to know what I was capable of.

"Well, well, I suppose at least you're preparing her for the war you created," said a masculine voice.

We all turned to where Quinn stood a few feet away with a sneering Cassar by his side. Locke was beside me before I could blink, and Kade moved closer to me, lifting to his full height. Asher gripped tighter onto his axes, and Darian slid all of his stars back into his belt except one and stood watching the scene unfold from behind us.

"Move along, shifters," Locke warned, his black claws extending from his fingertips. "We all need to train, and we've already explained we're not responsible for the war."

Quinn cut his pink gaze to my vampire, and I didn't like the calculated glint in his eyes. "Oh, we understand perfectly. Even if your little pet here isn't a spy and you haven't sided with the fae, it's your father who tortured the fae prince and created the outliers. For all we know, you were aware of his intentions to take over the city this whole time."

Lock's expression remained passive, the vampire not showing an ounce of emotion at his words. "Careful. I could take your heads before you've even shifted."

Quinn glared, and Cassar bared his teeth as tusks grew from between his lips.

"As fast as you are, you can't fight all of us," Cassar jeered. Like his words were some kind of silent command, the shifters from the House of Silat stopped sparring with one another and began to form up behind Quinn and Cassar. *Great. Well, this is just what we need.*

It was so fucking stupid. We were at war with the fae. We didn't have time to be killing each other.

"We saved your lives," I blurted incredulously. "When you were going mad from the poison in your veins, *we* helped you. We're not spies or accomplices, or whatever the hell else you think we are."

"Oh no, you're supposedly a dragon shifter who's going to be a great weapon to have on our side," Cassar mocked. "So far, I haven't seen anything to make me believe this. Everything bad that's happened has been since your arrival in Katakin, and I don't think it's a coincidence. Unlike some of the other monsters, I never thought you were a sign the curse would be lifted. I always knew you were a sign of something much more sinister. And to think, Losak had offered you a place in our house."

I frowned, entirely pissed off and tired of the situation. Didn't they know we had more important things like a *war* to plan for? I didn't like where this conversation was headed, and I definitely did *not* appreciate how the shifters were circling in on us like we were their next prey.

"Clearly, you're delusional, perhaps a side-effect from the poison, but I'll say this one last time," Darian said calmly, spinning the star in his fingers as he stepped up to Locke's side. "Turn around before you no longer can."

Quinn only smiled, his body beginning to shift as he attacked. In an instant, his clothes fell to the ground and white fur sprouted over his skin as his nose stretched into a fanged snout. Following his lead, Cassar and the other shifters did the same, some of them falling onto all fours as their bodies twisted and remolded into their monstrous forms.

I didn't bother trying to hold back my dragon as she roared internally in response to the threat to my males. Flicking my head back, I gave in to my creature, changing into the freaking badass monster I was. My large, scaled body pushed Locke and Kade to the side, my huge maw snatching up the white fox as it leaped into the air, its claws outstretched toward my demon. *Oh no you don't, you fucker.*

Cassar squealed, and I turned my head to see Locke slam the massive boar to the ground. Kade's fist slammed into the side of a bear shifter's head, and Darian's star lanced across an attacking leopard-shifter's eyes, momentarily blinding her.

The remaining shifters halted, no longer looking sure of themselves as they watched us through their creatures' eyes.

Quinn struggled, held firmly between my teeth, and I glared at the shifters as I tossed the fox to the side. I'd meant to throw him a few feet, but I underestimated my strength, and the fox flew to the opposite side of the training room and smacked into the wall before falling in a crumpled heap to the ground. *Oops.* A crack sounded as he landed, and I tried not to think about how satisfying the sound was. *Goddess, I've turned into a psycho.*

A shifter in the form of some massive gray animal with a huge, curved horn moved to my left, and before I could stop myself, I instinctually opened my mouth and roared. As I did so, heat bubbled in my belly and a stream of fire shot out across the space. The shifter dropped into a crouch, and the fire seared the air above his head, incinerating the hair off his small tail, and burning a large hole in the wall leaving an opening into the next training room. *Make that double oops.*

There was a commotion in the room next door, and the moment the fire stopped, two gargoyles peeked their heads through the hole. Their stony jaws slackened when they glimpsed me, and I breathed in, appreciating the scent of charcoal in the air.

I roared again, managing to keep back the fire this time, and the monsters around me winced at the noise. I didn't care for these insignificant creatures. All I cared about was my mates. I turned my head, my huge eyes taking in where Darian and Asher stood by my sides, and Kade and Locke stood beside a bleeding Cassar.

Asher stared up at me, his axes resting on his shoulders and a wide grin splitting his face. "Well now, sweetheart, next time you're goin' to have to learn to share."

I puffed a breath on his face in response, surrounding him in a cloud of smoke that dissipated quickly.

"You wanted to know the truth, and now you do," Darian said, stepping forward a few paces so he could see all of the monsters around the room. None of them took their attention from me. "Our lovely Raine is indeed a dragon shifter, and it just so happens that she's as intolerant of your bullshit as the rest of us. So, I suggest you get back to training and be grateful we're on your side because when we go up against the fae and the outliers you'll be glad we're standing next to you." When he finished speaking, an unspoken challenge glinted dangerously in his blue eyes as he twirled another star in his fingers.

A male who had turned into a bull huffed, but before I could think about roasting him, he began shifting until he was standing naked in his human form. Following his lead, the rest of the shifters did the same, changing back to their human forms. Cassar was the last to change, and he remained bleeding on the floor as he glared at us through his one eye that was swollen shut.

Kade rolled his shoulders as if he was trying to stop himself from shifting, and when he spoke his words came out more wolf than human. "The next monster to whisper untruths about Raine or any of my brothers will regret they ever opened their mouth."

Asher started stroking the scales of my neck, and instinctively I curled my tail around him and pulled him closer.

Despite the fact I was showing my demon affection, the shifters continued to watch us warily.

"What's going on here?" A male voice hissed, and I turned my attention to the doorway on our left, where Losak was entering the room beside Lyr and Dean. Lyr smiled, her eyes shining with approval as she admired my dragon form, but Losak shook with rage as he took in Cassar, Quinn, and the rest of his naked shifters.

"The members of the House of Silat were throwing around wild accusations," Darian answered primly, "and Raine was gracious enough to give them a taste of what she could do."

Lyr turned to the hole burned into the wall, and Dean raised his brows in surprise.

Losak turned his attention to me, his eyes becoming reptilian slits as he took in the four red horns protruding from my head, and the glittering gems that stretched along my scaled chest.

When he didn't speak, Locke added, "Keep your shifters in line, alpha, or you'll need to find yourself another second."

"Whatever they said, I assure you, I have no interest in fighting any of you," Losak finally hissed, addressing my vampire. Then he turned to Quinn and the others. "Shifters, go cool off elsewhere. We have a war to prepare for!" He paused, and then added, "And take Cassar and Quinn to get patched up."

The monsters jolted into action, a few shifters scrambling forward to help Cassar and Quinn limp from the room, while the rest filed through the doorway like they were keen to get away from me and my mates as quickly as possible.

"Well, I can see you've been having fun," Lyr mused as she sauntered closer with Dean by her side. I snarled, reminding her that she was not to touch any of my monsters. While her body remained relaxed, her eyes were alert as she analyzed me, like she was ready to react if I made any sudden movements.

Understanding that the tiger shifter wanted to talk, I focused hard, forcing my dragon back until I was shifting and again in human form. Asher looked forlorn that I was no longer wrapped around him, but he pulled his shirt over his head and held it out to me. I smiled but shook my head with a laugh. I wasn't about to yank the sweaty fabric over my head no matter how good it smelled. Instead, I rested a hand on a hip, not caring that I was completely naked.

I opened my mouth to finally disagree with Lyr's comment, but I closed it again when I realized she was right. It *had* been fun messing with the shifters, and after the incident with the fae scout, it'd been just the outlet my dragon needed. As if she could read my thoughts, Lyr's lips curved higher.

"Losak, you need to get your shifters under control, or the battle will be over before it's even started," Kade growled.

"He's right," Lyr agreed. "Without the House of Saceris and the House of Shadows, we're short on warriors. We can't afford to be fighting each other."

"I'll handle it," Losak replied. "Quinn and Cassar are still upset our house was attacked. Both of them lost friends to the outliers. We all did. But I'll make sure they're reminded that we need to be united. It'll take time."

"Time isn't something we have," Locke said coldly. "The presence of a fae scout proves just how serious the fae are. For all we know they could arrive any day now."

Lyr tapped her chin with her finger. "We need to capture Warrick, so we have him when the fae arrive. I still don't think King Adrien will be enough for them to accept peace. If we give the fae Warrick as well, and explain he was the one who tortured Prince Azaren, it might just be enough."

Asher scratched the back of his neck. "Yeah, does anyone actually think that'll work?"

"It has to," Lyr replied. "It's our only chance."

"And how exactly are any of us going to capture Warrick when he has an army of outliers at his disposal," Darian commented.

"I've been tracking his patterns when I can," Lyr said. "From what I've heard, he's planning to hold a meeting with the Taratun council tomorrow. They're gathering in the mountain."

"The council?" Kade growled in surprise. "I thought Warrick would have silenced them given his control over the city."

"No," Locke said, his expression hard. "Warrick will want to keep the Taratun council appeased for now. If only to enjoy their support."

"Right, so he's goin' to the mountain," Asher said. "That doesn't answer the question of how we grab him without triggering his monster beasts."

"We'd also need to neutralize him," I added.

Asher nodded. "Yeah, and that."

"Warrick won't be expecting an attack during the meeting, and it's possible he'll have fewer outliers with him in the confined tunnels," Lyr theorized. "As for neutralizing him, well that I haven't figured out yet."

"How did you entomb King Adrien?" Kade asked.

"That was through trial and error," Dean replied. "Some monsters have different weaknesses, and we discovered that a tomb made of stone, the very material he now consists of, was the only thing that would be able to contain him."

"Then we sealed the lid with magic," Lyr chirped, using an enchanted object we *borrowed* from the royal vault.

We gaped at the pair of them, in surprise.

"So again, how are we goin' to—" Asher began.

"Warrick's lab," Locke answered thoughtfully.

We all fell silent and waited for him to continue.

"We can visit Warrick's lab first," Locke went on. "When I would capture the outliers for Warrick, he'd provide me with a gray powder that he'd created in the lab. When inhaled, it makes the creatures unconscious. There may be more powder back at the lab, and we can use it on Warrick and any outliers he has acting as his security."

"So I'm guessin' that means you've just volunteered us for the job," Asher commented with a grin, looking pleased with the development.

"Yes, we'll bring Warrick in," Locke confirmed, his gaze darkening like he wished to do much more than simply capture his father.

CHAPTER 16

Four years ago

Xander ran his fingers lazily along my bare arm and kissed my shoulder. I smiled, all too ready to enjoy his company again, but as he pressed close the scratch of leather against my skin had me tilting my head back to look at him. *No.* "It can't be time already," I whispered.

He was fully clothed, his fighting leathers fitted tightly to his form, and his weapons belt already secured around his waist. I must have still been sleeping when he'd risen and dressed, and I peered at the watery light streaming through the window of our shared home. Xander had called his house *ours* for the past year, but whenever he was gone, I still went back to staying with Ode, preferring to be in the company of the pixie rather than in the empty glass structure.

Leaning down, Xander pressed a quick kiss to my lips. "You know I need to go. We've been through this."

He was right, but that didn't make it any easier. "I don't understand why I can't come with you. At least if someone gets hurt, I can help them right away."

"You are too precious to be out there with us," he murmured as he kissed beneath my ear, and despite the way my core clenched at the anticipation for more, I was still annoyed.

"I want to help," I protested.

He responded by clamping his teeth onto my earlobe drawing a gasp out of me.

"And you will. When we return," he replied, and I closed my eyes, focusing on his touch.

As the years passed and I'd remained trapped in Zalei, I'd come to accept my place with the Forgotten Fae. With my healing power, I now helped the seriously wounded when the Forgotten Fae soldiers returned from their battles with the king's soldiers. It felt good to be useful.

But I was now twenty-two, and it was only four years until Raine would have to participate in the Night of the Offering and stand in the line up before the monsters. Xander still hadn't found a way to send me home, and while I'd been able to tell myself that Raine was safe for the time being, lately I'd started wondering more about my powers and what it meant for my sister. When my magic had presented, Xander had explained that I must be part fae. It was the only explanation for what I could do, but I had no idea how it could be true. And if it was, did that mean my sister had powers, too? If the monsters who visited my island were the same ones who slaughtered the fae all those years ago, what would they do to Raine if they found out she had fae blood in her? I thought about bringing Raine and my father to live in Zalei amongst the fae. Perhaps this was where we belonged? Raine had always talked about wanting adventure.

Xander had assured me that there were tomes in the royal library that detailed all about portals and other worlds. That one day he'd get his hands on the books so he could help me find my way back to my island. But the battles with the king were becoming more vicious, and more of the Forgotten Fae were returning grievously wounded. I needed to keep Xander safe, and not just to save myself from a broken heart. If Xander died, he'd never be able to fulfill his promise to me.

Xander claimed my lips as his hand lifted to squeeze my breast, and I moaned into his mouth. "Please Xan," I pleaded when our lips parted. "Let me come with you."

But he didn't reply as he took my lips again and slid his hand lower.

· · · · · ● · ● · · · ·

"We can't," Ode hissed with wide eyes, pacing across the grass. We were alone in the forest, just outside the Forgotten Fae camp, and I was pretty sure no one had seen us leave. Xander and his select group of warriors had gone through a portal two hours prior, and I stood, my single knife bulging in my pocket.

"Please, Ode," I begged. "Every time the warriors go out on a new mission, they return with more serious wounds than they did the last time. The king is fighting back hard, and I need to be there to make sure Xander, Ellis, and the others don't get themselves killed."

Ode chewed her bottom lip. I knew it wasn't fair of me to bring Ellis into my argument, but it worked to sway Ode's mind. Besides, I'd grown rather fond of Xander's younger brother. If he was in danger, I would do everything I could to save him.

She let out a frustrated noise. "Fine, but if Xander asks, this was all your idea."

"It *was* all my idea," I pointed out to her with a grin, and she smiled back at me. In spite of what she'd just said, I already knew that no matter what happened, she wouldn't let me take the blame on my own, even though I wanted to.

"Do you know where they went?" I asked. All Xander had told me was that they were going to a small village further to the north where a group of the king's elite soldiers were said to have made camp. Apparently, Xander had received word that the soldiers were mistreating the village folk.

Ode bobbed her head. "I do, but it's been a long time since I've had to create a portal."

"Just take your time," I said giving her a reassuring smile. "You can do this."

She didn't look convinced, but she turned around and closed her eyes, blowing out a steadying breath. "All righty, a portal. Sure, I can do a portal. Easy peasy like pumpkin pie." She fluttered her wings, and shook her body, bouncing on her toes.

Pumpkin pie? The more she rambled, the more I began to second-guess my whole idea of following after Xander, but as Ode moved her arms in the air a large ring of blue fire began to materialize. When the circle of fire was large enough for us to step through, Ode snapped her eyes open, and squealed, giving me an ecstatic grin. "I did it!" she squeaked. "I didn't think I still had it in me, but whoa!"

I grinned, stepping up beside her. "If anyone could do it, I knew it would be you."

She beamed at me, but her smile soon fell. "You sure about this Cara? Xander never lets us go on any of the missions. Especially not you. If anything bad were to happen..."

She trailed off, and I grabbed her hand. "Nothing bad is going to happen to me. I'm a healer, remember? But you don't need to come. I'll pretend someone else made the portal."

She raised a brow. "Right, because Xander would believe that."

"He might," I defended.

"Nope. If you're doing this, I'm coming with you."

I squeezed her hand tighter, knowing there was no point in arguing. "Okay then. You ready?"

"No," she said, but she stepped into the portal with me.

• • • • • • • • • •

I don't know what I expected exactly. Maybe that we'd find ourselves standing in a village with dilapidated wooden cottages, dirt roads, and simply dressed villagers like back on my island. In hindsight, given my time with the fae, I probably should have known better.

I stood gaping at the tall glass houses on either side of us, the buildings even more elegant and colorful than the structures back at the Forgotten Fae camp. Flowers and greenery sprouted everywhere, including between some of the polished stones on the cobblestone road, and the air smelled like burnt toffee and spice.

"Where are we?" I asked Ode who was peering around, looking just as dazed as I felt.

"This is the village Qurea, home to the largest library outside of the Royal Palace."

I frowned, entirely confused by her statement. "A library? Is that why the king's elite soldiers are here? Is it something to do with the books?"

"I'm not sure," Ode replied. "All I know is that in the last few months, Xander has been talking about needing to get his hands on some rare texts. Ellis says he keeps ranting about it, almost like it's an obsession."

Texts? My heart began to race as I remembered Xander's promise to find a book about portals and the different worlds. Had he discovered the book he needed wasn't in the royal library but out here instead? Was Xander here because of me? Maybe there weren't even any soldiers.

"Look!" Ode said as she pointed above the buildings, and I lifted my gaze to where a trail of smoke had risen into the sky. Shouts and cries carried on the wind, and I took off running, fearful for the lives of the Forgotten Fae. Ode fluttered her wings, flying just above the rooftops and directing me through the maze of streets until we reached the heart of the village.

"What in the name of Falia?" I gasped as Ode dropped down beside me. On the opposite end of the village square, a massive structure burned, flames licking at the glass, and the roof close to collapsing. A symbol showing a stack of books hung just above the huge double-doors of the building, so I guessed it was the library. But there weren't any of the king's soldiers around, and Xander stood before the building with the Forgotten Fae warriors, watching calmly as the library was destroyed. *Something's not right.*

A group of fae I didn't recognize kneeled just in front of the doors of the building, their robes torn and dirty as they cried and wailed, staring in horror as the flames rose higher.

"We should go," Ode breathed, a hint of fear in her voice, but I was already jogging toward the Forgotten Fae.

"Xander!" I called out as I crossed the square, my boots slapping on the polished cobblestones.

He turned toward me in surprise. "Cara? What are you doing here?" His gaze went to Ode who was a few paces behind me. "You can't be here. You need to go back."

"What's happened?" I asked, gesturing to the library. "Did the king's soldiers do this?" I peered around, but I still couldn't see anyone resembling the king's elite. A strange emotion I couldn't place flashed across Xander's face before it was gone again, and I frowned.

"Please," a female sobbed from close by. Her face was covered in soot like she'd run from the fire, and she shuffled on her knees closer to Xander's boots. "I beg you, please stop this. We told you. We don't know where the books are. We don't know anything about curses! If we did, we would give the tomes to you!"

Curses? It took me a moment to register what the female had said, but slowly realization overcame me, and I stared at Xander in surprise. He wasn't there for a book on portals and other worlds. No, this was something else entirely. I understood then that there also weren't any soldiers coming, and it was possible this mission had nothing to do with the king's elite. Ever since Corak had been killed, Xander had stepped up as the leader of the Forgotten Fae in the Eastern camp, becoming more focused on the fight against the king every day. Still, I couldn't believe he would do this. "Xander," I said softly. "What's going on? No books can be worth this destruction."

Ignoring me, Xander stared at the female with indifference. "My sources say those books are being held here, and they're impervious to heat. You should have told us where they were when you had the chance." He tilted his head to a Forgotten Fae who stood close by, and fire shot out from the fae's hand, racing toward the library and climbing up the glass. The flames consuming the building crackled and popped as they grew larger.

"Stop this!" I shouted.

Xander's expression was hard, his blue eyes emotionless and nothing like the eyes of the male who'd shared my bed not long ago. "I told you to return to the camp," he said coldly.

I gaped, my heart pounding as I turned to the Forgotten Fae warriors. "You can't agree with this!" I said, but they didn't reply as they stood with stony expressions.

The wails of the fae villagers filled my ears, and for a moment I couldn't breathe. Clenching my fists by my sides, I forced myself to suck in a sharp breath. "I-I don't understand," I said, turning my pleading gaze back to Xander. He still didn't reach for me, and simply stood staring at the fire.

In a sudden movement, the double doors of the library burst open, and a tall fae male staggered out with a small boy in his arms. He walked down the steps and collapsed to his knees, cradling the child. Both of their silken robes were covered in ash and grime, the embroidered image of a stack of books only just visible beneath the soot on their chests. But while the tall fae male looked mostly unharmed, the boy was covered in burns, large red welts covering the flesh I could see, and his hair was burned to the scalp. "No!" the older male cried, his arms trembling as he rocked back and forth, tears streaking down his cheeks. "No, no, no!" The child's chest barely moved, and I stifled my own cry as I rushed forward, not giving myself a moment to think.

Startled, the older male simply watched as I dropped beside him and touched one of the boy's arms. Focusing my power, I let it rush out of me and into the fae child as I healed him. "It's all right," I said to the older male, my words a choked whisper as the boy's skin started to smooth, his burn marks becoming healed flesh, and his hair growing longer and becoming soft and silky. The boy's breathing became stronger, and his beautiful brown eyes blinked open as I felt the tell-tale gem forming on the inside of my arm. *Thank the goddess.* I knew it was a gem I would forever be proud of. I smiled, relief coursing through me as I stared at the child who was no longer fighting for his life.

"Father?" The child said, reaching up to rub his eyes as he stared at me in confusion.

The male who was holding the boy let out a strangled cry and sobbed louder as he clutched the child tighter. "Thank you. Oh, bless all the stars, thank you," he said to me, and I couldn't stop the tears rolling down my own cheeks. Letting go of the boy with one hand, the male went to reach for me, but strong arms pulled me backward.

"You shouldn't have done that," Xander's rough voice sounded from behind me, and I let out a startled cry, surprised by the way his fingers dug into my skin.

"Xander, stop!" Ode cried, and I spotted her pink hair in the crowd of Forgotten Fae. Ellis stood holding her back, his face full of regret as he kept her there.

"I don't understand why you're doing this," I said as Xander held me, forcing me to watch the destruction he'd caused. "These aren't the king's soldiers," I said, referring to the fae villagers still cowering on the ground. "You said the Forgotten Fae are there to help those who are in need around the realm. But you're not helping anyone."

Just hours ago, Xander had held me like I was the most precious being in the world, but now, he was acting like an entirely different fae. My heart shattered as a hundred memories flashed through my mind, and I second-guessed everything he'd ever said to me. All those years he'd told me he'd find a way to send me home. Had any of it been real?

"You think you saved that child, but you've only made this harder," Xander whispered in my ear, his voice so cold and so unlike the fae male I'd grown to love. "He can't be allowed to live. None of them can. Not now that they've seen just how valuable you are."

"Xander, please no!" I gasped, struggling against his hold as fear made my heart clench. They were all going to die because of me.

My gaze flicked wildly to the villagers. "You need to run!" I shouted, but none of them moved. Their fearful gazes remained watching the Forgotten Fae warriors.

Xander lifted his hand, ready to let out his magic, but I flung my head back, butting into his chin and startling him. "He's going to kill you! RUN!" I screamed at the villagers, tears filling my vision as the library continued to burn.

This time, they listened. Lifting to their feet, the villagers fled, some of them pushing past the Fae warriors who tried to stop them, and others letting out their own magic in their efforts to get away. It was obvious none of the villagers were overly powerful, but a female fae sent out a blast of wind, blowing back the two Forgotten Fae pursuing her and a few others. Another three villagers were killed as they tried to escape, but the boy I just healed managed to get away with his father, the pair of them fleeing down a street. The tightness in my chest eased a little at the knowledge they'd escaped.

Xander let out an irritated grunt, still gripping me. "Go after them," he ordered a handful of the Forgotten Fae.

The warriors nodded and split up, sprinting past the buildings in pursuit of the villagers.

Xander's lips brushed the side of my temple, and I flinched. "Once I find the books I'm after, you'll understand. Those texts contain ancient knowledge that will give us the ability to create curses. With a weapon that great, we'll be able to defeat the king once and for all. It might not seem like it, but I'm trying to free the realm."

"By burning down buildings and terrorizing the fae just as you said the king has been doing?" I scoffed. "You're right. It doesn't seem like it."

He clenched his jaw. "You'll come to understand. It's not like you have anywhere else to go." At that, he jerked his head toward where Ellis was still holding Ode. She'd become limp in his arms, her eyes red and swollen from the tears she'd shed. "You and Mason take them back," Xander ordered. "We'll return once we've located the books in the rubble."

"Will do," Ellis replied, and Xander pushed me into the arms of a fae male who I presumed was Mason. I should have fought it. Someone needed to be there for the fae villagers, but my chest ached and deep down I knew there was nothing I could do.

"Cara, I didn't know," Ode said beside me as we were led away, but I didn't look at her. It wasn't her fault, but I didn't have the energy to speak.

"Keep quiet," Ellis whispered to us, a trace of fear in his eyes as we turned our backs to the fire. "Don't speak while he can hear you."

Ode pressed her lips together, and we walked until we could no longer hear the crackling flames and shouts of the Forgotten Fae. A numbness settled over me, and I barely registered what was happening as Mason and Ellis led us into a portal, and we found our feet on grass again.

Back at the camp, the forest was quiet, and it wasn't until Ode and I reached the front door of her little house that Ellis turned to Mason. "I've got it from here."

Mason hesitated, eyeing me suspiciously like he expected me to run, but he eventually turned and strode away. Once he was gone, Ode opened the door and led us into the living room of her house.

"What the fuck was that?" she squeaked, spinning around to face us once the door was shut.

In answer, Ellis gently pulled her to him and pressed a kiss to her hair. "You shouldn't have gone there," he replied.

She batted him away, though her expression had softened. "You think? You said Xander was becoming obsessed looking for those books. You didn't tell me that meant he was burning down villages to find them!"

"Xander's changed since Corak was taken," Ellis replied. "The king has taken everything from him. From *us.*"

"But I thought we were the good ones," I said softly, finally managing to speak.

Ode bit her bottom lip. "We are." She elbowed Ellis lightly in the ribs. "Right?"

He didn't speak for a long moment. "Things will be better once we free the fae from the king's rule. You'll see. But you'd both better stay low for a while. Promise me you'll remain here until everything smooths over."

Ode sighed, but she nodded. Ellis turned his attention to me, but I only stared blankly back at him. Giving up on getting a response, he moved toward the door.

When he reached for the doorknob, I called out, "He never intends to send me home, does he?"

Ellis stilled, his shoulders tightening. "You have a rare gift, Cara. And Xander loves you," he replied over his shoulder, then he exited the house, leaving me to fall to my knees.

CHAPTER 17

~ Cara ~

Ode and I stayed inside her house for the next week, with Ode only venturing out to bring us some food. Xander and the Forgotten Fae warriors had returned from the village, but none of them had been injured so they didn't need my healing power. I kept thinking that Xander would search me out. That he'd find me and explain that everything had been one giant mistake. That I hadn't seen what I thought I had. But the days passed, and he never came. The only sign that he'd returned to the camp was the bouquet of wildflowers he left for me on Ode's doorstep every morning. Flowers that I refused to touch.

"He's not someone you want to be around right now," Ellis had explained during one of his visits. "We never found the books, and now that you've seen…" he sighed. "Give Xander time. He'll find you when he's ready. Just know that he's sorry about how everything played out at the village. I'm sure he'll try to make it up to you."

I'd nodded mutely as if I understood, but the truth was, I was glad he hadn't come for me. I wasn't even sure what I'd say when I saw him face-to-face. I was questioning everything he'd ever told me, and with each passing day, the urge for me to run from this place grew stronger. The urge for me to run from *him*.

"I saw Xander in the camp today," Ode said softly as I pushed around the fruit on my plate. "I think Ellis is right. He's not happy about what happened. He was just surprised that we were there and handled it poorly. He said he's going to come by later today to speak with you."

I lifted my gaze from my plate and finally looked over at her. "Speak with me?" My heart squeezed as panic rose up my throat.

"I know what we saw was bad," Ode said with a tight smile, "But Xander has assured me that he wasn't himself that day. I believe him, Cara. He's only doing what he thinks is right for the Forgotten Fae."

As much as I wanted to believe that, I couldn't. I could still feel Xander's fingers digging into my skin as he wrenched me away from the boy I'd saved, and Ellis's words rang in my head: *You have a rare gift, Cara. And Xander loves you.*

No, the only true love I'd felt was from my family. My father who raised me, and my sister, Raine. I had to get back to them, and if I couldn't trust that Xander would help me return to them, I needed to find another way.

Sliding the plate from my lap, I lifted to my feet.

"Cara?" Ode said in surprise, but I didn't explain what I was doing as I moved around the house, collecting a flask of water, wrapping some food in a cloth, and checking my blade was in my pocket. Reaching back, I braided my hair and strode toward the door.

Ode fluttered her wings, making it to the doorknob before I could. "You can't go," she said, her voice wavering and her eyes wide with alarm.

But I was tired of cowering in Ode's house and waiting for Xander to find me. "I have to. You've been a good friend to me Ode, but my family needs me, and if Xander doesn't intend to send me home, I have to find another way."

Her bottom lip wobbled. "What other way?"

"I don't know yet," I admitted. "But I can't stay here. I get it. There's a lot of history between the king and the Forgotten Fae, but after what I saw in that village, I don't want to be any part of it."

Ode blinked, and I knew she was trying to keep back tears. Reaching forward, I crushed her in a hug, struggling to keep down the emotions that threatened to overwhelm me.

"He won't be happy, you know," she whispered. "When he finds out you're gone. I know he messed things up, but I do believe he loves you."

I pulled back and swallowed hard, studying her face. I didn't want to talk about Xander. "You could come with me, you know?"

She shook her head, and I gave her a small smile. I didn't think she'd leave. Reluctantly, she moved away from the door.

"Goodbye, Ode." I said. "Take care of yourself."

Outside the house, a few fae were around, but I tried to blend in as I walked between the buildings and toward one of the barrier boulders which acted as a gateway to the camp. No one noticed as I slipped into the forest.

Years ago, when I'd first arrived in Zalei, I would have had no hope of surviving in the forest, but I wasn't that same girl anymore. I made my way quickly between the trees, careful not to leave tracks or make any sudden noises. Ode had often talked of the fae city that was far south of the camp, so I figured I'd head in that direction. I still had Samson's glamor over me, and now that I knew I was part fae, I wasn't too worried about trying to blend in with the citizens. I'd have to find a way to gain access to the royal library, or perhaps get information out of the scholars there, none of which sounded like an easy task, but maybe I could start by trying to get a job in the palace.

In any case, I first had to get away from Xander and the Forgotten Fae. It wasn't until I'd been walking for a good while that I could finally breathe easily again, and I slowed my pace to something that was more sustainable.

When night fell, I allowed myself to have a short rest and sat with my back to the thick trunk of a tree. Reaching down, I was about to pull out my flask of water, when someone stepped out from the shadows of the trees and lifted a blade to my throat. As if on cue, half a dozen more soldiers stepped into view, their silver armor gleaming in the moonlight, and they spread out in front of me, their weapons pointed in my direction.

I peered up at the male soldier who stood with his blade still pressed against my neck.

"Is this the one?" the soldier called out as if he was speaking to the forest, and as if in response, a gust of wind rushed by us, rustling the leaves of the nearby trees.

I lifted my hands into the air and worked a tremor into my voice. "Please, I-I'm from the city. I became lost in the forest, and I'm just trying to find my way home."

The soldier smiled kindly. "You don't need to lie to me," he said calmly, sheathing his dagger. "We know full well who you are."

My brows slammed down. "You do?"

He gestured with his head to the surrounding soldiers, and they lowered their weapons.

"You're the one who stood up to the Forgotten Fae. They say that the child was near death and somehow you managed to save him. His father keeps raving about you."

I blinked in surprise. "He does?" I cleared my throat, realizing I made a mistake by exposing my power, but also not able to regret having done it. *They managed to get away.*

"From the sounds of it, no other healer would have been able to save him, but you did. You then also helped them escape by the sounds of things. King Chalir is very interested in speaking with you, and when the nymphs said they spotted a fae female of your description traveling through the forest alone, guess who got charged with the job of bringing you in."

"What does he want to speak about?" I asked, unable to hide my fear.

"It's not my job to ask questions," the soldier answered, holding out his hand and helping me to my feet. "But I don't think you have anything to worry about." With that, he stepped away from me and moved his arms, concentrating until a circle of blue fire appeared. "Portals are strictly forbidden, so the king must think you're very special to task me to use one to ensure you make it to the palace."

Forbidden? Xander had never mentioned that using portals was forbidden in Zalei. Was it just another thing he hadn't told me about? My heart hurt as I thought of the fae leader, and I stared at the portal. I needed to go to the palace, but I hadn't thought I'd get there like this. For all I knew, the king could want to imprison or execute me. However, that seemed unlikely if my power was as rare as the soldier said. No, more likely he was hoping to use me.

"Cara, don't!" A male roared, and I spun around to see Xander, Ellis, and two more Forgotten Fae behind us. They burst from the trees, their weapons out as they charged forward. They collided with the royal soldiers, their swords clanging and magic aiding the fight.

I gasped. "Xander?"

The soldier beside me cursed. "Rebel scum." Turning to me, he held out his hand. "We'd better go now, or we might not make it."

I hesitated, my gaze going from Ellis to Xander. Xander's blue eyes flashed with anger as he cut down a soldier and stepped toward me, only to be stopped by another soldier.

"Don't go!" Xander called out to me, his voice strained and eyes wide and afraid. "Please, Cara. I know what you saw looked bad, but you can't trust the king. We need those books, and I wasn't thinking!"

Indecision warred inside me, but I couldn't go back. For years I'd stayed with Xander, hoping he'd find a way to send me home. I gave the fae my heart, and now that it was broken, words weren't enough to fix it. Even if I hadn't been desperate to return to my island, and going to the palace wasn't possibly the only way to get me there, I couldn't stay with the Forgotten Fae. Not now that I'd seen the truth of what happened on their so-called missions.

"Goodbye, Xander," I said softly, and I grabbed the soldier's hand before I could change my mind. He led me into the portal, and Xander's anguished cry was the last thing I heard as I stepped into the blue light.

CHAPTER 18

"It's too quiet," Kade commented as we trekked through the forest, his wolf ears twitching every so often as we moved silently through the trees. "It's almost as if..."

"All of the animals are gone," Locke finished, his body tense.

I noticed it then. The lack of birdsong or the scratching of rodents in the underbrush. The forest was eerily quiet, and dread made my throat dry. "You don't think he's turned all of them into outliers, do you?" I asked quietly. "How would he even capture them all?"

Asher shrugged. "Who the fuck knows. Maybe some of his outliers are good at huntin' and retrieval?"

The thought of outliers capturing animals for Warrick to experiment on creeped me out even more, and a shiver went down my spine. If a single rat could be turned into a terrifying monster, I hated to know what else he'd created in recent nights. He now had control over most of the city. Were there houses filled with his army of monsters?

"You should have stayed back at the camp," Locke said beside me, his steps matching mine.

"And here I thought you were starting to love my company," I quipped back with a smile.

His onyx gaze slid to me, still devoid of amusement. "There is no guarantee any powder remains at the lab. For all we know, Warrick may have gutted the space, and if he detects our presence and captures you…" His expression darkened, rage hardening his features.

My smile became tight. "Then I'll burn his face off." The words came out as a joke, but I was deadly serious. I had no intention of letting the vampire get his hands on me again. I mean, we needed him for the peace offering with the fae, but did King Chalir even know what Warrick looked like? Would it matter if the vampire turned up a little charred?

"Start with his wings instead," Asher said with a chuckle, nudging me from my other side, but Locke still stared at me, his expression livid like he was imagining his father torturing me again.

"Hey," I said, and he finally blinked. "The plan will work. We're going to get that asshole and deliver him to the fae. You don't need to worry about me."

• • • • • • • • •

We made it to the mountain without encountering any monsters. Situated at the base of the massive landform, stood a metal door that was battered and dented as if something or *someone* had crashed through it. Whoever came along after to repair it, obviously hadn't cared enough and did the shittiest job possible.

Asher joked to Kade about him still needing to fix what he broke, but I wasn't listening. I took a deep breath. I hadn't been back to the mountain since the night Warrick's outliers had attacked everyone in the ballroom.

"You all right, lovely?" Darian said beside me, his fingers brushing over my back.

"Never better," I replied with a forced smile. It was hard to believe that I'd once thought the mountain was all there was in Katakin, but that was before I'd seen the sprawling monster city and traveled to a land ruled by the fae. For so long all I'd dreamed about was rescuing Cara and taking her back to our island, but as I stood there with my males, my *monsters*, who'd captured not only me but my heart, I couldn't help but think about how my life on the island seemed so small and sheltered in comparison to the world I now knew.

"You know, those trials we put you through..." Darian began.

"You don't need to apologize for it," I said. In comparison to how Warrick had tortured me, and almost being executed by the fae, the trials hadn't been that bad. I could remember Darian singing to me for the first time, his body pressed against mine. Would I kick his ass if he tried to trick me again? Well, hell yes. But I wasn't going to lose any sleep over what happened. Especially now that I knew they were only doing what they had to. "I'm all right, and we'd better move before someone spots us."

They all shuffled uncomfortably like they wanted to say more, but Kade settled with gesturing toward the door and saying, "If things get bad in there, Raine, you shift and get back to camp."

I stared at him incredulously. I was definitely *not* going to leave without them, but I didn't say anything as he wrenched the door open.

We filed into the tunnel, and the torches on the walls ignited, blue flames lighting up the darkness as our presence was detected. Locke moved to the front of our group, quickly leading us into the depths of the mountain where Warrick's lab was situated. The more the tunnel wound down, the colder the air became, but fire burned in my stomach, warming me from the inside and banishing the chill.

Locke's shoulders relaxed in the darkness, and he led us down one tunnel after another, stopping every so often to listen intently before we rounded a bend.

Before long, we came to a stretch of tunnel I remembered all too well. Rows of thick iron doors lined the tunnel on either side of us, but unlike the last time I'd been there, the cell doors were all wide open. Marks had been gouged into the doors and walls of the cells, and bits of fur and broken bones were scattered along the ground.

"I don't remember it stinkin' this much," Asher groused, scrunching his nose, and I peered into a cell that had a pile of decaying flesh and gnawed bones that reached a few feet off the ground, mixed with animal excrement.

"Yes, it rather reminds me of the time you ate that rotten fruit despite my warning," Darian mused thoughtfully.

"Quiet," Kade growled, his head jerking to the side every so often as he listened for any signs of danger.

As we approached Warrick's office, Locke inspected the opening in the wall that I'd made the last time I was there.

"Huh. I thought they'd have fixed that by now," I commented.

All four of them turned to look at me in surprise.

"What?" I replied innocently. "If Warrick wanted to keep people out, he should have designed it better."

Asher grinned. "And to think we ever believed you were human."

Inside Warrick's office, drawings of outliers were still covering the walls but everything else had been cleared out. The cabinet that had once contained the reports of Warrick's subjects, had been emptied, and the drawers were left open as if Warrick had been in a hurry when he'd taken the files with him.

The lab next door looked much the same, though vials of blood still covered the wooden shelves around the room. The stone slab where I'd found Prince Azaren still held the cuffs I'd helped pry open, and blue blood was covering a portion of the floor like the fae prince had tipped over the bucket of his collected blood in his haste to escape.

Asher whistled as he eyed the drawings on the walls. "Well, this ain't fuckin' creepy at all."

Locke moved quickly, rummaging through a selection of vials on one of the lower shelves until he found a few filled with a distinct gray powder. "We're fucking lucky," he said as he pocketed them.

"Great," Asher said, turning from the drawings. "Now that you've found what we needed, let's go get the asshole."

The rest of us didn't quite share Asher's enthusiasm, but we exited the lab and began making our way up the mountain again. Kade heard noises coming from one of the tunnels we were about to travel up, so we ended up taking a detour. The rocky tunnel opened up to a massive cavern with a large pit in the middle of the space.

"Is that what I think it is?" I asked, stopping to stare down into the massive black hole.

"The Pit of Reask," Darian confirmed.

I paled.

"If you're guessin' the hole we tossed you down when you first arrived here, you'd be right, sweetheart," Asher answered, watching my face.

I scowled, though my expression didn't hold any real menace. "You four really were dicks, you know that, right?"

Darian placed a hand on his chest like he was offended. "In our defense, lovely, I was waiting below to ensure you didn't all drown."

I grinned. "I thought that was you in the water."

"And right you were. We're not barbarians," Darian replied with a devilish smirk.

Asher smiled, baring his teeth. "Speak for yourself."

Looking back down into the black hole, I frowned. "But if that's the pit, it would mean the portal..." My words trailed off as I spotted the ring of blue fire burning close to the edge of the pit on the opposite side of the cavern. I scurried over and stopped close to the portal, my heart racing. My monsters followed.

"I can't believe I'm standing here," I said. There was a time when all I could think about was finding Cara and bringing her to this very spot. But that was before I'd realized how foolish I was being. Before I'd discovered Cara wasn't even in Katakin City, and that she might not even want to leave.

"I'd thought it would be so simple, saving my sister," I murmured, staring at the flames. "That by now we'd be back on my island. I was so stupid."

"No," Darian said, curling his arm around my waist and placing a kiss on my cheek. "If your sister was in the city,

I have no doubt you would have found a way to bring her here."

I leaned into his touch, and my lips twitched. "So...you're saying you wouldn't have stopped me from escaping?"

Asher grinned and gestured to the portal. "If you managed to get through there, nothing could have prevented us from goin' after you. But I'm sure you would have kicked our asses for it."

My smile grew wider, but my expression sobered when I noticed a glowing blue handprint close by on the rocky wall.

"What's this?" I asked, pulling away from Darian and moving to inspect it.

Kade came up beside me. "When Queen Izla cursed this land, her handprint remained from where she infused her power into the rock."

"This actually used to be part of the old treasury in the palace," Darian added.

"Wait, her handprint has been here this whole time?" I said, my brows lifting.

"Like the portal, it appears to be indestructible," Kade replied.

I don't know what compelled me to do it, but before I could stop myself, I reached up, placing my palm on the glowing handprint.

And that's when the world disappeared.

CHAPTER 19

~ Raine ~

The scene blurred into focus, and I stared at my strange surroundings. I appeared to be in some kind of royal vault surrounded by shelves lined with jewels, golden vases, and priceless artifacts. And I wasn't alone...

A tall guard with ebony hair stood with a sword protruding from his shoulder, the blade lodged between the plates of his armor. As the man staggered backward, a male dressed in a golden robe with a crown circling his hair, snarled and lunged for him. From the male's attire, it was obvious he was royalty, either a king or a prince. Before the royal could reach the wounded guard, a female with long white hair darted forward, intercepting him, and the two sprawled to the floor. I gaped in surprise when I recognized the snow-white hair and glittering blue eyes.

Lyr?

"I said, STOP!" someone shouted, and the ground trembled as if in answer. Ancient weapons and treasures toppled from the shelves, clanging as they collided with the stone floor. It took me a moment to realize that I was the one who'd yelled. Well not me, but...I glimpsed my reflection on the golden surface of a vase. I had long beautiful azure-colored hair, a similar shade to Prince Azaren's, delicate features, and small ears that curved into pointed tips.

Holy goddess, am I seeing through Queen Izla's eyes?

"You will not slaughter my people," Queen Izla said to the king, her voice eerily calm. Her gaze softened when she peered at the wounded guard, and then to Lyr who was on her feet again, crouched low in a fighting stance. I couldn't just see through the queen's eyes, I could feel her emotions. Her regret and sadness twisted inside her like barbed wire caging her heart, and then she reached her hand out, her palm pressing against the stone wall beside her. The floor shook more violently, and items continued to fall from the shelves.

I noted Lyr's human form. Great Mother Falia, is she about to create the curse?

"What is this?" the male in the golden robes bellowed, and I understood now that he was likely the king who had ignited the war between the fae and the monsters all those years ago. The king lifted to his feet glaring at Queen Izla as the words tumbled from her lips.

"I curse you, King Adrien, ruler of the human Kingdom of Katakin," she said in a frightening voice that sounded ancient and unnatural. "You will become the monster you so fear my people to be. All portals to my kingdom will close to you, its treasures will be lost, and you shall spend your days unable to die and unable to live. No longer a human, but a walking disease upon this land. Your heart will become stone, as that is what it is."

Where her hand was touching the wall, blue flames ignited, filling the room with blue light. The fire absorbed into the stone, sinking into the mountain, and a separate line of blue fire shot out from her hand, racing along the stone until it reached King Adrien's golden boots.

King Adrien stepped backward in fear, but not before the blue fire had begun to climb up his legs, consuming him until it sunk into his skin, disappearing into his body. I watched in horror as the king convulsed, falling to his knees and screaming as his skin turned the color of ash, and he transformed into a monster made of stone.

"What did you do to me?" King Adrien roared when the transformation was complete.

Queen Izla pulled her hand from the wall as she watched her furious husband. Where her palm had been, a handprint of blue remained. The color dimmed, but before it disappeared entirely, flames shot out from it again, and streams of blue fire speared across the floor in all directions.

"No!" Queen Izla cried as the fire reached the others in the room, and they began to fall and writhe just as the king had.

Queen Izla's frantic gaze went to Lyr. "This wasn't supposed to happen."

The guard who had been wounded let out a pained cry, and Queen Izla ran to him and fell to her knees, pulling his head onto her lap. "Vasken. No, Vasken. This curse wasn't for you," she cried.

"You little fae demon," King Adrien shouted. Turning, he lunged for her.

"Izla," Lyr gasped in warning, but before the queen could move backward, King Adrien's stony arm smashed across her chest, sending her to the floor. She cried out and sniffed, blue blood trailing from her nose.

King Adrien grinned, watching as she slowly rose to her feet, her body trembling, but his smile fell when a circle of burning blue fire appeared behind her. She spared one last regretful glance at Lyr and Vasken, and then with a hand pressed protectively to her abdomen, she stepped backward and into the portal.

• • • ● • ● • ● • • •

Light engulfed my vision, and I drifted in the endless blue as if I were stuck between worlds. *What is this place?* As if in answer, a picture began to materialize in front of me, and I focused on the illustration of a winged beast depicted on the left page of an ancient book. I'd seen the image before, but it took me a moment to realize it was in the book Prince Azaren had in the fae realm. The book he'd had open when he'd implanted information about the curse in my mind.

The image then changed as if I was flipping through the pages of the book, but this time instead of fae text inscribed under each illustration, the symbols shifted, forming into words that I could read.

One of fae, blood so blue,
One who's cursed, but bold and true,
Forgive the past, pay the price,
Surrender to the sacrifice.

The book closed then, and Prince Azaren's voice filled my mind along with the image of his face. He appeared just as he had before the assassin had attacked him, with his neat azure-colored hair and vibrant blue eyes, but there was a severity to his expression that he hadn't had when we'd seen him in person.

Raine, if you're hearing this, you must have found a way to unlock my message as I knew you would. I'll get right to it. By now you should have read the secret to breaking the curse placed over Katakin. While I can't be certain what the words mean, I can only guess that someone with pure fae blood must forgive the monsters for their past transgressions and be willing to give up their life for the monsters, and similarly, a monster must be willing to do the same for the fae. At present, I cannot think of any fae who would be willing to do this, so unfortunately and regretfully, I believe your group may be on a fool's errand.

There was a pause, and I thought the message was over, but then Prince Azaren's voice sounded again.

But there's more. I told you the magic over you was made with love and about protection, and that's true, but I wasn't honest about all I discovered. The four monsters you travel with have been bound to you as part of a protection curse. My aunt has scribbled notes about such a curse in one of her books, and I believe she adapted it so it would be placed on your bloodline rather than an individual. I can only guess that it was intended so that if, for any reason, a member of your bloodline was forced to go to Katakin, their life would be tied to the first monsters they encountered in turn creating monster knights who would protect rather than harm.

And when I say your bloodline... Raine, I believe Queen Izla placed it on her bloodline. There was another pause before the message continued. *And if that's the case, it would mean you have royal ties to the Kingdom of Aestas, Realm of Zalei. It would mean you're possibly a descendant of both my aunt, Queen Izla, and King Adrien, the cursed human king. Even now as I embed this message in your mind, I can feel your power calling to mine. I hadn't understood what it meant the first time I felt it, but now I do. We're family, dear. I couldn't tell you this in front of your monster friends, especially as you all seem quite...attached, but if you're back in Katakin when you hear this, you must find a way to return to Zalei. You are clearly not a full-blooded fae and there is no hope for you to break the curse over Katakin. If you return to Zalei, I can break your bonds with the monsters, and perhaps, I can help you figure this all out.*

· · · ● · ● · ● · · ·

"Raine," Kade's worried voice sounded in my ears as he shook me lightly, and I blinked my eyes open to find all four of my monsters crouched over me.

I coughed, my mouth feeling bone dry, and even though I couldn't hear Prince Azaren's voice anymore, his words echoed in my mind. *Family. Sacrifice.* I already knew I had fae blood, but the idea that I could have royal blood made my stomach churn. Could I be the descendent of King Adrien, the cursed king? I thought of the way Queen Izla had touched her belly in my vision, and my coughing turned to gagging as I fought to keep down the bile rising up my throat. I swallowed, determined to hold it together. I couldn't lose my shit. Not even if I was the descendent of the cruel king.

"Thank the Devil Enzal," Darian commented as I calmed and peered at them. He lifted my hand to his lips and kissed it gently.

"You gave us a fright there, sweetheart," Asher said with a grin, though his face was still a shade paler than usual.

I groaned, and Kade helped me to sit up. It was only then that I noticed my ass wasn't on the cold stone but on the wolf shifter's warm lap.

"What did you see?" Locke asked from my other side, his body rigid and his features taut like he was still concerned for me.

I wrinkled my brow. "How do you know I saw something?"

"You're not the first one to touch Izla's handprint, Mahare," Kade answered with a serious expression. "It calls to all of us, and many have pressed their palms against it over the years. Everyone who does enters some kind of trance. Most say they see visions of nightmares come to life, though some simply pass out and wake a short while later unable to remember anything other than having touched it."

"Asher here has experienced it firsthand," Darian commented.

"He has?" I asked, cutting my gaze to the demon.

Asher shrugged. "I had to know what the fuck everyone kept goin' on about."

Darian shook his head at the demon, but I didn't take my attention from Asher. "And what did you see when you touched it?"

My demon became thoughtful. "There weren't any nightmares if that's what you're wonderin'. But I do remember seeing a burst of color. Come to think of it, it kinda reminded me of the forest in the fae realm. Can't say I remember much more than that. It was years ago, after all."

My brow scrunched as I took in the information.

"So, what did you see, Raine?" Locke prompted.

I stared at the monsters who all had a place in my heart. My mates in every sense of the word, even though we hadn't yet marked one another. I didn't want to keep secrets from them, but would they even believe me? I mean, did *I* even believe it? And if they did, how would they feel about the discovery that I was a descendant of the king who led them into darkness? I was already part fae, telling them that I was also the king's descendant was just...a lot.

"You're not easing our worries here, lovely," Darian said with a small smile when I still didn't speak.

I took a deep breath and went on to tell them of the scene I'd witnessed through Queen Izla's eyes, and then the words Prince Azaren had embedded in my mind describing the way to break the curse. Steeling myself, I was about to tell them the other part of Prince Azaren's message, but Locke cursed and drove his boot into a nearby boulder. The rock careened into the pit, impacting with the wall before shattering into smaller pieces that fell into the darkness below.

"Locke," Kade growled in warning. "We're not meant to be drawing attention to ourselves."

My vampire clenched his fists before turning to us. "No pure-blood fae will ever sacrifice themselves for the monsters."

Darian lifted a finger. "Not yet perhaps, but in time if we can foster the relationship between the fae and the monsters, who knows?"

"Yeah, even I know that's not gonna happen," Asher commented with a skeptical expression.

"Raine, is there something else?" Kade asked, and I blinked my attention away from Asher and turned to my wolf shifter who was watching me carefully.

I bit my lip. "What?"

Kade's golden eyes were attentive. "Was there anything more in the prince's message?"

I peered at where Locke stood with a defeated gleam now in his black eyes. I had intended to tell them everything. To come clean and hope for the best, but now, well I wasn't so sure. As much as I told myself my monsters would understand, I couldn't help but wonder if that was true. Out of all of them, Locke hated being a monster the most. How would he feel if he found out I was of the same bloodline as King Adrien? *No, later. I'll tell them everything, just not right now.* Besides, we were there to capture Warrick. Hearing that extra bit of news would just be another thing playing on their minds. No, it was better to wait. Or at least, that's what I told myself.

I stared at the portal that burned close by. I understood it all now. The queen was pregnant with King Adrien's baby when she'd escaped to my island, and somehow, she'd given birth. *My ancestor.* Did anyone else on my island know about this? Know about *her?* Realizing Kade was still waiting for an answer, I shook my head. "No, sorry. That's all I've got."

He stared at me for a moment longer before he nodded, and his shoulders relaxed. "Well, at least we now know about the curse. Looks like we won't be able to break it."

"So I guess we'd better focus on stopping this war," Darian added grimly.

"The council must be about to convene," Locke muttered. "We'd better go."

CHAPTER 20

~ Locke ~

We can't break the curse. I was going to remain a fucking vampire forever. No pureblood fae would ever sacrifice themselves for us monsters. I wanted to destroy something to release my rage, but I couldn't lose control now.

"Did Lyr say where the council would be meeting?" Raine asked me as we made our way further up the winding tunnels and away from the portal. She had been mostly silent after our discussion about the curse, but I knew she could sense my anger.

I forced myself to let out a long breath. "They have a history of meeting in one of the higher rooms, formed from part of the old castle," I answered. "If they follow tradition, as I suspect they will, I can take us where we may be able to listen in on some of the meeting without being detected."

She nodded, and no one said anything else as I led them through the mountain. Every so often I would stop, carefully listening for the tell-tale sound of a heartbeat or claws scratching stone, but aside from two detours, the mountain appeared to be relatively empty.

When we made it to the tunnel I was after, I led everyone into a small cavern and closed the door behind us. Then I went straight to the opposite wall and pressed my hands against the stone, tapping into the magic of the mountain. I shaped the wall until the rock turned the color of steel, shimmered, and then became clear like glass, allowing us to see what was happening in the adjoining room.

"Holy goddess, can they see us?" Raine said, jumping back as the Taratun council came into view. The members all sat around a large table conversing with one another, and a line of guards stood in a ring against the walls, the golden bands on their biceps contrasting against the blue light from the torches on the walls.

"No," Darian said with a smile. "But we would be wise not to make any loud noises in case they pick up on our close proximity. They are monsters, after all."

I stood staring at the spineless bastards who had turned their backs on their own kind, and Raine and my brothers all took up positions near me, observing the council.

"Wait," Raine said looking thoughtful. "Have you four ever spied on me like this?"

Asher chuckled and draped an arm across her shoulders. "Would you be offended if we hadn't?"

She narrowed her eyes. "Is that a 'yes'?"

Darian waved a hand dismissively. "Not since the beginning. We had to watch all the newbloods undertake the trials."

"Unbelievable," she muttered, but despite her unimpressed expression, she looked like she was trying to restrain a smile. Staring back at the wall, she stretched out her fingers in front of her. "Hold on. Now that I've turned into a monster, does that mean I should be able to do this too?"

Asher shrugged. "Don't see why not."

"Huh."

We all abruptly fell silent as Warrick entered the room, sweeping in like he was a damn king or something. I tensed, my back going ram rod straight as he glided to the head of the table. Two demon dogs trailed after him, and they sat on either side of his chair, their bodies so still they would have looked like statues if it wasn't for their glowing red eyes carefully watching the other members around the table.

I recognized everyone who was there. All members of the Taratun council were in attendance, including my mother Perene. Sitting in the position on Warrick's right, she inspected her painted red nails and leaned back. I wasn't surprised the council members were all so weak they agreed to support Warrick even though by now it must have been painfully clear he had no interest in being an equal member of the council.

"Wait, none of you have actually told me who the council members are," Raine whispered then. "Are they alphas?"

"Many could have been," Kade responded. "In the early days when the monarchy was destroyed and the council was formed, some of Katakin's strongest fought to become members even though it meant they wouldn't be alphas to their own houses. They craved power and believed being a member was an even more desirable position."

"And others found more creative ways to become part of the council," Darian added.

"Ri-ght," Raine said slowly, looking back at the monsters in the next room.

Warrick cleared his throat and took Perene's hand, placing a kiss on her pale skin. "You look stunning as always, my dear."

She smiled as he dropped her hand but didn't reply.

As Warrick turned his attention to the other members around the table, his lips twisted into a dark smile. Some of the monsters blanched and shifted in their seats when he glanced their way.

"Thank you all for coming," Warrick said smoothly, leaning forward in his chair and resting his elbows on the table. "I know your time is valuable, so I won't keep you long. You all know of my intentions to rid ourselves of the vermin who call themselves the fae, but I have called this meeting as I have great news to deliver. It seems we won't have to trouble ourselves by finding a way to enter the fae realm because our enemies are coming to us. Just hours ago, one of my beasts took down a fae scout in the heart of our city."

"Fuck," Asher commented under his breath.

There were quiet gasps and whispered curses around the room, and more than one monster gazed at Perene as if they wanted to speak, but they believed she was the only one who could do so without drawing Warrick's unwanted attention. Perene's throat bobbed. In the past, my mother had been the one leading the discussions during the Taratun council meetings, but now she looked uncertain, like even she didn't want to speak. She wet her lips nervously before peering at Warrick. "We have not seen the fae for quite some time. Is it possible this was an imposter?"

Like he expected the question, Warrick reached into the pocket of his cloak and threw something onto the table. The small medallion gleamed in the dim light, the silver metal and intricate patterns etched into the armored cuff distinctly fae.

More whispers erupted, and Perene stared in horror at the cuff which proved a fae scout had indeed been in Katakin. Straightening, she regained her composure. "But why would the fae choose to attack now? My love, is it possible the soldier acted on his own?"

So, Warrick didn't tell her about the fae prince. I wasn't surprised to hear she knew little of what had happened over the past weeks. Warrick would only tell her and all the council the information he wanted them to know. Admitting that he had captured a fae and had been running experiments on them without the council knowing wasn't something he was likely to divulge.

Warrick cocked his head. "That soldier was following a direct order from his king. As you all know, I have long since believed that if we don't eradicate the fae first they will one day try to take over our world. We've all heard the rumors about my son and his...*friends* going to the fae realm. I think it's safe to assume that the fae were somehow reminded that we are still a threat."

I clenched my fists at my sides, though I shouldn't have expected anything different from the vampire. Blaming me and my brothers for the war was easy for him.

"What an ass," Raine hissed under her breath, and just her voice eased the red that had begun to creep over my vision.

"Has our Locke returned?" Perene asked, looking stricken, but I wasn't delusional enough to think she was truly worried about my well-being.

Warrick peered back at her with black eyes. "Quite so, my dear." I wondered then whether my dear old mother knew that Warrick had tried to end me when his outliers had us cornered in the ballroom. Then again, she'd never cared much when Warrick had harmed me in the past.

Warrick stared at the members around the table again. "After interrogating the fae scout, I discovered that King Chalir of the fae has declared war on Katakin following the attempted assassination of his son, the crown prince. It seems Locke and his friends were quite busy while they were away." His dark smile grew wider like he was proud of me for being the one to reignite the war.

Perene gasped, bringing her hand to her mouth, and there were shocked expressions around the room.

"If the fae attack in full force while our kind is divided, it may not end well," said a minotaur from the other end of the table, the monster clearly unable to keep silent in light of the news. Morlos was one of the oldest members of the council having already been in his seventies when the curse claimed us all. "Years ago, we defeated them in battle because we were able to unite our power against a common foe. Last I heard, the majority of the high houses have sided against you and remain in hiding."

Warrick cut his gaze to the minotaur, his black brows drawing down. He lifted his left hand, and the outlier to the left of his chair began growling, the beast's attention fixed on the council member like it was preparing to attack.

"N-not to offend," Morlos stammered as if he'd just remembered who he was speaking to.

Warrick smiled and lowered his hand, and the beast ceased growling.

"It doesn't matter whether there are some who cannot see my vision," Warrick said calmly, though from the tick in his jaw I was sure it was irritating him that not all of the monsters had fallen to their knees before him. "As you know, I have been preparing us for when we must fight against the fae. My army is now thousands strong and growing every night." I didn't think it could be possible, but the faces around the room paled even further.

"Thousands?" Darian muttered in disbelief.

Warrick continued, "It is of no consequence if the monsters of Katakin are united, as my army will sweep through, ridding us of the fae..." He paused before adding, "and those who wish to see this city fall."

"He's fuckin' talkin' about us and the other rebels," Asher growled, looking like he was ready to smash through the wall and take Warrick down.

"Indeed," Darian agreed with a tense expression.

I moved closer to Raine, unable to help myself now that Warrick had spoken his threat so plainly. Not that it was news. He'd already tried to kill her once, and I would make him pay with his life if the opportunity arose. We needed to keep him in one piece so we could gift him to the fae, but if the fae rejected our offering, I planned to take Warrick out myself.

"Surely, they can still be persuaded," Perene reasoned, giving him a weak smile, but Warrick ignored her.

"The House of Saceris, House of Nesarin, and the House of Faren are with us along with a portion of the lower houses. Our enemies will stand no chance against a force so great." Everyone continued to remain silent, clearly understanding that this was never meant to be a discussion but merely a transfer of information from their new ruler. "Go and prepare yourselves. The scout indicated that the fae army has already mobilized and will likely be here within days. I will call for you when it is time for battle."

"But my love," Perene spluttered, looking as perplexed as many of the members around the table. "You can't expect *us* to fight as well? Isn't this why you created your... your... animals?" she asked indignantly.

Warrick turned to her, his expression dismissive. "We must all fight or we must all die. For too long, this council has merely used its voice to carry out petty punishments in the name of maintaining order. This is our chance to show our power and be at the forefront of our enemies' minds."

More of the council members looked like they wanted to argue, but no one dared to speak as Warrick stared at them all again and lifted to his feet, gliding from the room.

"We need to reach Warrick before he gets to the city," I said quietly. He only appeared to have two outliers with him, and our best chance of capturing him would be before we were anywhere close to his other beasts.

"This has to work, Locke," Kade growled, and from his tense expression I wasn't entirely sure if he was referring to the fact that Raine couldn't be taken again, or the fact that we needed Warrick now more than ever to barter for peace.

A vial of powder was already in my hand, and I rubbed my thumb over the smooth glass until I could feel the cork stopper at the top. "It'll work."

I wasn't surprised my father only had two outliers with him. The council members had all clearly been successfully terrified into submission, and Warrick would have wanted to show that he didn't need a large portion of his outliers around him at all times.

None of the council members looked like they were too eager to leave the room, and I could only guess they were purposely biding their time to make sure Warrick and his outliers were long gone before they started their own journeys back to their houses. Which suited us perfectly.

When I felt as if we'd waited enough time ourselves, I started moving towards the door. As I went to yank on the iron handle, I turned to Raine who was behind me. Before I could speak, she held up her hand and blurted, "If you're about to tell me to hang back save your breath. I'm not going to sit by while you guys do this."

I closed my mouth again because I had been about to say just that. Instead, I nodded once and wrenched the door open.

CHAPTER 21

Days. That's how long Warrick thought it would be before the fae army arrived. We'd already guessed as much after we'd encountered our own fae scout, but we hadn't been able to get any information out of him before he'd disappeared through the portal.

"Well, that wasn't fuckin' good," Asher commented as Locke and Kade led the way through the mountain. Kade had picked up Warrick's scent and the vampire was moving downward quickly.

"We can't let the outliers distract us. If we do, Warrick will be gone before we've even had a chance to take them down," Locke said as he strode ahead of me.

"Those dogs will smell us as soon as we get close," Kade warned. "We'll need to be fast."

Fast? I grimaced. I mean, it made perfect sense. When Locke wanted to, he could move incredibly fast, and I could only imagine that all vampires were the same. But as much as my dragon loved the sky, on land, speed was not exactly my biggest monster strength. Especially not when maneuvering around tight tunnels in a mountain.

"Warrick's getting close to the base of the mountain," Kade said. "If we're going to move, we need to do it now."

Darian pulled me close, pressing a kiss to my lips. When he pulled back, he smiled. "Time to catch a vamp, lovely."

I bit my lip, hating the words that were about to come out of my mouth, but I wasn't going to be the reason Warrick got away. "Yeah, I think you all might need to go on ahead. I'll, uh, catch up."

"I'll carry you," Asher offered with a grin, but I scrunched my face. "Just get the vamp. I'll be right behind you."

My monsters all shared a reluctant look.

"I don't like this." Darian commented.

Kade's furry ears twitched, and he growled, "Neither do I, but if we don't go now, we might lose him. You sure you'll be right behind us?" He stared at me with his golden eyes, and I smiled reassuringly.

"Yep."

As if that was the final push they needed, they all glanced at me one last time before sprinting away.

• • • •• • •• • • •

My monsters were out of sight within seconds, and I rolled my shoulders, ready to race after them. *Maybe I'm underestimating myself, and I'll get there in time to see Warrick be incapacitated?* Truthfully, I hadn't tested to see how fast I could run now that I was a shifter but considering how fast my dragon moved while on four feet, I wasn't holding my breath. I was willing to bet that my dragon enjoyed being able to roast things so they couldn't run away before eating them. Why run when you can shoot fire across a room?

I was about to lunge forward when my back prickled with awareness. I spun around, my alert gaze taking in the flickering shadows behind me. If I'd still been human, I was sure I wouldn't have noticed the slender female slinking in the darkness some distance away. Undoubtedly, she'd waited until Locke and the others were gone before coming closer. *Just my luck.* I was suddenly regretting my decision not to let Asher carry me.

"Perene," I whispered under my breath, and the vampire smiled before moving incredibly fast and coming to stand in front of me. Her black hair remained in a perfectly styled bun, and I had to wonder how she managed to move so fast without looking like she'd just had a romp in the sheets.

"So, the rumors are true," she purred, one hand resting on her bony hip, and her long red nails vibrant against the black fabric of her ankle-length dress. "Our unusual newblood has finally turned into a monster." Her eyes shone with confidence, making her seem like an entirely different monster than the one we'd seen speaking during the Taratun council meeting.

I glared at her, remembering how she'd threatened me the last time we'd spoken during the Week of Orash. If she was about to warn me again to stay away from her son, she was about to be sorely disappointed. "What do you want?" I asked, glowering at her as my creature snarled internally. Something told me the vampire wouldn't look so confident when my dragon was staring her down, and the urge to shift made my skin itch.

Like she could read my thoughts, she lifted her hands in a placating gesture. "Please relax. I'm only here to talk. From the sounds of things, I would be a fool to attack you. What had they called you..." She tapped a finger against her temple, "a dragon?"

From the way she was speaking and analyzing my movements, I got the distinct feeling she was fishing for information. Like she didn't quite believe the rumors about what I was, and she was hoping to find out for herself. It was yet another display that Warrick wasn't telling the council everything he knew. If he had, she'd know exactly what I was and what I could do. I wondered whether it was in part because he didn't want the council to know the rebels had such a big weapon on their side. Not that I was trying to get a big head or anything, but my dragon *was* physically large.

"If you want to talk, spit it out," I said coldly, not about to just give information away freely, and entirely irritated that this conversation was keeping me from going after my monsters. For all I knew, Warrick had more outliers around than we thought and things had gone horribly wrong. I tried to remind myself that Locke and the others could take care of themselves, but just the thought had a puff of smoke trailing from my nose.

Like seeing the smoke was the sign Perene had been hoping for, her lips curled into a smile. "Well, that *is* new," she commented like she was delighted, and I was simply another newblood she wanted to train.

A low growl slipped from me, and her smile wavered. "Talk, Perene," I repeated, not in the mood to stand around if all she wanted to do was ogle me.

She waved her hand in the air, though she was watching me carefully. "Oh, I just want to confirm that you are indeed still with my son and that the rumors about your new abilities are true."

"What? Why would you ask me that?" Perene had already made it clear that she believed the vampire newblood, Lana, would be a more suitable mate for her son.

Her gaze darted around the tunnel like she wanted to make sure it was still all clear before she spoke. "Oh, well my darling Warrick has always had his way of seeing things. The vampire is a visionary and it's why I love him, but lately things have been...tense." Her smile fell, but as if she realized she'd let her guard down, she beamed at me again.

I raised a brow, entirely surprised by the conversation.

"Well, come now, Raine." She said my name like we were friends rather than enemies, or at best, acquaintances. "Surely you can understand. I may be a monster, but I am a mother. Warrick tries to be a good father, but even I can admit he went too far by trying to kill our son. From what I hear, you saved Locke then, and with your new...abilities, I'm hoping you may be just what Locke needs. It's obvious you care for him, and he must care for you or he wouldn't be staying with you like he has been, *despite* me trying to set him up with a more suitable match."

I bristled.

"But if the pair of you are going to insist on being together, the least you can do is persuade Locke to sit out on the coming battle," Perene continued to prattle. "Take him into the mountains somewhere until the war is over. In the meantime, I'm sure I can convince Warrick to let you all back into the city. And when the war is over and you and Locke have had your fun, my son can finally take over the House of Nesarin and select a suitable mate. After all, the rules do say you must only mate with a monster from your house and one who is of the same kind."

I gaped, unable to believe what I was hearing, and she went on.

"I know you five listened in on the council meeting. And if you were paying attention, you now know that when the war begins it's not only the fae who will be obliterated. You heard him, my husband has thousands in his new army. If you fight against Warrick you will all die, and for what? The fae deserve to be defeated. I know my son doesn't wish to ally himself to his father, but in time, he'll see it was the right choice."

Anger had fire bubbling in my belly, and I was finally able to overcome my shock enough to speak. "You say this like you care what happens to Locke. Your husband is a maniac who tortured children. He even conducted experiments on his own son! We won't ever side with him."

Perene looked taken aback, but she powered on. "Warrick loves Locky in his own way, and so do I." She looked like she was about to say more, but she promptly pressed her lips together and cocked her head like she was listening to something. I strained my ears, hoping to pick up on whatever she'd heard, but she turned her attention to me again. "If you want the best for Locke, you'll think about what I said." Then before I could answer, she was gone.

I wasn't sure what had spooked her, but I didn't waste time as I started sprinting for my mates, desperately hoping that I'd find them with an unconscious vampire and that they weren't wounded or worse.

Don't think about it Raine, just run. By the goddess, for Warrick's sake I hoped they were all right.

CHAPTER 22

~ **Kade** ~

Leaving my Mahare while we went to capture Warrick wasn't ideal, but we had one shot to get the bastard and I wasn't about to let him get away. I'd always detested the cruel monster, but after what he did to Raine, I was looking forward to sinking my fangs into his neck.

Matching his speed to the rest of us, Locke kept pace so we could attack as a unit. My vampire brother kept his hand clenched, a dose of powder in his grasp. We had one chance to render Warrick unconscious. If it didn't go as planned and Warrick was able to call on more of his outliers, we were fucked.

We rounded a bend, my paws scratching on the stone, and Warrick and his beasts came into view. The outliers detected us first, snarling as they launched at us, but we were ready.

Locke and I darted around the beasts, going straight for Warrick, while Darian and Asher went for the creatures. Locke reached Warrick first, but Warrick swung out his arm sending Locke flying into the tunnel wall. Before Warrick could retreat, I clamped my teeth onto his leg, and he fell as I dragged him backward.

Warrick reached up, his clawed hand positioned to strike my head, but Locke appeared beside me and blew gray powder into the male's face. The older vampire's eyes fluttered shut instantly, and he fell hard to the ground.

I released Warrick's leg and paced around him, watching as the vampire's breathing became steady. The urge to make him *permanently* incapacitated made me snarl and slaver.

A howl pierced the air, and I turned my head to see one of the outliers calling for its brethren before Asher silenced it for good. A moment later, answering howls came from somewhere beyond the mountain, and I knew that wasn't a good sign.

Darian and Asher strode toward us, their chests heaving, and blades drenched in blood. Asher hoisted Warrick onto his shoulder, and we sprinted back up the mountain the way we'd come.

We were halfway up when we ran into a red-faced, panting Raine. She stopped when she spotted us and let out a relieved sigh, but before she could say anything Locke lifted her into his arms, and we continued without slowing our pace.

My ears twitched as the howling became louder, and it was clear there were more outliers in the mountain.

"Is that what I think it is?" Raine asked as the tunnels blurred by, but none of us answered as we followed Locke to one of the training rooms and onto a balcony. It was one of the larger platforms, with a long-curved railing, but I had no clue whether it would be big enough for Raine.

Locke stretched out his wings, looking like he wanted to keep Raine in his arms and launch into the air, but he didn't. His muscles rippled as he set her on her feet.

"The outliers are coming," he told Raine bluntly. "If I could carry you all I would."

She bounced on the balls of her feet. "Not to worry, I've got this." Cracking her neck, she let out a long breath, and then her body was shifting and growing in size until her dragon occupied the majority of the balcony, pushing us to the side.

Locke took Warrick, and I changed back into my human form and climbed onto her back behind Darian and Asher. More howls rang out, and Locke didn't waste time. He flapped his wings, rising into the air with Warrick in his grasp. The balcony groaned, the railing twisting as Raine's talons hooked onto the metal and she pushed off, her massive wings spreading as she followed after him.

We dipped, falling closer to the ground before rising again, her head angled toward the sky. Her scales were warm against my bare skin, and I held on tightly as we lifted higher.

More howls erupted from behind us, and I peered back as the outliers came into view, dozens of the beasts swarming onto the balcony. Two of the creatures slid on the stone, unable to slow their movements and pitching over the edge of the balcony through the gap Raine created when she destroyed the railing. The remainder of the outliers howled and snapped, watching with red eyes as we headed toward the sun, their paws scrabbling on the stone.

CHAPTER 23

I fought against the instinct to arc around and burn the monsters howling on the balcony. The monsters who dared to think they could hurt me and my mates. Fire burned in my belly, and I was about to change direction when Asher began stroking me appreciatively, his hands brushing along the scales of my neck.

"Damn, they're so smooth," my demon murmured like he was completely oblivious to the threat that was behind us. I wasn't sure if he had intentionally tried to distract me, but it was enough that I blinked, my focus going back to Locke who flew ahead of me.

Huffing out smoke, I banished the outliers from my mind as I followed my vampire high into the clouds before we came down again, careening toward the ground quickly until we were below the forest canopy and landing on the ground.

Kade, Asher, and Darian jumped from my back, but I stayed in my dragon form, not ready to shift back into my human form just yet. If Warrick somehow regained consciousness, I wanted to be ready to take him down.

"We'll walk from here," Locke said from beside me. "That way we hopefully won't accidentally lead anyone to the location of the hideout."

At that, we started forward, making our way through the trees.

"Well, I'd say that went rather well," Darian commented as he smoothed his hair, tying it back into a neat ponytail.

Kade grunted like he was still in wolf mode, and Asher grinned. "I gotta say, I doubted we could pull it off, but I'm feelin' rather good about this."

I opened my mouth, momentarily forgetting that I couldn't speak while in dragon form, and instead of words, a stream of fire shot out, igniting a nearby tree. *Oh, fuck.* Growling, I scurried forward as the tree toppled, already turning to ash, and I patted the ground with my massive paws, carefully putting out the fire before I burned down half the forest. When the flames were out, I turned around to find all four of my mates staring at me.

Rolling my eyes, I forced the shift, shrinking to my human form until I was standing butt-naked in the pile of ash. "What?"

A stupid smile crawled across Asher's face as he blatantly admired me. "What'd I say? Raine being a shifter is better than the time Darian got with the succubus who had a fetish for feet."

"How dare you," Darian retorted. "That succubus planned our encounter before I'd even arrived at the party."

"And you were defenseless to stop her," Asher countered with a grin.

Darian shrugged. "You would have done the same had she chosen you to be the object of her desire for the night. Besides, I do have rather supple feet."

I stared at the pair of them, not really sure why they were talking about *feet* in that way. Stepping from the ash, I decided to take a position between Kade and Locke, and we walked further into the forest, leaving Asher and Darian to follow behind. My demon and siren could explain that one later. Or you know, not.

We were still a short distance from the rundown cottage that marked the location of Lyr's rebel camp when Kade stopped abruptly and placed an arm around me protectively. "I hear shouting," he growled in warning.

Locke cursed, gripping Warrick tighter in his arms. "What is it?"

Kade sniffed the air. "I'm not sure. Something feline."

Asher and Darian grabbed out their weapons as we continued forward, and Kade shifted, padding alongside me. Locke hung back with Warrick in his arms, but I don't think he was happy about it.

When the familiar cottage came into view, the trees opened up to a clearing and I finally managed to get a good look at what was causing the commotion.

Lyr, her mates, and a couple of wolf shifters from the House of Worzel had circled a beast with a lion's head, long horns, and a tail ending in a snake's head. *Vasken?* The chimera roared, his jaws opening wide before he snapped them shut and lunged for Lyr. Dean's hand shot up, vines springing from the ground and winding around the creature's front paws before it could reach her. The monster snarled, tearing through the green restraints before swiping at Lyr again. She dropped and rolled back, avoiding his claws.

I frowned in confusion, surprised that Lyr wasn't shifting, but then I took notice of what she was saying. She lifted her hands, facing her palms toward Vasken. "We're going to give King Adrien to the fae, Vas. He got us into this mess, and we can use him to try and forge a peace treaty once again."

Vasken's creature roared in response like hearing her explanation only infuriated him more.

"You sure he can understand you?" One of the wolf shifters asked skeptically as Vasken lunged toward him and he only just managed to dodge out of the way, missing the chimera's claws.

"Yes," Lyr hissed. "He understands."

"Or at least, we think so," Dean added, wrapping more vines around Vasken's hind legs.

Vasken set his sights on Dean, but then he stopped to sniff the air. In the next moment, he tore through the vines and was bounding in our direction.

Lyr's eyes widened when she caught sight of us. "Vas, no!" she shouted as the chimera sprinted across the clearing.

"Oh, fuck," Asher said, grabbing his axes and moving in front of me as Darian went for his stars. Kade growled and sprang forward as I shifted into my dragon form. My wolf shifter met Vasken halfway across the clearing and the pair of them became a mess of claws and teeth. One of Vasken's paws lashed out, managing to clip Kade's face, and my wolf went tumbling to the ground. Kade was on his feet again in an instant, but I roared, letting the sound vibrate through to the very ground at my feet.

Moving around Asher and Darian I lumbered forward, my talons flicking up the dirt. Vasken hissed and snarled, no longer advancing as he stared at me with wild eyes. Every instinct I had was telling me to destroy the shifter. To make him pay for touching my Kade, but as I moved forward, the image of Vasken writhing on the floor while Queen Izla stepped into the portal filled my mind, and my dragon's rage and desire to squash the little pest was soon replaced with a sad clarity. This was Queen Izla's friend and someone she had cared about. Someone my *ancestor* had cared about. I still hadn't had much time to digest this newest discovery about myself, but the knowledge was enough to temper my beast. Vasken paced in front of me before snarling and leaping into the air, his front paws outstretched like he wanted to scratch out my eyes. I flicked my head, driving my snout against his side and sending him flying into the dirt.

Before he could rise again to his feet, I was there, a large paw pressed firmly against his side as I held him down. He scrabbled in the dirt, determined to free himself from my hold, but I opened my mouth, fitting his head between my teeth and he fell still, his heart thundering.

"Don't!" Lyr cried out, but I stayed as I was, letting the little creature know just how fucking lucky he was that he was still alive.

My mates appeared by my side, followed by Lyr, her mates, and the other shifters.

"He doesn't know what he's doing," Lyr said, her pleading gaze going from me to my monsters like she knew that if anyone could stop me it would be them.

Locke didn't look the least bit upset at the idea of me eating the male, but Kade and the others watched me intently.

"Raine, lovely, I think you'd better let him go," Darian said calmly beside me, but I didn't move. I mean, I wasn't stupid. If I released Vasken, he might attack my monsters again, and I wasn't about to let that happen.

"He's here for the king," Lyr explained like she thought if she kept me talking it would distract me enough that I wouldn't eat her friend. "He wasn't trying to hurt anyone."

Vasken remained still in my hold, and with every passing moment, his heart rate slowed a little more. *That's it.*

Lyr took a step closer to me, but Locke lifted his hand and she halted. "Wait," he said. "Let's see what happens."

Vasken started scrabbling in the dirt again, but I huffed a puff of smoke onto the chimera's face, and he stilled, his chest heaving. I stayed like that for a long while, and slowly Vasken's heartbeat continued to slow.

No one moved around us like they were afraid that any sudden change in their position would startle me into tearing the chimera's head off, but that's not what my dragon wanted. It wasn't what *I* wanted.

I closed my eyes, thinking of how I'd seen Vasken in the vision, bleeding as Queen Izla dropped beside him in anguish. He meant something to her, and he'd lost himself without her here. It was no wonder he was obsessed with the idea of keeping the king trapped. After what I'd seen, the king was obviously a monster on the inside before the queen changed his physical appearance.

I'm not sure how, but as I thought of that image, I could feel the chimera's mind close to mine. I focused on sharing the image with him. Locke had spoken about how the gargoyle, Garan, could send mental messages to him, and I tried to do the same with Vasken.

I felt the moment our minds touched, and Vasken let out a pained sound in my hold. It was as if seeing the memory had actually harmed him. Lyr shot forward, panic flashing in her eyes, but I released the chimera and stepped back before she made it to me.

No longer restrained, Vasken roared and whined, but he didn't lift from the ground. Asher rested his hand on my side as we all watched the chimera's skin begin to ripple and shift. The chimera's snake hissed before it disappeared, and then there was a naked man on the ground instead of the giant beast.

Vasken sobbed quietly in the dirt, his bony shoulders shaking, and I shifted back quickly, not wanting my massive dragon form to be the first thing he saw while in human form.

"Vas?" Lyr said softly, slowly dropping to her knees beside him as Dean, Soren, and Nic stood guard over her. She rested her hand on Vasken's shoulder, and he turned his head to her, wincing up at her in the bright light. "Shadow girl," he rasped, his voice scratchy from disuse.

"Thought we wouldn't see you again for a minute there," Soren said with a tentative smile.

Dean dipped his head. "You are a welcome sight."

Vasken's eyes were vacant like he still couldn't make sense of the scene around him, but as they helped him stand, his gaze landed on me. My monsters shuffled closer like they were still afraid he would attack, but I returned his stare knowing it for what it was. He wasn't exactly thanking me, but there was acknowledgment there as if he knew what I'd done for him, and he was glad there was someone else out there who understood his pain.

I smiled, feeling a little proud that my dragon had done something good, and Lyr linked her arm with his and led him away.

CHAPTER 24

~ Raine ~

"What is it that you're tryin' to do again?" Asher asked, looking completely bewildered.

I stood with my arms raised toward him, my brow furrowed in concentration, but when nothing happened, I groaned. "Seeing Locke use magic to create that mirror wall in the mountain got me thinking about my own abilities. Since turning into a dragon, I haven't used my magic."

"And you're afraid your powers are gone," Darian said as he watched me with inquisitive eyes. "Could it simply be that you haven't needed to use them?"

Dropping my arms, I turned to him. "I mean, maybe?"

Darian rubbed his chin. "Every time you've used your magic in the past it's been when you were in a dire circumstance. There's been less of those instances since you obtained your creature form."

I realized my siren was right. Now that I had my dragon form, I didn't have the same fears as I had before, and I hadn't really been in any life-or-death situations. Of course, we'd had to fly from the outliers at the mountain not too long ago, but I needed my dragon to help with that, not my magic.

"That's true," I started, "but we need all our tricks if it comes to all out war." And that included me being able to use my fae magic *and* my monster abilities.

Since returning with Warrick and the news that the fae would arrive any day now, most in the rebellion had been training twice as hard, while other monsters made armor and weaponry tirelessly day and night. With Warrick and King Adrien ready to be gifted to the fae, there was hope we wouldn't have to fight at all, but we still planned for the latter.

Monsters from the lower houses in Katakin City continued to join our ranks, but there was no more news from the House of Saceris or the House of Faren. Still, so many monsters had joined the rebellion that even the surrounding caves had become crowded, and monsters had begun camping in the surrounding forest, sheltered by the tree canopy.

Despite the overcrowding, this time me and my mates had a training room all to ourselves. I was sure our private room mostly had to do with the fact that no one wanted to be around me when I went into dragon mode, especially after what had happened with Losak's shifters. But that suited me just fine.

Lifting my hands again, I concentrated, trying to use wind power to blow Asher across the room, just like I'd blown back the Dazra when they were attacking us in the fae realm, but...nothing happened. I could hardly sense the spark of power that I usually felt when I focused.

Letting out a frustrated noise, I dropped my hands, almost ready to shift and burn something, when Darian stepped in front of me and grabbed my hands in his. Gently, he leaned down and pressed a kiss to my forehead. "Burning this place isn't going to help you find your magic again," he said with a smile like he knew exactly what I'd been thinking. "I think it's time for a break."

"What?" I asked incredulously, though I was already beginning to lean into him, my body subconsciously starting to calm. "We found out that Warrick basically plans to kill us all, and everyone's working their asses off, so I need to as well. We might have him unconscious, but who knows what that means for his outliers." With Warrick passed out rather than dead, Lyr's scouts had noticed that the outliers were dormant in the city, like they were waiting for his next command, but we still didn't know what would happen in the nights to come.

"You'll be no good to anyone if you exhaust yourself," Darian reasoned. "This war doesn't all come down to you."

I knew he was right, but I couldn't help feeling like I'd let everyone down. "When Prince Azaren had embedded the information about the curse in my mind, I'd thought that at least we had the answers we needed," I said softly. "That even if the fae didn't accept another peace treaty, somehow we would find a way to end the curse."

Darian's fingers brushed over my cheek. "Whether we remain monsters or not doesn't matter, as long as I have you. And I'm growing rather fond of your dragon side, I have to say."

One of fae, blood so blue. How had I been so stupid to think we might find a way to break the curse? I gave him a weak smile. "But Warrick's outliers... You heard him. He has *thousands* of the creatures. What if we can't defeat them? We need to survive this. If we don't, I'll never find my sister."

Darian pulled me into his chest and rested his chin on my head. "We will find her. I promise you. When the war is over. And right now, Warrick is safely sleeping and contained just like King Adrien. Locke has been dosing him up with that gray powder every few hours, and he's restrained and under constant watch. He's not going anywhere. If the fae don't accept our offering of peace, we'll end Warrick's life ourselves. The outliers might still be in the city, but without him controlling them, at least they won't be organized."

What Darian was saying made sense, but I couldn't shake the feeling that everything was going to go horribly wrong, and that by the time the war was over, it would be too late to find Cara. Asher came closer to us just as the door opened. Noise rushed in from the commotion of the monsters beyond the training room, and I turned my head as I recognized Quinn's voice. "Hands off, goblin," he snarled, to which another male responded. "Those weapons aren't for you, shifter. They've already been requested by the alpha, Borren."

"The House of Thorem got the last set you made," Quinn protested. "I think they can wait until the rest of us get our share before receiving more handouts."

Darian let out a suffering sigh, and I didn't get to hear any more because Kade and Locke entered the room and closed the door behind them, striding toward us.

"Sounds like the monsters are gettin' along," Asher commented sarcastically.

"From the moment we shared the news that Warrick is intending to murder us all, things have gone downhill," Kade growled. "No one believes the fae will accept our offer, and it's way too crowded out there for this many fucking monsters. Even my wolf is getting agitated."

Locke adjusted the collar of his black coat. "Which is why Lyr has announced that we're all to take the night off. We'll be useless on a battlefield if we can't stop ourselves from being at each other's throats. A group of monsters snuck into the city and managed to grab some supplies including a few barrels of liquor. We have orders to put down our weapons for a few hours."

Darian perked up, his eyes brightening. "Well now, I've always known Lyr was a clever one. I agree. A good drink is just what we need."

. . . . ● . ● . . .

~ Asher ~

The main hall was cleared for the party, and the celebration spread from there through to the larger rooms of the hideout. I sat with Raine and my brothers as Darian topped up my goblet with more wine.

Putting down the jug, Darian leaned back, and his lips stretched into a smile. "Remind me to thank the tiger shifter the next time I see her."

Kade frowned. "Don't thank her just yet. All it'll take is one monster saying the wrong thing, and we'll be brawling."

I followed Kade's gaze to where he was staring intently at the monsters relaxing around us. Despite Lyr's request that everyone try and get along, the monsters mostly remained in their respective house groups, keeping separate from one another.

"Speak for yourself. I have no intention of fighting anyone right now," Darian said, tipping back the rest of his wine and letting out a satisfied sigh. "Unless of course, they try to touch our lovely Raine. Then they might lose a hand or two." He grinned, baring his teeth in an uncharacteristically sadistic way for my siren brother. A female goblin passing by must have thought he was smiling at her because she batted her lashes back at him and started walking with a saucy sway to her hips.

I turned my head, interested to see how our possessive little dragon would feel about the attention Darian was getting. Raine's goblet was pressed to her lips, but as her eyes narrowed on the goblin, flames beginning to flicker in her amber gaze, she...choked? Raine pulled her goblet away from her mouth and coughed, her eyes watering. "Wrong hole!" she wheezed.

Rubbing her back, I leaned down to stare at her reddening face. "You all right there, Sharachi?"

She nodded enthusiastically. "Yep, all good," she replied, her words strangled as she tried to clear her throat, but the next time she coughed, fire shot from her mouth, burning the back half of the goblin's dress. I grinned when I realized it was the same goblin who'd been giving Darian an appreciative look and was swishing her ass from side to side as she walked. With a startled cry, the female ran off, the flames spreading and her dress turning to ash as she fled.

"Oops," Raine commented with a wince when she spotted the fleeing goblin, her naked ass now on display. "Goddess, should I go after her and try to help?" Raine looked genuinely remorseful as she coughed a few more times, managing to keep her fire contained.

I grinned as I pulled her into my arms and settled her on my lap. "I always knew you would be fun," I chuckled, and dragged my lips across her neck. Her skin warmed at my touch, and her heart began to race as my hands slid across her stomach.

"The monsters know what you mean to us," Kade growled like the goblin had gotten off easy. "She should have known better."

"And I dare say now she does," Darian said with a smirk, like he was delighted at the turn of events.

Raine still looked like she was contemplating going after the goblin, but I kissed along her shoulder, distracting her. "If you follow the goblin, you'll only terrify her more. Leave her be," I murmured.

Raine still didn't look convinced, but I trailed my kisses up and along her jaw, and she turned her head to me, pressing her lips against mine. I groaned as her tongue dipped into my mouth, and she wiggled her ass, making my cock so hard it ached. *Fuck.*

"You'd better stop, sweetheart, unless you want an audience," I said, pulling my lips from hers. She only rubbed her ass harder, enjoying how it tortured me.

I could feel my brothers watching us, all of them just as ready as I was. With the whirlwind of events these past nights, none of us had been able to enjoy her company nearly as much as we would've liked.

It wasn't just my brothers who were enjoying the show, either. A small group of demons strolled past us, and my gaze flicked up in time to see one of the demons give me an assessing gaze, lust shining in her bronze eyes. Raine didn't notice the female's lingering stare, but Darian raised a brow, and his gaze locked with mine.

I easily read the question in his eyes. Over the last few nights, it had become obvious that things were shifting. Unlike in the past, monsters were no longer keeping their distance and ignoring my existence. Females who once refused to acknowledge me were now trying to catch my gaze, and even some of the males were beginning to treat me with more respect.

It seemed that capturing Warrick had made the monsters a little more accepting, and even, appreciative. Also, since Raine had become a monster, it was as if everyone wanted to know about the fiery dragon shifter and the males who had her attention. I didn't give a shit about what any of them thought about me. I never had. But it was an interestin' development. Whatever the monsters used to believe about me bein' potentially detrimental to their fucked up social status or mental health, was quickly facing.

"She'd better stop ogling you, or she'll end up like the goblin," Raine said with a smile, and I wasn't sure if she was joking or not.

Grinning, I lifted Raine, spinning her around and spreading her legs so she was facing me. As her thighs slid to either side of me, her eyes popped wide. "As far as I remember, you only have one of those. Unless there's something you haven't told me..."

My grin widened, and I reached beneath her leg, taking out the weapon I'd hidden in my pants and handing it to her. She stared at it in surprise and pulled the dagger from the leather sheath. "It has a dragon," she breathed in awe, inspecting the tiny metal creature that decorated the hilt. A small red gem was embedded in the dragon's chest, and its spiked tail curled around, reaching close to its face. "Goddess, its beautiful."

My hands slid up her waist. "I had it made for you. To replace the dagger I took."

Her eyes met mine. "Wait, does this mean you're not giving me my dagger back?"

My lips twitched as I thought of the makeshift blade that was still in my room in the mountain. The one I'd confiscated from her after she'd stabbed it into my shoulder. "I was hopin' we might be able to trade," I replied with a smile.

She grinned, her eyes sparkling. "I'm not sure if it's a fair exchange given the time I spent crafting my blade, but I'll allow it."

Her fingers brushed over the dragon again.

"Does that mean you like it?" I asked, my heart pounding, though I wasn't sure why I was so nervous.

"That depends, are you going to mind if I get blood on my new blade?"

I wrapped my arms tighter around her, sliding my hands down until I gripped her ass. "I'd be offended if you didn't."

Smiling, she twisted and peered around like she was searching for a target, and as her gaze fixed on something in the distance her eyes lit up. A few yards away, a round wooden training shield had been left propped against the wall. "How about I start with that?" she suggested eagerly.

I didn't doubt she could hit the target, but I gestured my head to her empty goblet resting on the table in front of us. "Are you sure that's a good idea seein' as you've been drinkin'."

Locke, who had been mostly silent all night, folded his arms across his chest. "If she's going to carry it around, she should know if the blade is balanced correctly."

"Exactly," Raine said, her expression becoming serious. "This baby looks like she'd be better at stabbing, but I'm sure I can hit..." she trailed off as she drew her hand back and flicked her wrist, sending the blade spinning in the air. It flew across the room and straight into...

Cassar let out an animalistic grunt as the blade sunk into his right ass-cheek. "What the fuck!" The shifter had walked right in front of us as Raine had thrown the blade. A female shifter from their house stood beside him, and she gaped at Cassar as he yanked out the blade and looked around murderously for his attacker. I couldn't help the belly-aching laughter that exploded from me.

"Sorry!" Raine called out, giving me a reprimanding look and scrambling to get off my lap. Cassar's face hardened when he noticed us, but despite his glare he didn't move toward us. Instead, he eyed the blade and smiled broadly. The bastard went to slide Raine's dagger into his pants like it was some sort of consolation prize.

Fucking asshole. I lifted to my feet, but Raine was already moving toward the shifter.

"Oh, fuck no," she huffed under her breath, but Locke made it to Cassar first.

Locke's stare was as cold as ice as he eyed Cassar and held out his clawed hand. "Thank you for collecting Raine's blade, she would have been...upset had it gone missing. Now, if you wouldn't mind..."

Cassar gaped at Locke like he thought the vampire had gone mad, and I sat my ass back down, content to watch the scene play out.

Getting over his initial shock, Cassar smirked. "If she wanted it so badly, she wouldn't have been throwing it away."

Raine looked like she was preparing herself to do some damage if Cassar didn't change his mind real fuckin' quickly, but before she could act, the blade was in Locke's hand and the shifter was flying backward. Cassar landed hard, his back cracking into the wooden shield Raine had first been aiming at and breaking it into two.

Locke wiped the blade on his pants and held it out to Raine who took it from him.

"I would have handled it," Raine groused light-heartedly, and Locke's black eyes flashed.

"I know," he answered, then he lifted her in his arms and the pair were back with the rest of us within a heartbeat. Locke dropped beside Darian with Raine on his lap, and she sheathed the blade and tucked it into her pants.

"I'm sure this isn't going quite as Lyr hoped," Darian commented with amusement as he watched Cassar grunt and lift himself from the floor. Cassar's body hunched as he stared at us, his eyes glowing and tusks protruding from his mouth as if he was about to shift, but the female with him grabbed his arm, and he let her pull him along.

"What is it with monsters trying to steal a girl's weapons?" Raine mumbled, and I grinned, again thinking about her makeshift dagger in the mountain. I still planned to give it back to her...eventually.

CHAPTER 25

~ **Raine** ~

Despite Lyr's good intentions, the night didn't play out how she'd hoped. While some of the monsters were able to get along for a few hours, fights broke out between the groups. It didn't matter how much wine we had, no one was forgetting about the fae or Warrick's outliers anytime soon, and the tension remained high.

Luckily for me and my monsters, we still had our own private room, and we retreated to have our own fun away from the drama. All four of my monsters took complete advantage of the fact I wasn't training, pleasuring me until I fell asleep in their arms.

When I awoke, I slid from where I was cocooned between Darian, Locke, and Asher, and stumbled from the bed. Kade wasn't in the room, and I pulled on a shirt and pants and padded across the room. Opening the door, I blinked into the dim light.

By now, most of the monsters had retired, returning to their usual sleeping locations in the bunker, caves, or surrounding forest. Some were passed out on the couches and scattered across the floor, and a few were still staggering about, laughing and dancing to imaginary music. I picked my way past the intoxicated monsters, heading for one of the tables with jugs of water. I drank until my throat no longer felt dry and sticky, then I walked around, searching for my wolf.

Lately, Kade and Locke had disappeared a few times to talk to Lyr and her mates or the other alphas about the war, weapons, and training, but unease went through me as I traveled from room to room, unable to find my wolf shifter.

I was about to move to search the next room, when I noticed a figure huddled at the far side of the dining hall. The male sat tucked into the corner with his back against the wall and a half-filled jug of wine by his side. He seemed to stare at nothing, his gaze empty and cold. *Vasken?*

I watched the male carefully as I approached, my heart twisting when I replayed the scene with him and Queen Izla in my mind. When Vasken didn't react to my presence, I dropped down, sliding my back against the wall as I sat beside him. For a long moment neither of us spoke. I knew the male likely wanted some alone time, and I'd just invited myself to his solo party, but it felt wrong to simply leave him there like that. Taking a breath, I said softly, "It must be hard. Adjusting, I mean."

He still didn't respond, and I tried not to think about how awkward I felt as I went on. "Losing someone you care about—"

"You know nothing dragon," he growled, cutting me off.

So he does recognize me. I pressed my lips together, silent for a beat before speaking again. Truthfully, he was right. I hardly knew anything of what he'd been through. But the image of his tortured face as the queen stepped into the portal haunted me.

"I understand you were one of the queen's most trusted guards," I said slowly. "When she went through that portal... It can't have been easy for you. You had a duty to protect her."

"Her guard?" Vasken mused with a chuckle that was devoid of humor. Reaching over, he grabbed the jug from the floor and downed the remaining wine before pressing his head back against the wall and letting out a long breath. "I know you saw what happened when she created the curse." His jaw clenched, despair entering his eyes. "I failed her. I failed *them.*" He picked the jug up again, bringing it to his lips before realizing it was empty. Letting out a grunt of frustration, he tossed the jug away, sending it rolling across the floor.

"Them?" I frowned as I watched the jug collide with a table leg and stop rolling.

Vasken turned to me, his glassy eyes struggling to focus on my face, and the smell of wine on his breath made me want to wrinkle my nose. His long unkempt hair fell in knotted waves past his shoulders, and despite the fact he looked to be in his thirties, his expression was weary as if he'd already lived a thousand lives. After a long uncomfortable moment, he slurred, "She was pregnant."

I sucked in a sharp breath. "I know."

His expression shuttered, his despair taking over his entire face.

"But the curse and what happened to Izla wasn't your fault," I said quickly, not sure why it bothered me so much to see him like that. "I saw what King Adrien did. It's not your fault he was terrible at caring for his family."

Vasken shook his head, his eyes filling with tears. "The king didn't know," he rasped, his throat clogged with emotion.

My brows lifted. "What?"

"About the baby," Vasken said, staring at a section of the wall across the dining hall. "And he didn't know that it wasn't his."

The world stilled as I stared at the shifter, his words settling into place. I took in his ragged appearance, and the grief in his eyes. It wasn't just because he had been the queen's personal guard.

I couldn't breathe, couldn't speak as I waited for Vasken to confirm my suspicion that *he* was the father, but as if he'd decided it was too painful to talk about, he lifted from his position, grabbed the empty jug from the floor and left the room.

I watched him leave, a part of me wanting to call after him. To demand that he tell me the full story, but I didn't. The shifter was hurting, and I wouldn't add to his pain.

My head was still spinning as I lifted to my feet. I had to tell my monsters everything I knew. But first, I needed to find my wolf.

CHAPTER 26

I had searched most of the hideout and the adjoining caves, and I was about to see if Kade had returned to our room, when his scent of sandalwood and coffee filled my nose. Curious, I followed the scent through one of the underground tunnels that led into the forest. The wolves from the House of Worzel were among the monsters who had chosen to camp under the stars, and I slowed my steps when I overheard Kade speaking with a familiar female. Keeping hidden behind a large oak, I stayed silent, though I knew it was only a matter of time before they picked up my scent. The fact they hadn't detected my presence already showed just how engrossed they were in their current conversation. Kasey, her mate, Tristan, and Kade were speaking, while a group of wolves listened intently.

"You're our alpha," Kasey said with a biting edge to her words. "We need you."

Standing with his feet wide, Kade folded his arms across his broad chest. "This is a difficult time for all of us. The pack is doing well with you leading them."

Kasey scoffed. "I'm not an alpha, Kade. You defeated Zacal, and it's your responsibility to step up. After what Zacal confessed, you should have been leading us this whole time."

Many of the wolf shifters who were scattered around them nodded their heads, agreeing with Kasey's statement, but there were a few who still looked unhappy about the whole situation.

"We're weak without our alpha," a shifter with a bald head and brown eyes called out. He stood with his arm draped across a female's neck, and it wasn't hard to guess they were mates. "What happens if we have to head into battle?"

Kade's expression hardened. "We have King Adrien and Warrick to offer the fae, and if they see reason it won't come to that."

Growls and sniggers erupted from the wolves.

"Only a fool would believe the fae will accept peace," Tristan said, stepping closer to his mate. "We've been patient with you, alpha, but the wolves need you. Every day the tension between our houses rises. Why do you think we stay in the forest? Monsters of different breeds aren't meant to live together."

Kade ran a hand through his shaggy brown hair. "You just need to hang in there a while longer." His eyes suddenly sharpened, his nostrils flaring ever so slightly as he breathed in, and for a moment I thought he'd call out to me, but he didn't turn my way.

I realized now that all those times Kade had disappeared during the past nights, this was likely where he'd been. With the wolves. *His own kind.* My throat grew tight as I thought about what the wolf had said just before. That monsters of different breeds shouldn't be together. Monsters like demons, vampires, sirens, wolf shifters, and...dragon shifters.

"You shouldn't be out here, beautiful," whispered a low voice. Icy breath puffed on my ear, and I shivered as I spun to find Locke crowding over me. My mouth popped open in surprise, but before I could utter a word Locke lifted a finger to his lips and curled his arm around my back, leading me further into the forest. We remained silent as we made our way through the trees, moving away from the secret tunnel entrance that led back to the underground hideout. I was about to comment and ask how far we were traveling, when Locke finally turned toward me. In a swift movement, he spun me around, pressing my back against the trunk of a nearby tree.

"It's not wise to spy on wolves," he pointed out as he leaned down and brushed his lips against mine.

I sucked in a sharp breath before clearing my throat and forcing a disapproving look to my face. "I wasn't spying. I was checking to see if Kade was all right. With you both disappearing so much these past nights, I was worried when I woke and he wasn't there."

Locke's lips curled upward, and one of his hands gripped my waist and slid higher, his claws dragging against my shirt. "I told you, I've had to speak with the gargoyles. And the wolves aren't wrong about the tension in the camp. It isn't natural for the different houses to work together like this."

"I know. It's just—"

"We're not trying to keep secrets from you. The gargoyles have always kept to themselves, and since losing most of their kind to the outliers...well, they're not doing so well. As for Kade and the wolves..." Locke sighed. "He's in a tricky position."

"But why? Zacal admitted to lying about the fae being behind all those wolf deaths. He's the rightful alpha to the pack. Doesn't Kade know I understand that? It's obvious they need him."

"If I officially take my place as alpha, they'll expect me to be with the pack at all times," Kade growled, stepping from the trees behind us as if he was materializing from the shadows. His golden eyes glowed as he pinpointed where Locke had me pressed against the tree, and my mouth became dry. "Locke is right. You shouldn't have been eavesdropping. It's lucky the wolves were so distracted."

I lifted my chin. "But if your place is with them..."

Kade narrowed his eyes as he came in close, boxing me in from the side. Goddess, I'd never seen him so serious. "My place is with you, Mahare. And Locke, Asher, and Darian. There was a time when my pack meant more to me than anything. But things have changed. I still have loyalty for the wolves, but they're not the family they once were." He blew out a breath. "If there was another wolf who I believed was strong enough to lead the pack, I would step down again in a heartbeat. For you. Kasey is proving to be worthy, but only time will tell."

My heart pounded at the intensity of his gaze. "What? No, you can't step down." I knew how strongly Kade felt for me, but I also remembered the guilt he had carried when he thought he'd failed the wolves. He cared for them, and he would be a great leader.

"There are rules in Katakin set by the Taratun council, and one of them is that you can't take a mate unless they belong to the same house and are of the same breed," Kade explained.

"Yeah, since when have you obeyed the rules?" I retorted. "You're already defying them by not being a part of any house right now. And I'm pretty sure no one gives a shit what the Taratun thinks given our current situation."

"While that's true, beautiful, the wolves want Kade to become a member of their house again to fulfill his role as alpha," Locke replied. "And even without interference from the council, they wouldn't be willing to accept an alpha who—"

"Had a dragon shifter as his mate," I finished for him, voicing the worry I'd already been obsessing over. I swallowed hard. I didn't want to be the reason Kade couldn't be with his house.

Locke stepped back, giving Kade space, and my wolf shifter closed in on me, staring at me with golden eyes that held me in place. "You might not yet be willing for us to mark you as our mate, but I know you're mine, Raine. And your dragon knows it, too. So, until I'm sure that the wolves will accept you by my side, I won't step up. Nothing could make me risk you like that."

A part of me wanted to remind him that I was a dragon shifter now. That I wasn't as easy to kill as I once was, but I was so wrapped up in his words and the emotion in his gaze that my eyes blurred with tears. Kade leaned down, pressing his lips to mine like he was desperate to remind me just how much I meant to him. He kissed me like we were already marked, and I let him have me, claiming his lips just as badly as he was claiming mine.

My arms wound around his neck, and his hands slid across my back pulling me away from the tree. Lowering me gently to the grass, he moved between my thighs.

"Give in, Raine," he breathed when he broke the kiss. "Let us mark you. Let us show the world that you're ours and nothing can change that. Not even when war is on the horizon. Fuck the Taratun council. We'll kill them all if we have to."

Locke laid beside us, and he grabbed my hand, trailing kisses up my arm. His teeth grazed along my skin, and I swallowed hard. My wolf shifter grinded his hips against me, and I squirmed as warmth pooled between my legs.

"You know I can't," I rasped. "Not until I find my sister."

I yelped in surprise as Kade tore my pants off me, tossing them to the side with a growl that made my insides clench. *Uh, yes fucking please.* But...I couldn't mark them. Not yet.

Kade's ears shifted, becoming pointed as he tilted his head to the side like he was listening, but then he turned back to me, his ears rounding again, and his eyes softening. "When we find her, your sister will see you're meant for us," he growled as he moved back and took off his pants.

Locke was now already naked, and he pulled me to my feet as Kade laid on the ground. Lowering myself, I straddled Kade, sliding along his length to tease him. A growl rumbled in his chest, and I smirked as my dragon preened on the inside. *My mates.* Locke dropped down behind me, and as the tip of Kade's cock pushed inside me, Locke's teeth clamped onto my neck.

"Fuck," I gasped as I drove my hips down, taking all of Kade as Locke's venom made my head spin. *Seriously, fuck.* I moved faster until the pleasure became too much, but before I could shatter, my vampire pulled back, hissing as he licked his lips.

"Locke?" I panted.

He nipped my ear and growled. "You're so fucking delicious."

I grinned, but my smile fell as Kade gripped my hips hard, thrusting into me so fast that all I could focus on was the pleasure to the point I struggled to remember my own name.

"Well now, this is much better than finding you three battling outliers as Asher suggested," a familiar voice commented with amusement, and I peered over to find my siren and demon striding toward us. They both grinned as they took in the scene and began stripping off their clothes.

Darian swayed as he crossed his arms, pulling his shirt over his head, and I half wondered whether he'd found more wine to consume while they'd been out searching for us.

"What took you so long?" I teased, but my smirk turned to a gasp when Locke's finger slowly worked its way into my ass.

Darian and Asher dropped down, moving to either side of us, and their gazes heated as they watched. Kade slowed his thrusts, and Locke removed his finger and lined himself up.

I gasped at the intense feeling of both of them inside me. I'd never had a cock in my ass, much less one as big as Locke's, but my body shifted slightly, until it was just enough that the pair of them could move in tandem, only the thin wall separating them.

Pleasure unlike anything I'd ever felt made me cry out, and both Kade and Locke groaned, thrusting harder. Darian moved close enough that I could twist my head to take him in my mouth, and I reached out, stroking Asher with my hand.

The orgasm shattered through me, making me moan around Darian's cock, and Kade and Locke found their release as well. Before I'd even recovered, someone was moving me from my wolf shifter and vampire, and then Asher was inside me.

My demon drove deep, his piercings rubbing me deliciously with every thrust until I exploded again. I panted heavily as tingles pricked over my skin and light flashed before my eyes. Still, I didn't get a reprieve. It wasn't until Asher was roaring his release and Darian had spilled himself over my chest that they finally pulled back, lifting me into their arms as they kissed every part of me, reminding me that they were my mates, whether we found my sister or not.

I was curled against Asher and Darian, with Locke lazing close by and Kade sitting near my feet, when I spoke. "I saw something else," I said softly, not wanting to ruin the moment, but also knowing I couldn't hold back any longer. "When we were in the mountain, and I had a vision of the queen."

My monsters stiffened, but no one spoke as they waited for me to continue. "Queen Izla was with child when she went through the portal. And I can't be sure, but I think Vasken was the father."

There was a long moment of silence, but then Locke was the one to speak first. "That would explain Vasken's behavior."

I nodded, and licked my lips before adding, "And I think I might be descended from both of them." I was glad I didn't have to say I was descended from King Adrien, but my heart still pounded as I waited for their response.

All four of them stared at me, none of them looking the least bit surprised.

I lifted my head. "Wait, you knew?"

"We suspected the queen might have been pregnant," Kade answered. "And that you might be her kin. It was the only explanation that made sense when we found out you had fae blood."

"However, this information about Vasken is new," Locke added.

Darian rested his head on his hand. "You came from the island that Queen Izla escaped to, darling," he drawled. "It wasn't hard for us to guess how you could be part fae."

"And none of that...bothers you?" I questioned, wondering how they were so relaxed about it all.

Asher snuggled in closer. "Nope. Queen Izla was loved before the curse. It was King Adrien who fucked everything up."

"And even if you had been descended from the king, we don't choose our blood relations," Kade growled.

Locke's black eyes were on me, and even though he didn't voice the words, I knew he was thinking about Warrick and Perene. I only hoped he knew the same thing applied to him.

CHAPTER 27

Two more nights passed, and the celebration hadn't done much to improve the monsters' morale and ability to get along. My monsters and I had been in the dining hall, finally having a meal after spending the first part of the night training, when Nic materialized beside Asher's chair.

Instinctively, Asher drove his fork into the wraith's abdomen, but the cutlery passed straight through Nic's incorporeal form. The chunk of steak on Asher's fork fell to the ground between the wraith's legs, and Nic glared at him unimpressed.

"Fuck. Ever heard it's not good to sneak up on monsters like that?" Asher grumbled as he tossed his fork onto the table.

I pressed my lips together to try and suppress my grin, but Darian smirked. Before my siren could make a smart comment, Nic addressed all of us. "There's an emergency meeting in the hall. All are to attend, especially you five."

"What's this about?" Kade asked, but Nic had already disappeared.

My stomach dropped, and I pushed my plate away, suddenly not interested in shoving more meat and cheese into my mouth.

"Anyone else think we're about to get some bad news?" Darian commented before drinking from his goblet.

Locke pushed back his chair. "Let's go. It's about time we heard something."

When we reached the hall, the room was already filled with monsters. Lyr, Dean, Nic, and Soren stood in the middle of the space, and Locke led us to the only unoccupied armchairs that were left. Dropping down, he pulled me onto his lap, and Darian sat beside us, crossing one leg over the other.

Lyr smiled when she spotted us and whispered something to Soren. Soren stretched out his large red wings before tucking them in again. "Everyone quiet!" he shouted.

When a few of the alphas continued to chatter, Nic growled, "Shut the fuck up or you'll be the first in line to fight against the outliers if it comes to it!"

At that, there were grumbles around the room, and the chatter finally ceased.

"Now, that's how you demand attention," Darian said with appreciation, and I grinned. The alpha's liked to show they were tough, but when it came to it, no one wanted to fight Warrick's outliers.

Lyr took a step forward, her blue eyes scanning the crowd. "As you no doubt have guessed, the fact we've called you here is a sign that things have changed. I wish I could stand here and tell you otherwise, but the fact is we knew this was coming."

"So, it's true," a wolf shifter from a lower house called out. Ure, I thought his name was. "The fae are here!"

All attention went to the tiger shifter.

"It is," Lyr replied, her brows dipping low. "Last night one of our own followed a fae scout from the city. The fae didn't return through a portal as expected but trekked through the forest to a rocky space between the mountains." She licked her lips and took a breath, as if she hated what she had to say next. "Thousands of fae are already in Katakin."

"We believe they've been amassing there for the past two nights," Nic added, before the monsters could call out questions. "It's as if they're using some kind of illusion magic to hide themselves. You can't see the camp unless you pass through the magical barrier they've created and are within a few yards from the first tent. So anytime our scouts have circled from above, they've seen unoccupied land."

At that, cries went up around the room, and Lyr yelled above the noise. "But we're in the best position we can be! With both Warrick and King Adrien in our custody, a small party of us will go to the fae and propose a peace treaty as planned. As far as we're aware, since Warrick was rendered unconscious, the outliers have remained mostly dormant not attacking in the city unless provoked. If we can foster peace with the fae, there's a chance we may never head to battle."

There were snorts of disbelief, and angry chatter from the monsters, but Lyr kept going. "We need at least ten to volunteer to go to the fae camp."

The room finally quieted as all of the monsters stared at one another, waiting to see who would be the first to step forward. Lyr's gaze swept around the room, and it wasn't until Kade began growling that I realized she was staring at *me. Oh, fuck.* Locke's arms tightened protectively around my waist.

"I'll go," called out an orc alpha, drawing the attention to him. Kenric was the leader of the high house of Axeran, and one of the few monsters who always seemed to be smiling. He jerked his head and elbowed the female standing beside him. "And so will Jade." I stared at the female who was a head shorter than her alpha, with thick ginger hair, and a mace at her side. I'd seen her fight and take down most of the orcs in their house, so I wasn't surprised when she shrugged her agreement.

Lyr bowed her head in appreciation. "And who else will join them?"

Again, her gaze fell on me, and I wiggled uncomfortably under her stare. It's not that I didn't want to volunteer, but it didn't seem like the best idea given that King Chalir likely still believed my monsters and I were behind his son's assassination.

"Don't you even think 'bout it, sweetheart," Asher warned from behind me, and I flashed him a grin even though I had no intention of putting my hand up. By now, more had volunteered including Ure, the wolf shifter who had spoken earlier, Borren, the alpha of the high house of Thorem, and another demon, Sophie, from a lower house.

By the time, Lyr's gaze fell on me for a third time, I couldn't have put my hand up even if I wanted to, because Locke's arms were like a vice as he kept my ass on his lap, and my hands in front of me. "What are you doing?" I hissed back at him.

"They can do this without us," he replied calmly. "If we show our faces to King Chalir, who's to say he won't attack at the first sight of us."

It was the same thought I'd had, but I was starting to wonder if we might be wrong. "Or he'll be more likely to accept a peace treaty if we show we're genuinely remorseful for what happened with Prince Azaren?" I countered.

"I don't know if you've forgotten this, lovely, but it wasn't us who assassinated the prince," Darian drawled.

I gave him a flat look. "Of course, not. And by being the ones proposing a peace treaty, he'll see that we're not trying to hide. If we were guilty, we'd never willingly walk into his camp."

"While that's an interesting thought, lovely," Darian began.

"It's a terrible idea," Kade finished. "We're not letting you near the fae king."

I understood what they were getting at, I did, but the more I thought about it, the more I realized we had to do this. Lyr had obviously already come to the same conclusion, and why she didn't share this with us was beyond me.

I hadn't really tested my strength while I was in my human form, but all it took was a little effort and my right arm was free from Locke's hold and shooting into the air. "We'll go," I blurted before Locke had even realized what had happened.

My vampire's icy breath tickled my neck. "You've been holding out on us."

I smiled smugly, enjoying the fact that I'd managed to surprise him.

"That settles it, then!" Lyr called out with a smile, not sparing my mates a glance as she clapped her hands together. "The volunteers will gather their things and leave immediately. May the devils spare you."

. . . • . • . . .

My monsters armed themselves heavily, but I kept it light, only carrying a few knives, and a sword at my side. If we were in any real danger, I would likely shift, and anything I was wearing would only be discarded. But if all went well there'd be no reason to shift anyway. The trek to the fae camp was estimated to take us a couple hours to walk, and I filled up a pack of provisions including rations of food and water. Before I could lift the strap over my head, Asher plucked the bag from my fingers and gave me a wink. "I'd better take that."

I grinned. "Probably a good idea."

As he went to grab another ax, I tipped my head to where Borren was fastening his leather armor across his chest. "Are you going to be all right traveling with him?" From what Kade and the others had told me, as alpha of the House of Thorem, Borren was expected to keep the demons of his house in check. When Asher's mom became unwell, Borren should have intervened, but he didn't. When the alpha finally acted, he decided the only way to help her was by taking her life. In the time that followed, Asher ran from the house and was ostracized by the monsters. No one actually said Borren was responsible for how the monsters treated Asher, but even if he wasn't, as alpha, he could have spoken up for Asher. I glared at the alpha and wondered what kind of monster found it so easy to turn their back on a child and his mother.

Asher smiled, but there was no warmth in his eyes. "Don't worry, sweetheart. It was a long time ago. Provided he stays out of my way, we'll get along just fine."

I almost wanted to protest, but if Asher had managed to forgive the alpha in some way, then I had to respect that. "He'd better stay out of my way too," I commented, watching as Borren slid a sword into the scabbard at his side. The urge to roast the demon had smoke puffing from my nose, but I turned away, grabbing another knife and adding it to my collection instead.

By the time we were ready, we met up in the cell where an unconscious Warrick was chained to the floor beside King Adrien's stone tomb. Borren, Kenric, Ure, and Kade carried the tomb, and Asher handed the pack to Darian before unchaining Warrick from the floor and hefting the vampire over his shoulder. We made our way out of one of the underground tunnels from the hideout, scanning the forest as we walked in the direction of the fae army camp. Everything was silent around us, and I shivered, still unnerved by the lack of animals in the forest. Warrick bobbed on Asher's shoulder, and I only hoped King Chalir would make the vampire pay for what he'd done.

"Lift it higher," Borren snapped at Ure who walked in front of him, the tomb balanced on his shoulder. The wolf shifter scowled, but he straightened his back so the tomb leveled again.

I was just wondering if I should offer to help when Jade sidled up beside me, her mace resting on her shoulder, the spiked ball swaying and the chain rattling. Her ginger hair was braided close to her head, and the thick muscles on her arms were almost as large as Kade's. I could feel the eyes of my monsters on me.

"So a dragon shifter, huh?" Jade commented. "Must have been crazy for you when you first turned. I'm Jade, by the way."

I stared, shocked by how casually she was speaking to me. "Uh, yeah it was," I finally replied. "But everything's been strange since I arrived here."

She nodded like she understood what I meant.

"I'm Raine," I said, not wanting to presume she knew who I was, even though I was sure the monsters had been gossiping about me.

Her lips curled. "Oh, I know who you are. Everyone does."

"Right." I shifted uncomfortably and went back to staring at the passing trees. Another beat of silence passed, and I'd thought that might be the end of our conversation, but then Jade started speaking again. "Still remember the day I turned. It was my sixth birthday and I'd been in the middle of changing clothes because ma had ordered me a new dress from the tailors. I was supposed to be getting ready for my big party, but I hated frills, so I'd been dragging my feet. I'd finally put it on, and that's when the pain had started."

She shrugged before continuing, "Of course, back then I didn't understand it was because of the curse the queen had placed on us. I'd been convinced it was the dress somehow hurting me. When I finally managed to stand again, I'd turned to the mirror, and screamed my little heart out. I'd thought I was staring at a monster." She chuckled and added, "Well, turned out I was right. I just didn't realize at first that the monster was me."

I wasn't sure how to react to her story, but I turned to her and asked, "So, the dress was that bad, then?"

Her grin grew wide, her vibrant green lips peeling back to reveal her teeth, and she laughed. When her laughter died down, she said, "Thankfully, that monstrosity had been torn off me because the threads had burst when my body had increased in size. Guess that was my silver lining."

"I bet your mother had a fit."

Jade adjusted her hold on her mace. "She turned into a troll, and suddenly getting her unruly daughter to wear a frilly dress was the last thing on her mind."

I returned Jade's grin, already liking the orc though we hardly knew each other.

"So what was yours?" she asked. "It can't have been easy. Remaining human for so long."

"My silver lining?"

She nodded. "Perene and the council make it seem like all the newbloods are grateful to become part of our world, but I wasn't born without a brain. You must have had a family and friends where you came from, and this curse always takes before it gives something in return. So what's the thing that's helped to keep you sane?"

My gaze slid to where my monsters were pretending they weren't eavesdropping on our conversation. My silver lining was *them*. That I could be with my monsters without them having to worry they might hurt me. Because I was a monster just like they were. My lining was that I could be a weapon in the fight against Warrick and his outliers instead of being a liability. And maybe, just one day, if we survived the fight, I'd be able to find my sister. But I didn't tell Jade any of that. Instead, I said simply, "Flying."

"Flying?"

"Yeah," I said with a soft smile, not really realizing how much I meant it until the word had come out of my mouth. "It's incredible being above the world and having the wind buffeting my wings. Up there it's like I could go anywhere."

Jade whistled low. "Well, that's better than my answer."

"Oh, I don't know. That dress of yours sounded pretty bad."

Her lips twisted to the side. "You're a lot of fun, dragon. We need to have a drink when this shit is over." Her expression darkened then, and I followed her gaze to King Adrien's tomb and Warrick's limp form.

"Think the fae will accept them?" I asked, honestly curious as to how the orc felt about the whole situation.

She adjusted the mace again on her shoulder, and I had the distinct thought that I wouldn't want to be opposing her when she wielded that weapon. After a moment, she replied, "They'd better."

CHAPTER 28

~ Darian ~

"We're getting close. Everyone keep your senses peeled for any fae scum," Borren said with a sneer as we neared the edge of the forest, trekking toward the mountains in the distance.

"There could be fae scouts watching us as you speak," I commented from where I was walking beside Raine at the head of our group. "I suggest you keep any insults to yourself for the next while." That I even had to remind the demon alpha of this fact was ridiculous.

"And sheath your weapons," Kade growled. "We don't want them thinking we're here for a fight."

Grumbling, all of the monsters except Borren put their weapons away. I stared pointedly at the demon alpha until he cursed and finally sheathed his sword. Devils if I knew why the demon alpha was allowed to volunteer.

There were only small patches of trees and boulders scattered around us now, so finding cover was becoming an impossible task. When we reached the end of the tree line and stepped out into open land, I moved closer to Raine, not liking our precarious situation.

None of us spoke the closer we got to the fae camp, and soon all I could focus on was the buzzing of insects and the warm night air that made my skin prickle with sweat. It was too quiet for my liking.

"Ow, you little bastard!" Asher cursed, shattering the silence as he reached around with his free hand and slapped his shoulder.

We all turned to him, and he looked up with an unapologetic expression. "What? It's not my fault mosquitos fuckin' love me."

I shook my head and followed Raine to move closer to Ash.

It wasn't until we'd passed the first mountains that Locke said in a low voice, "Remember we're here for peace. No one is to draw their weapons unless the fae attack first. This is our one chance, so don't fuck it up."

Not that we needed the reminder. We all knew full well what was at stake.

Kade stopped abruptly as his ears twitched, and he growled low.

"What is it?" Ure whispered, sniffing the air. "Can you sense something?"

"The opposite," Kade replied, still balancing the tomb on his shoulder. "There are less scents than there should be. Like the land ahead holds...nothing."

I squinted at the expanse of bare dirt and grasses ahead of us. The unoccupied land stretched on, winding through the mountains, but there was a humming noise in the air, and an unpleasant metallic taste coated my tongue. I frowned, though I already knew what it was. *Magic.*

Locke moved in front of Raine, Asher and me, and led us forward. I noted the distinct sensation as if I were moving through a sheet of rain, except instead of water droplets pattering delightfully onto my uncomfortably warm skin, tingles washed over my body making my senses go on high alert. We had to be passing through the illusion Nic and the others had spoken about, which meant things were about to get very interesting.

The air shimmered as we pierced the illusion, and I found myself staring at a hundred armed fae soldiers. They stood in defensive poses in front of seemingly endless rows of small tents like they had been waiting for us. *Sweet Toros, there has to be thousands of tents here.* We all knew King Chalir would bring a sizeable force, but this was more than I think any of us had imagined. I moved in front of Raine, all too ready to use my body to shield her if it came to it.

"Easy," Locke said to our group, lifting his hands in a placating gesture.

My throat bobbed as I eyed the soldiers in their gleaming silver armor. Could I sing fast enough to entrance them before they used their own power?

In the middle of the semicircle of soldiers stood a familiar male with sky-blue material beneath his armor and a large image of a dazra etched onto his breastplate. I instantly recognized the arrogant male's pale gray eyes and his distinct jawline exposed by his helmet. *Captain Pezar.*

The captain stepped forward, the only fae before us without a weapon in his hands. His gaze went to the tomb and Warrick, and when he recognized my brothers, Raine and me in turn, a smile crawled onto his face. "The escaped assassins. Why does it seem so fitting that you five are among the first monsters to greet us now that we're in your realm?" He spoke like we'd just made his day. Which didn't surprise me considering recapturing the monsters who'd escaped execution would likely make him look favorable to his king.

Speaking of... I peered around, trying to glimpse King Chalir and spotted a tent in the middle of the camp that was ten times the size of the other tents. *Ah yes, of course.*

"You mean his returned guests," I countered the captain's statement with a gracious smile. "The incident with our dear friend, Prince Azaren, was merely a misunderstanding. And everything after came down to simple self-preservation. I'm sure you can understand."

"Oh right, the prince's *friends*," Captain Pezar said, emphasizing the word 'friends,' then his smile fell, and he spat on the ground. "I knew what you were the moment I set eyes on you, and the fact that the prince trusted you simply showed just how ill-equipped he is to rule."

Raine bristled behind me, and I had to wonder how Prince Azaren had turned out to be a kind-hearted royal when he'd had to deal with the likes of Captain Pezar. The male would make anyone sour.

"And don't you even think of trying to entrance us with whatever perverted magic you used during the execution," Captain Pezar went on, oblivious to my scrutiny. "You'll be down before you've even sung your second note."

I smiled broadly, but I didn't point out to him that one note was all I needed. One note would be enough to bring on the confusion, but admittedly I would need more than that to fully entrance them.

"We're not here as a threat," Locke said coldly. "Go tell your king we're here on a mission of peace. We come bearing gifts with the hope that we can mend the rift between our kind."

Captain Pezar stared for a long moment, and then he tipped his head back and howled with laughter. His body shook, and the soldiers around him seemed uneasy.

Locke's temple pulsed, and for a moment, I worried my vampire brother might simply snap the fae's neck, but the captain's laughter eventually died down.

Captain Pezar sneered. "You don't honestly expect me to believe you're here for peace after all that has happened between your kind and ours. Especially in light of recent events."

"It has been a long time since the fae fought against us," I pointed out. "There have been…developments, since then. King Chalir might think he knows what he's up against, but for the sake of the thousands of lives that will be lost if it comes to battle, I implore you to advise your king that we wish to speak. Much thought has gone into this encounter in the hopes we can avoid the bloodshed."

"Lives will be lost," Captain Pezar agreed. "But the fae will be the victors. Our numbers are great."

"If you do not announce us, the blame will go to you when the battle turns." Locke added, his voice so cold even I felt the chill of his words.

Captain Pezar pressed his lips together and shifted uncomfortably under the gaze of the vampire.

Jade took that opportune moment to lick her lips as she stared at the soldiers closest to her, and I had to stop myself from smiling when the soldiers blanched, their grips on their spears loosening ever so slightly.

"Despite what you think, we admire the fae," Raine said, my lovely dragon predictably stepping to the side, so I was no longer shielding her. In truth, I worried less about her well-being now that she was a monster just like we were, but that wouldn't stop me from doing everything I could to protect her. "Give us this chance to try and avoid a war that will wound both our kind."

Captain Pezar's gaze lingered on her, and it was clear he was displeased about having to make such a choice. As much as I disliked the fae, I could sympathize with his predicament. If he didn't announce our intentions to his king, he risked being responsible for pertinent information not being received, but if he did and we attacked the king, he'd be the one responsible for jeopardizing the king's safety. I smiled as I enjoyed the captain's discomfort. Finally, Captain Pezar dipped his head in agreement, and turned to the soldier closest to him. "Tell the king of our unusual visitors."

The soldier nodded frantically and scurried off, racing between the tents, and kicking up dust with his boots. We all stood awkwardly as we waited. It was a long while before there was a commotion further in the camp. It was hard to see much beyond the wall of soldiers still in front of us, but then I heard the shout, "Make way for the king!"

The soldiers and Captain Pezar opened the semicircle, moving to the side as King Chalir strode forward flanked by another twenty soldiers who I deduced were likely the king's personal guard. The guards moved in unison, their armor clinking as they took up their positions behind their king.

King Chalir's white hair hung loose below his jeweled crown, and he was strapped in fine armor fitting for a monarch. He glared at us with disdain, like we were merely the dirt beneath his feet. It was a far cry from the welcome we'd first received from him in the fae realm.

His hate-filled gaze took in the tomb and then Warrick's unconscious form, before he turned his attention back to us. Irritation crossed his features, and I couldn't help but feel the tiniest bit of satisfaction. Undoubtedly, the king had been hoping his army's presence in our world would remain undetected until the fae attacked and took us by surprise. Luckily for us, they thought wrong.

"So, we cross paths again," King Chalir mused. "I'm told you're here on a mission of peace. You must have something incredibly valuable to offer for you to even consider you can come to my war camp and return to your kind alive, let alone with an agreement of peace."

"The value of an offering is determined by the needs of the one receiving the gift," I returned with a steady smile, all too aware of Raine and the others around me. One mistake. That's all it would take, and this situation was going to go very badly for all of us.

"True words," King Chalir agreed. "And what is it you think I need, other than to rid us of the threat of your kind?"

I indicated to the tomb. "We offer you the one who started the war between the fae and the humans of Katakin all those years ago. The one who killed your father, King Jazrec, and dishonored our Queen Izla, your sister. The king who failed his people. It was his actions alone that led to the curse being placed on us, and everything that has happened since."

King Chalir's eyes widened with shock before an intense hatred gleamed in his eyes. "I'll admit it would give me great pleasure to finally see my family avenged. Still, it wasn't only King Adrien who slaughtered the fae soldiers who came here to fight two-hundred years ago. And he wasn't the one who attacked my son in mere days past."

I maintained my strong stance. "We were following the orders of our king and defending ourselves when your soldiers arrived that first time. The entire situation was regrettable and would have been avoidable under different leadership."

There were curses and scoffs of disbelief from the fae soldiers, but none dared speak up more than that.

"As for the assassination, we have already explained it wasn't us who attacked the prince." I gestured my head to Asher, and he swung Warrick from his shoulder, letting the vampire fall to the dirt with a thud. "But Warrick here, was the one who captured and tortured your son when the prince visited our realm."

King Chalir glared at Warrick on the ground. The vampire was still unconscious, and his skin was deathly pale.

"So," King Chalir began. "You expect me to simply take these two as a gesture of your goodwill and lead my army back through the portals to our realm?" He scowled. "As if the execution of these males could make me forget all that has happened between our kind. No, my sister finally saw you for what you are, and I will not turn away now that I have made my decision."

"No," Raine protested, her eyes burning as she stood tall. "We don't think it'll make you forget. We hope it'll make you remember."

King Chalr cocked his head, surprised by her words.

"There was a time when Queen Izla was a kind ruler of this land," Raine went on. "She fostered a connection between the humans and the fae and was loved by many. It was King Adrien who betrayed her love and, in turn, his own people. We shouldn't all be judged because of his mistake. Now it's Warrick who wishes to control the realms just like King Adrien." Raine peered around at the king and the fae soldiers who watched her intently. "We want you to remember the time when there was peace. When the humans and fae were able to learn and grow together. You think we're monsters, but we're nothing compared to the tortured creatures Warrick has created. If we engage in all-out war, we'll all die. That's why we've tried so hard to bring him to you before it comes to that."

Everyone was silent for a long moment, and my heart swelled for my mate. She spoke as if she'd always been one of us. As if she personally knew the queen, her ancestor. Would the fae care if she revealed her heritage?

Opening his mouth, King Chalir went to speak, but before he could utter a word the world exploded into chaos. A clink sounded, and Warrick, who had been lying still at our feet, was no longer there. The vampire ripped the stone lid of the tomb away, sending a cloud of dust into the air.

I grabbed Raine, instinctively pulling her away as my brothers moved into action. Before they could reach Warrick, the vampire hissed, taking a syringe and squeezing a black substance into the open, screaming mouth of the motionless stone king.

Locke moved like a blur, snarling as he grabbed Warrick's shoulder and sent the vampire flying.

Warrick landed in a crouch, his lips curling into a cruel smile as his gaze went from Locke to King Adrien.

Before Locke could go after the vampire, a fae cried out, "I-It's alive!"

Locke turned his head in time to see the stone king open his eyes. His gray pupils flickered black before turning to a glowing, blood red, and he burst from the tomb, tearing apart the stone and sending chunks flying in all directions. A large piece smashed into Locke's chest sending him careening backward.

When I turned back to Warrick, the vampire was gone.

"Contain him!" King Chalir shouted, pointing to King Adrien, but the fae's spears couldn't penetrate the king's stone body. We watched in horror as the monster grew five times his size, his lips bulging and spikes covering his body. A stone crown sat atop his head, as if when the curse was created, his crown had become a part of him. We stepped back as we stared at the monstrous king, the fae soldier's arrows and blades bouncing off his stony exterior and falling to the ground.

"How long has Warrick been awake for?" I muttered in disbelief. I eyed King Adrien who appeared to be some perversion of an outlier. *Warrick has discovered how to turn monsters into outliers.* The realization was chilling.

Smoke trailed from Raine's nose, but I pulled her further back. "Don't, lovely. If you turn, the fae will see you as the monster that King Adrien is."

King Adrien stepped forward, his red eyes blazing as he moved his giant arms, swiping through the lines of fae and sending them flying.

The other monsters fought to bring King Adrien down, but they were flung in all directions. Some of the fae outstretched their hands, finally coming to their senses and reaching for their magic, and the wind picked up, howling around us as magic sizzled in the air.

King Adrien swayed on his feet, but he remained standing as he fought against the buffeting wind.

"We need to go," Kade shouted.

Jade let out a cry as she ran at King Adrien, swinging her mace into the giant monster's foot. King Adrien cackled, his thunderous laughter making the ground vibrate.

"We can't go," Raine hissed, her eyes wild. "We need to help them! Dar, you can entrance him!"

"There will be no peace treaty now," I told her rationally. "The fae will believe that we led Warrick and King Adrien here to infiltrate their camp."

"But we didn't," she protested.

"I know," I told her, but I indicated to the wounded fae soldiers, and the others rallying to fight King Adrien. More fae were running toward us from the tents with their hands outstretched.

"They'll manage to overcome him with their magic, and then what do you think they'll do to us? Helping them with this will only mean we're next in line for their latest execution. And I won't let them harm you."

Her mouth opened and closed like she wanted to say more but the words wouldn't come out. Finally, she nodded, her gaze defeated.

Lifting Raine into my arms, I jogged away from the fae and the stone king, and my brothers ran around us, ready to defend. We fled across the stretch of bare land, and when we reached the cover of the forest, I peered back to see King Adrien was on the ground, a legion of fae surrounding him as he thrashed and struggled against whatever hold they had over him.

But there wasn't any time to wait and see what else would happen. We sprinted through the trees, not slowing until we reached our camp. Because there was no stopping the battle now.

CHAPTER 29

Present day

All right, Cara, you've made it to Katakin, now you might just get some answers. I mixed my bowl of oatmeal for what had to be the twentieth time, but I still didn't eat. *Or...you could die here and Raine and Father will never know what happened to you.*

I sighed and put down my bowl. Four years had passed since I'd ignored Xander's cries and walked through the portal that would take me to the fae king. Four years, and I was still questioning whether I'd made the right decision. I'd believed going to the palace and meeting the king was the only way I'd be able to find a way back to my family, but I'd soon learned the king was just as the Forgotten Fae said he was. He cared little for his kind and focused his time throwing lavish parties and building his army. I knew from the moment I stepped into his court that he was never going to let me leave. Not when he declared I was a hero and announced I was a rare "jewel" in Zalei.

At first, I was able to come to terms with my new arrangement because he allowed me to help some of the less fortunate fae, but as the years passed, he began to keep me hidden away. Healing others drained my energy, and even though my magic always replenished after resting, he became possessive. With the more frequent attacks from the Forgotten Fae leading him to become more concerned for his own well-being, he declared that my real duty should be to him, my king, and he didn't want to share. What would happen if he needed healing, and I was unable to help?

On the bright side, I was able to visit the royal library and study many of the texts. Eventually, I was able to teach myself to create portals, even though it was forbidden. But as much as Xander had lied to me about many things, he hadn't lied about it being nearly impossible to create a portal to an island without knowing its exact location. Every time I created a new portal, I'd strap myself with weapons and head through. Sometimes, I'd find I'd accidentally created portals to places within Zalei. Other times, from the strange surroundings or unusual animal life I encountered, it was clear I'd created portals to other worlds. Either way, the result was the same. I couldn't find my way home.

But when the monsters visited Zalei I realized I'd been thinking about it all wrong. The Katakin monsters knew where my island was *and* how to get there. So I just had to survive this war, and hope that when I finally found my way back home it wasn't too late. I had to hope that Raine hadn't been chosen during the last offering...

"Lady, the king needs you," a frantic voice interrupted my thoughts, and I turned to see Flynn had lifted the flap of my tent and was peering inside. Of all the guards King Chalir had assigned to watch me night and day, Flynn was my favorite. He never made me aware of his presence unless necessary, almost giving me the illusion of freedom.

"What is it?" I asked, jumping to my feet when I noticed a soldier standing beside him with blood splattered across his face and coating his hands. *Has the battle started already?* My face hardened, and I pulled my hood low as I strode to the opening of the tent. "What's happened?"

The soldier stared at my exposed chin as I drew close, undoubtedly staring at the artwork of gems covering my skin, but then he blinked and jerked his gaze away, gesturing with his head to the camp behind him. "The king is injured. You must come quickly."

He began leading us between the tents, and Flynn and I followed, keeping up with his brisk pace.

"The monsters came saying they wanted peace," the soldier explained. "But instead, they unleashed a beast within our barrier. Before we could contain the stone giant, it fled the camp, but many have been wounded and killed." Horror filled the soldier's eyes, and fear trickled down the back of my neck. *Stone giant?* On my island, the elders who told stories about the Katakin monsters always spoke of how terrifying and cruel the creatures were, and in Zalei, the tales about the beasts hadn't been any better.

I wanted to ask the soldier more about the monster, but shouting pulled my attention to a commotion up ahead. I walked faster and gasped when the scene came into view. Fae lay on the ground bleeding, some crushed and others with wounds to various places on their bodies. Tents had been destroyed, the wooden posts broken and splintered, and huge footprints were indented on the ground. I started to move toward a fae who was bleeding profusely from his chest, but the soldier who was with me lifted his arm, stopping me from moving any closer.

"The king has ordered me to bring you directly to him, lady," the soldier explained, though his face was tight as he stared down at his wounded comrade.

I clenched my jaw, but I pivoted and followed the soldier to where King Chalir was propped on a chair outside one of the intact tents. One of the king's personal guards stood fanning his face, and I frowned when I took note of the king's good health besides a deep gash on his arm.

"Your highness," I said, bowing low.

King Chalir's eyes brightened, and he smiled. "Ah, my jewel, I was hoping you would come."

"Of course, my king," I replied blandly, though we both knew I didn't have a choice. Moving forward, I inspected his arm with my gloved hands. The wound was deep, but nothing a fae couldn't heal from in time.

Squeezing my eyes shut, I concentrated, focusing on the smoothness of my gloves against his skin, and the power building within me. In the beginning, I hadn't used gloves, but the silky fabric made it easier to control the rate of healing. I felt the exact moment a tiny gem formed on the inside of my arm, adding to my collection. I had hundreds of them now. Countless gems covering my skin, reminders of the times when I'd healed others. In recent years, many were from times when I'd healed the king, usually from wounds he could have easily healed from naturally in time, and the thought of them covering my body made me sick.

With my work complete, I stood. "If that's all, I shall tend to some of the other wounded," I said softly.

Before I could step away, King Chalir grabbed my arm. I stared at where his long fingers curled around my sleeve before lifting my attention to his face.

"You are to return to your tent," he ordered, the smile falling from his face and revealing the cold, calculated king I'd come to know. "We battle at sunlight, and I need you to be well rested."

"But your highness—" I began, my heart skipping a beat as I peered at the other soldiers who were grievously wounded, many who wouldn't make it past the next few hours without my help.

"Flynn, escort her to her tent," King Chalir snapped at my guard, though his gaze stayed on my face. From the glint in his eyes, I knew the king was admiring the colored gems that lined the bottom of my jaw. Gems that all appeared after I'd healed him on numerous occasions. Rage began to course through me, and I tried to focus on the azure-colored gem under my right eye that had appeared when I'd saved the fae prince.

Prince Azaren had been near death when they'd brought me to him days ago. The guards said monsters had tried to assassinate him, but I recognized the poison in his veins. No, it was a Forgotten fae who tried to claim his life, and the thought made my heart ache.

The kind prince had been my only friend in the palace, even if we were only able to speak briefly. Sometimes we would encounter one another in the library and escape into one of the rooms where we could speak without having to worry about those listening in. He was a better fae than his father, always passionately speaking about the importance of education in the pursuit of peace, and he would make a great king. I could have used a friendly face right then, but the prince remained in Zalei, seeing to the kingdom in King Chalir's absence.

Perhaps it would be better if I let the king die on the battlefield?

"This way, lady," Flynn said, coming up beside me, and I blinked, my heart pounding as I reminded myself that even thinking about the king's death in that way was heresy.

"My king," I said curtly and turned, following my guard.

CHAPTER 30

I leaned against Darian's chest, breathing in his scent and letting it ground me. Kade and Asher stood by my sides, and Locke was a couple steps in front of us. My vampire paced angrily, his claws extended, and wings folded behind his back. My blood still pounded in my ears from our wild dash through the forest, and scales sprouted on my arms before I pushed back the change.

Darian brushed my hair away from my neck and kissed beneath my jaw. "Easy, lovely."

I tried to focus on the smooth tones of his voice and not the fact that the fae were likely preparing for battle as we stood there. The great hall of the hideout had been nearly empty when we'd burst in, but monsters were now filling the space.

"We're not ready," protested a goblin in the middle of the hall.

Locke stopped pacing. "The fight is here, whether we're ready or not."

"And how did this happen, anyway?" one of the alphas shouted. "Where did the syringe come from?"

"We searched Warrick's clothes when we first brought him here and didn't find anything," Locke defended.

"Sounds to me like someone fucked up," shouted one of the shifters.

"How it happened doesn't matter," Lyr interjected.

"I still think we should let Warrick and his army take care of the fae," Kasey spoke up.

"We don't know how long Warrick was awake," Kade replied. "He could know the location of our camp. And even if he doesn't, it's only a matter of time. He'll head straight for us after he defeats the fae. Our best option is to fight on the battlefield and hope the fae come to their senses and join with us after they see the monsters Warrick has created."

Kasey frowned. "And if they don't?"

"We can't hide from this," Kade growled. "If we want any hope of reclaiming Katakin and having a life without Warrick or the fae controlling us, we need to fight."

There were grumbles around the room.

"We don't have time for this," Lyr said. "We need to prepare ourselves."

The goblin from earlier held up the swords bundled in his arms. "Many still don't have adequate armor or weaponry!"

"Then we make do. We are monsters are we not?" Lyr replied, standing tall.

Kenric took a step forward. "If it's true what you're saying and Warrick can turn any of us into one of his outliers, then this battle is lost before it has even begun."

There were murmurs of agreement and defeated expressions around the room, but Lyr shook her head. "We don't know if Warrick has any more of the serum he used on King Adrien. It's possible he hasn't had the time or resources to formulate more."

Nic folded his arms across his broad chest. "I don't know about you, but I'd rather die fighting than wait for Warrick to turn me into one of his puppets."

At that, it grew silent around the hall.

Lyr stared at the monsters around the space. "Now, if you're all done talking about how we've already lost, how about we start talking about how we can win."

• • • ● • ● • ● • • •

I strode into the room we'd been using and whirled around as my monsters filtered in behind me and Asher closed the door.

"They're right to question this," I said, my throat tight as I indicated with my head to the monsters beyond the door. "We all saw what happened to King Adrien. If Warrick can turn us like that, we have no hope of surviving the fae and the outliers." I didn't want to believe that we might lose, but I'd seen King Adrien's eyes as they'd turned red. "We can't fight him if he already controls our minds."

"Then we only attack Warrick if we're together and fighting as a unit," Kade pointed out. "He can't change all of us at once."

I bit my lower lip, and Locke stalked toward me, wrapping me in his arms. "I won't let him touch you," he growled.

Smoke trailed from my nose as my chest heaved. "It's not me I'm worried about," I admitted, all of the emotion from the past few hours catching up with me. I wanted to burn the sky, to hunt Warrick down and make him pay for all that he'd done. I wanted to slap King Chalir and force him to see that we would only survive this if we united, but I couldn't do any of those things.

My monsters crowded around me, and when Locke dipped his head, I brought my lips to his, desperate to remind myself that Warrick wasn't going to take him from me. We had to leave within hours, but I needed this. I needed *them.*

Locke slid his arms to the hollow of my back, and he pressed me against him as he kissed me back, devouring my mouth like he was just as desperate to taste every part of me. Like he'd unravel if he couldn't remind himself that I was his. We kissed like the world was ending, and when Locke's touch became gentle, a tear slid down the side of my cheek. My vampire swiped the tear away with his thumb and carried me to the bed.

Asher, Kade, and Darian stripped as they followed us, and Locke pulled off my clothes, his gaze locked on me as he peeled away the weapons and layers. Every move slow and methodical. When I was completely naked, he set about undressing himself, and Kade moved onto the bed.

"You don't need to worry about us, Mahare," Kade growled softly as he nudged my neck and pressed soft kisses to the side of my face. "All we need is for you to live."

"But that's not all I need," I whispered, and my heart ached at how true those words were. From the moment Cara had been taken from me, all I'd cared about was finding my sister. I had to make sure she was all right and finally apologize for being the reason she was taken, and if she wished, to help her return home. But my heart had grown since then. Locke, Kade, Asher, and Darian. They'd become a part of me.

I leaned across, claiming Kade's lips as I finally admitted to myself that these monsters weren't just my mates, they were my *family,* and I'd fight for them just as hard as I was willing to fight for Cara. The last barrier around my heart shattered, and I let them in. *Completely.* Because there was no life for me without my growly wolf, my mischievous demon, my sweet siren, and my broody vampire. My heart would be theirs. Always.

"Sweetheart," Asher croaked, his throat raw with emotion as my gaze locked with his, my eyes blurry with tears. He moved closer to me on the bed, and I gasped as his tail flicked out, wrapping tight around my thigh.

Darian, who'd been busy kissing my inner thigh paused and pulled back with an intrigued expression. "Now, now, Ash, I'm not sure if you know this, but I've already claimed this spot right here."

Asher grinned, his violet eyes glowing. "Luckily for me, I know you like to share."

Darian's lips curled upward into a sensual smile, and suddenly I was laughing.

I lifted my hand but hesitated. "Does this mean that I can touch your tail?" I asked uncertainly, watching Asher's expression.

My demon's grin fell, and he looked as bewildered as I was, but he guided my hand to his tail, letting my fingers brush along his smooth skin. As I touched him, he shuddered, the glow in his eyes brightening. "Only you, Sharachi," he breathed, his usually amused gaze now intensely serious. "And it'll always only be you, if you'll have us."

My bottom lip trembled as I realized what he was truly asking. He wanted to mark me. To claim me as his mate. And this time...I was ready.

"Yes," I replied, my words barely above a whisper. "Always."

Asher's smile grew so wide, and my eyes watered as he kissed me, his soft lips warm and gentle. I kissed along his jaw to a place beneath his ear, and as his tail burned against my skin, I harnessed a part of my dragon that I'd been too afraid to use. I breathed a small amount of fire onto his skin, leaving a mark of blue flames that glowed in the light. The pain in my thigh soon disappeared, Asher's mark on me now tingling rather than burning, and somehow, I knew that even when he wasn't around me, I would always feel his skin pressed against mine. *My demon. Mine. Always.*

Asher's tail released my thigh, and I ran my fingers over the violet mark remaining on my skin like a tattoo. My *mate's* mark.

Kade kissed my shoulder. "I'm next," he growled.

I frowned. "But what about your pack?"

He tucked a stray strand of hair behind my ear. "You are part of my pack, Mahare. And if the House of Worzel don't want me because you're by my side, then so be it. There is no life for me without you, my mate."

I swallowed hard, but I nodded. Kade left a bite mark to my neck, and I breathed fire onto his collarbone until blue flames marked his tan skin. He ran his fingers over the mark I'd left on him, a low satisfied growl rumbling from his chest.

"My turn," Darian said with a sensual smile as he marked me, pale blue stars tingling all the way up my arm as I left blue flames on his chest.

"A fitting mark for you, my darling," Darian commented as he admired his sparkling stars. "Because even in the darkness you shine brighter than any monster I've ever known." His eyes softened. "And all I want is to be with you."

I couldn't stop the tears from rolling down my cheeks, and then I was laughing while Darian kissed up my arm, pressing his lips to each star.

When my siren released me, I turned to Locke, my heart already feeling so full I thought it might burst. His onyx eyes watched me carefully as he drew closer, his fangs already extended.

"Are you sure you want this?" he asked quietly.

My heart raced at his words as I momentarily panicked. "Don't you want to mark me?"

He smiled, his dark gaze so intense I couldn't look away. "More than anything, *beautiful*."

"Then what are you waiting for?"

Locke snarled as he took me in his arms. His punishing kiss was like fire, and when he sunk his teeth into my neck, on the opposite side to where Kade had marked me, I moaned loudly, enjoying the burn and the sensation of his venom entering my system. He hissed as he pulled back and licked the wound until it healed and tingled.

I held him as I marked the skin above his heart, my flames striking against his pale white complexion.

And then he moved me, and my back was against the bed as he kissed and licked down my body. My mates closed in on me, more monsters than men as they claimed every inch of me just as possessively as I claimed them.

Because nothing and no one could take this from us. Not Warrick. Not the fae.

We enjoyed each other like the moon wouldn't rise again, and when I finally curled into their arms on the bed, I smiled, knowing that no matter what happened during the battle, I would always have them.

Asher wrapped his tail around my thigh, over the spot where he'd marked me, and I stroked his soft skin. His cock jumped, instantly hardening and pressing against my side like his tail was a direct connection to the appendage.

"Fuck," my demon chuckled. "Now, I understand all the hype I've heard over the years."

"That good?" I asked with a grin.

He winked. "You are, sweetheart."

CHAPTER 31

My mates remained close to me as they fitted their armor and loaded themselves up with weapons. I began adding plates of leather armor to my arms and shoulders, and Kade helped me tighten the straps.

When he finished, my wolf shifter's golden eyes met mine. Neither of us spoke. In fact, no one around us did either. We all readied ourselves in silence, the tension thick in the air as we collected our weapons and prepared ourselves for the fight to come. The battle we'd hoped to avoid was here, and none of us knew if we'd survive it.

Asher grabbed two massive axes and his muscles flexed as he slid them into the holsters behind his back. Darian collected his stars, a bow and arrows, and a selection of blades, and Locke slid two long swords into the scabbards by his sides. My mates were like works of art, their lethal bodies crafted as if they were made for this fight, but worry still twisted in my gut.

Locke peered over at me, and I could read the promise in his eyes. He'd die to protect me. They all would. But I'm not sure if they realized that I'd never let it come to that. Goddess help any outlier or fae who tried to take my family from me.

My gaze swept around the hall to the other monsters who were preparing themselves. Clumped together in house groups, the clang of metal, shuffle of boots, and scent of leather filled my senses along with the tang of brimstone.

Cordelia and the House of Saceris hadn't joined us, and neither had Mabel and the House of Faren. We had four high houses, the House of Silat, House of Worzel, House of Thorem, and House of Axeran. We also had over half of the lower houses from the city, many of which were camped in the caves and forest. No one knew if it would be enough.

Lyr and her mates walked between the different groups, checking on their progress, and goblins scurried around with their arms full of weapons and shields.

And then we were marching through the forest, thousands of boots crunching the leaves under our feet, and moving past trees as we made our way toward the battleground. Rebel scouts had informed us that the fae army had assembled on the stretch of bare land between the fae camp and the city, so it seemed that's where we would fight. *And where many will die.* I tried not to think about it.

My monsters walked beside me, and no one around us commented on the marks now covering our skin. No one said anything about us not belonging to a house, or that we weren't supposed to mark monsters who were of different breeds. None of that mattered right then. My mates glared at anyone who came close to me, and the monsters stayed at a respectful distance, careful not to crowd into our space.

Before long, we exited the trees and marched forward onto the plain. My heart caught in my throat when I took in the fae army, fully assembled and spread across the land in front of us almost like they'd been waiting for us to arrive. The soldiers stood in neat formations, their silver armor gleaming under the light of a full moon shining high above us. Heat bubbled in my belly as I eyed the rows of soldiers that extended far and wide. *There has to be over twenty thousand of them.* Twelve fae sat on silver horses at the back of the army, and I could only guess it was the king and his closest guards and generals.

I wet my lips nervously as the rebels moved forward in their house groups, forming neat lines, and unsheathing their weapons. My mates and I stayed at the back following the plan Lyr and the other monsters had put forward. As the largest shifter, I was to be the surprise weapon, and my mates refused to leave my side.

Kasey stood leading the House of Worzel with Tristan, and her gaze found Kade across the stretch of monsters between us. Kade didn't acknowledge her pleading stare, and unease went through me. The wolves hadn't said anything about the fact Kade had marked me, but Kade still refused to lead because he wouldn't leave my side. I turned to my wolf shifter, though I wasn't exactly sure what else I could say. I didn't *want* him on the front lines, but the wolves needed him. Before I could utter a word, the ground began to shake, making my body vibrate.

"What the fuck did that used to be?" Asher breathed as a massive outlier with six legs, two heads, and a long-spiked tail crested over the hill to our right. The creature had holes where I imagined its ears were supposed to be, and massive black horns that twisted into the air. Warrick sat atop the beast's back, firmly planted on a lavish black saddle.

"Perhaps, a gazelle or a warthog?" Darian suggested like he was discussing someone's new pet rather than the beast that was undoubtedly going to try to kill us.

Monsters from the high houses of Saceris, Faren, and Nesarin marched behind Warrick along with monsters from dozens of the lower houses. The members of the Taratun council were also there, their billowing robes fluttering in the wind. Even from my position I could make out their red eyes, and a shiver clawed its way down my spine.

"He's turned them all," I breathed, watching as the monsters moved in perfect unison and stopped in neat rows by Warrick's sides.

Locke cursed.

"No wonder they didn't join us," Kade growled.

Anger lit up Darian's eyes as he stared at the sirens. "I warned Cordelia to get them out." Abruptly, he jerked his head toward me and the others. "Unlike me, the sirens usually struggle to entrance more than one individual at a time, but if they sing with one voice controlled by Warrick, I can't be sure of their abilities. We need to find a way to take them down from a distance."

I furrowed my brow. "Take them down?" I'd been holding onto the hope that the monsters from the other houses in Katakin would all eventually side with us once they saw what Warrick was capable of.

"Yes," Darian replied bluntly, regret evident on his face. "There's no hope of them changing sides now."

Asher adjusted his grip on his axes. "Fuck."

I was still staring at the sirens of the House of Saceris when outliers began streaming over the hill, snapping, snarling, and howling as they ran. The smallest outliers came first, thousands of them sprinting through the ranks of the Katakin monsters and forming up to become the front lines of the army. The larger monsters were spread out, lumbering slowly, and taking up their positions. King Adrien was last as he strode forward with a cruel smile on his stony face and took up a position close to Warrick. His red eyes stared gleefully at the armies before him, and I sucked in a sharp breath.

"The fucking fae didn't take him down," Kade growled as he stared at the king.

I turned my attention to the back of the fae army, where the silver horses were pawing the ground in agitation.

"You think he's regrettin' his decision?" Asher asked, gesturing with his head toward the fae king.

Darian let out a long breath through his nose. "Even if he is, there's no turning back now."

A part of me wished King Chalir would see sense and open portals, letting his soldiers flee, but his army stood firm.

Three armies faced each other in the night, all of us knowing that no matter the outcome, our worlds would never be the same again.

Lyr and her mates went to the front lines of the rebel forces. Like me, leather armor was strapped across her body, and her waist was heavy with weapons. She held an iron shield with one hand and lifted her sword with the other. "Monsters of Katakin!" she shouted as she walked along the front line. "Too long have we been ruled by the Taratun council and the curse. Too long have we accepted the rules of our world without question. But not tonight!

We will not bend to Warrick's rule, nor will we surrender to the fae. We either fight or we die." There was a pause as every monster in the rebel army watched the tiger shifter. "Well, I for one choose to fucking LIVE!" she yelled, and at that, the monsters around us howled and roared, lifting their weapons into the air.

Lyr's fearsome face contorted with anger as she went on, "We deserve to control our own fates, and when the fae are bleeding at our feet, when the outliers are no more, we will make the fae remove the curse that's plagued us for too long!" The screams became louder, but I stayed silent. I didn't know if the curse would be broken if they forced a fae to sacrifice themselves, but I didn't want to contemplate it. For now, we hadn't told anyone of what we'd discovered about the curse. *First, survive, Raine. Survive and protect your mates.*

An uproar came from the fae, and the army parted in the middle to allow a fae rider through. A silver horse galloped across the plain, the rider moving past the front lines of the fae and continuing onward. Lyr and her mates started forward as if to meet with the soldier and discuss whatever terms he wanted to offer, but before the rider made it any further, an outlier swooped from seemingly nowhere. The creature's black leathery wings outstretched as the beast descended from the night, reaching out with gangly legs, and picking the horse up with its talons.

I gasped. "What the hell is that?"

The outlier was much smaller than my dragon, but still large enough to easily lift both the horse and rider into the air. My heart lurched as the horse whinnied in alarm. I tensed, and Locke slid his hand down my back. I couldn't shift and save them in time, and I'd simply be giving away our advantage of surprise. This was only the beginning of the horrors we would witness.

High in the sky, the outlier screeched before releasing its captives. A handful of winged fae lifted into the air as if to save them, but both the rider and horse plummeted, impacting with the ground before the winged fae could reach them. The outlier soared through the sky, screeching again as it disappeared back into the night.

The world stilled, the silence deafening, and then King Adrien's bellowing laughter sounded across the plain, loud, and abrasive. Like the sound was a signal, foot soldiers at the back of the fae army trumpeted their horns, and the first ranks of soldiers surged forward. The sea of silver split in half, with soldiers heading for the rebel forces and others moving toward Warrick and his outliers.

Lyr lifted her sword into the air, letting out a battle cry as she pointed her blade at the attacking fae. She started to run, and the rebels moved with her, picking up speed as they went. Some of the shifters opted to begin the battle in their human forms, but others surrendered to their beasts, wolves, bears, stags, and countless other creatures sprinting through the rebel ranks and leaping into the air as they clashed with the first lines of the fae, their claws outstretched and antlers as sharp as spears. The tang of blood filled the air as the clang of metal rang out.

Vasken ran with Lyr and her mates in his chimera form, his large feline body moving with terrifying grace. He leaped and clamped his jaws onto a fae, tearing the soldier's head off, helmet and all.

I clenched my jaw so tightly my teeth ached as the world turned to a scene of blood and death, and cries of pain that would haunt me forever. Like the goddess herself was weeping crimson tears, a hue of red washed over the battlefield, and I peered up.

"A blood moon," Kade growled. "It's a bad omen."

"Well, we all knew this wasn't going to end well," Darian commented, his sharp blue eyes watching the battle unfold.

Kade let out a breath, his gaze fixed on where the wolves of the House of Worzel were fighting, most of them now in their wolf forms. "We underestimated the forces of both Warrick and the fae."

"Knowing accurate numbers wouldn't have changed anything," Locke replied.

"We should be out there," I said, my heart pounding as adrenaline coursed through me.

Locke's face remained hard. "Not yet."

I turned my gaze to where Warrick sat atop his beast, watching as the fae fought his army of outliers. The

Katakin monsters remained beside him, their eyes glowing red as they remained silent and unmoving in their lines. As the larger outliers lumbered through the ranks of silver, sending fae flying, ranks of fae soldiers moved away from the fight with the rebels to battle the creatures.

A group of fae used their wind magic to push back a giant outlier, and the creature overbalanced and toppled to the ground. The fae swarmed the beast, soldiers attacking the outlier, and the creature howled before it was silenced.

I turned my gaze to where the wolves of the House of Worzel were being overrun. A fae soldier lifted her hands and trees burst from the ground, creating a wall behind the wolves and giving them nowhere to retreat. Kade growled as lines of fae soldiers advanced on the group.

"Fight," Kade muttered under his breath, his knuckles turning white as he gripped the hilts of his swords.

The wolves snapped and snarled, trying to attack, but the fae continued to push them back until they were close to the trees.

"Why aren't they working together?" Kade snarled, cursing under his breath. "They could get out of that if they moved as a unit."

My chest heaved, my panic rising because I knew why, but I didn't want to have to say it. "They need their alpha," I rasped. "They need a *leader*."

Kade's golden gaze connected with mine, his body tight. "I won't leave you, my mate."

I shook my head slowly. "You're not leaving me. You're saving *them*." I moved my hands, unfastening my weapons belt so it fell to the ground. "And like hell are you going without us."

I was done waiting. Whatever moment Lyr had wanted us to wait for, this was it. Around us, the rebels were falling. Borren and the demons of the House of Thorem cried out as they fought an overwhelming number of fae, and two massive outliers crossed the battlefield attacking the shifters of the House of Silat.

A howl rang out as another wolf from the House of Worzel fell, and I stepped back a few paces and surrendered to my dragon. My skin rippled, hard scales forming like plates of armor as my body grew in size. When the change was complete, I opened my maw and roared, satisfaction going through me as the sound rose above the noise of the battle. Fae and monsters glanced in my direction, and there were cheers and answering roars from the rebels.

"We're with you," Asher told Kade as he held his massive axes. "Now let's fuck some shit up."

Kade's golden eyes flashed, and then he was shifting as well, his limbs changing and sleek brown fur sprouting over his body until he was the large wolf I'd come to love. Darian and Locke gripped their weapons, and Kade stared at me one last time before he started to run.

We moved as one, joining the battle, and I crashed through the trees that had blocked the wolves. Together, my mates and I started to push back the fae. I moved my massive body, sending soldiers flying backward, and Darian let his stars loose. Asher and Locke worked in tandem to take down a large outlier that barrelled through the demons of the House of Thorem and toward us.

Kade growled as he jogged past the wolves, his large paws flicking up the dirt. The sound was a command from their alpha, and the wolves formed up, regrouping and launching back at the fae as a unit, their teeth tearing through flesh. With renewed strength, and Kade's massive form leading them, they moved as a pack, taking down fae soldiers and outliers with lethal precision.

A screech sounded from above and the flying outlier from earlier swooped down from the sky, materializing from the darkness like a wraith. A black blur in a sky of red. I narrowed my eyes as it drew closer, its talons outstretched as it targeted my wolf. *Mine. My treasure. My mate.* Kade continued forward, unaware as he used his teeth to tear off an outlier's arm.

The flying creature swooped lower, and heat bubbled in my belly, but there were too many rebels around me. And too many fae. Before the outlier could grab my wolf, I let out a deafening roar and the creature veered away, picking up a fae soldier instead. The fae cried out as he was lifted into the air, and I moved, my wings unfolding.

Darian jumped onto my back before I launched into the air. I would kill the creature that tried to take my wolf. A small voice in the back of my mind screamed that I should stay with the rest of my mates, but all I could think about was how the outlier would taste as its blood slid down my throat.

· · · ● · ● ● · ● ● · ·

~ Asher~

One glimpse, that was all I could spare as Raine and Darian flew away. One glimpse, and then two more outliers were coming at me. Locke cut through one, and I hefted my axes cleaving through the other.

My vampire brother peered up at where Raine's blue fire filled the sky, momentarily blocking out the red moon.

"Go," I shouted at Locke.

Indecision flickered across his face, but then he shook his head and cracked his neck. "Raine and Darian can handle that outlier, but I'm not so sure about them."

I lifted my head to where he was staring at the demons of the House of Thorem, and the orcs and trolls of the House of Axeran. The monsters were surrounded by outliers and separated from the main rebel army.

I stared at the demons who had turned their backs on me long ago, and Borren, the alpha, who'd taken my mother's life. An outlier struck Borren across the face, and he fell hard to the ground. As the creature stepped forward with its huge, clawed paws, intending to crush him, he rolled to the side and jumped to his feet.

"It's your call," Locke said giving me the choice as his twin swords cut through another outlier. "We fight here or there, makes no difference to me."

I hesitated only a moment. Kade and his pack were still tearing down the outliers and fae in their path.

"He doesn't need us for now," I yelled, indicating to the wolves. "So, let's go have some fun with the demons."

Locke's pale lips twitched upward. "All right then, brother."

We ran toward Borren and Kenric, cutting down the outliers in our path and making our way to the circle of trapped monsters. Just as an outlier was about to sink its fangs into Jade's throat, I let one of my axes fly through the air, slicing the monster's head off.

Jade pivoted toward me and flashed me a grateful smile, blood coating her teeth. "Thanks!" she shouted, and rolled before jumping up and swinging her mace, smashing her weapon into the face of another outlier.

I grinned as I collected my axe, but my smile fell as a large creature with a reptilian head and thick horns charged toward Borren. The demon alpha turned too late and braced, his face slick with sweat, and I jumped, driving my axes into the outlier's scaled neck. The creature's massive head rolled along the ground, its slitted eyes going pale as its body slumped.

Borren gave me a grim nod, but I didn't do it for him. I'd already seen what happened with the wolves. The demons needed their alpha to lead them. With Borren now at my back, the pair of us fought like monsters possessed, taking down any outlier that drew close. Locke flapped his wings, gaining height to take down some of the larger outliers that circled the group.

Borren's back bumped against mine. "Down," he ordered, and I dropped into a crouch as a clawed paw of an outlier swiped above our heads. The massive creature now facing us was twice the size of a bear, and four times as thick, with saliva dripping from its maw.

Borren and I attacked the beast, coming from both sides to confuse the creature and we soon had it on the ground bleeding at our feet.

The demons of the House of Thorem and monsters of the House of Axeran rallied around us, but the outliers kept coming. Like a swarm of fuckin' insects, they surrounded us, a never-ending mass of claws, and teeth, and red eyes. Another stream of blue fire lit up the sky, and I thought of my mate as I fought the outliers. *Thank fuck Raine is away from this shit.*

I took down two more outliers, breathing heavily as their bodies fell. And that's when I realized the silence. Instead of attacking, the outliers swarmed around our group, a thick mass of ravenous beasts waiting as if they were observing us.

Locke dropped down beside me. Folding his wings behind his back, he held his swords that were dripping with blood. Borren clenched his jaw, eyeing the writhing swarm.

"What are they doin'?" I muttered under my breath, but even before I'd finished speaking, I spotted them. Three huge outliers lumbered toward us, their bodies covered in strange spikes the size of daggers. The little bastards were waiting for the big guys to join the fight.

"You're right to think I failed," Borren said unexpectedly, his gaze still on the outliers.

"Yeah?" I asked, holding my axes as the large outliers lumbered closer. We would have to avoid the spikes as we took them down. "The battle's not over yet, alpha."

Borren's throat bobbed. "No, you're right to think I failed Saskia."

I frowned, anger coursing through me at the sound of my mother's name. "You don't get to speak about her," I said, not willing to hear his bullshit. Not even now while death was staring us down. "You don't get to apologize for what you did."

The smaller outliers snapped at each other and growled, slavering as they watched us.

"I know that," Borren replied gruffly, surprising me. "Your mother needed help, and I was too fucking weak."

My nostrils flared. "I said, shut up."

"At first, it was easy to ignore there was a problem," Borren continued, ignoring me. "But by the end, fuck, I should have listened to her."

He should have—? I took my gaze from the larger outliers to glance at the demon alpha. "What are you talkin' about?"

Sorrow softened the features of the arrogant male. "There were times when we were together, times when she was lucid, that she asked me to end it. She knew she was a threat to you, to the house...to me. But I couldn't, not until..." He swallowed hard. "And when it was over, you were gone. The demons found out about my relationship with Saskia and were beginning to question my role as alpha. So, when they turned their anger on you..." He dipped his head. "I was too weak once again."

I stared at the demon beside me, a sharp ringing starting to drone in my ears. For years, I'd believed he was simply a cruel alpha who'd cleaned house when my mother became too much of a mess, but had he... *cared* for her?

"You can explain yourself later," I told him, but he didn't appear to be listening.

"I'd always thought she'd gone mad, but that wasn't it at all. I simply hadn't pieced it together until now." He chuckled darkly, and his lips formed a sad smile. "Forgive me, Saskia," he muttered under his breath, and his face contorted with anger as he turned his head to where Warrick still sat on the massive beast, hundreds of yards away. The vampire was still watching the battle unfold from relative safety. With a anguished cry, Borren ran in Warrick's direction, toward the outliers that stood like a sea between them.

He'd only made it two steps when spikes shot out from the large outliers that were headed for us. I swung my axes, diverting the spikes headed for me, but two spikes pierced into Borren's chest, puncturing his armor, and driving deep. Borren staggered, and blood trailed from his mouth as his knees slammed to the ground.

The cries of the outliers became frenzied, but they didn't attack as they continued to watch us.

"Alpha!" I dropped to Borren's side as he pulled out the spikes. Blood gushed from beneath his armor, flowing onto the ground.

His gaze remained on me as he gripped my shoulder. "Saskia wasn't broken," he rasped, blood gurgling in his mouth. "It was always because of him. I didn't realize it until I saw what happened with King Adrien and everything finally made sense."

The outliers shot out more spikes, but I was too distracted to react. Locke diverted the ones away from me, but a spike buried into Borren's throat. The demon alpha slumped to the ground, blood pooling in his mouth, and I turned to find the demons of the House of Thorem all staring at me grim-faced.

"Well, what the fuck are you waitin' for?" I roared, the ringing still loud in my ears. "Let's kill these bastards!"

The demons lurched into action, and we surged toward the outliers, carving into the lines of the beasts. Locke fought beside me, taking down the creatures with his inhuman speed. But I knew we wouldn't survive this. There were too many of the fuckers, and not enough of us. Still, my axes sang as they connected with flesh, taking down Warrick's monsters.

Saskia wasn't broken. It was always because of him. The words echoed in my ears, mixing with the sharp ringing, as a memory resurfaced in my mind. A memory of Warrick talking to my mother and giving her a vial filled with a dark liquid. She'd refused to let me touch it, and when I'd questioned her, she'd merely said it was a payment she owed. My kind-hearted mother had always been in touch with others' emotions, and when she'd turned into a monster, the sense had heightened to the point she would say she could feel others' emotions like they were her own. When I reflected in the years after, I'd thought it had been the source of her madness.

Another three outliers fell by my hand, one managing to rake its claws along my collarbone before its head rolled.

I forced myself to think about the moment when my mother had advanced on me as a child, her eyes wild and a blade in her hand. She'd said she was going to make us human again, but... I pictured my mother's eyes. Eyes that had been the same violet as my own had flickered to red as she'd strode toward me, the color a crimson shade that had terrified me. But it wasn't until now that I realized what it meant.

"WARRICK!!" The cry that left me contained a fury that tore apart my insides, burning its way through me piece by piece. I would tear the vampire apart.

CHAPTER 32

The outlier dropped the fae soldier, and I flew after the creature as it flapped its wings and soared high into the clouds. The creature banked left and then right, its wings spread wide as it narrowly avoided my jaws, but I wasn't letting it get away. Opening my mouth, I let my fire light up the sky, and the beast turned to ash before my eyes.

Satisfaction hummed through me, but Darian's warning had me snapping to attention.

"There are more!" my siren shouted as he let two stars fly, blinding one of the winged outliers that appeared from the thick clouds on my right. The creature shrieked and clawed at its face as another five outliers attacked me from all sides, their taloned feet aiming for my wings.

Darian reached for his bow and shot a series of arrows at one of the creatures that angled toward me on my left. I stretched my neck and closed my jaws around another outlier, tearing the creature in two. Blood filled my mouth, and I roared, my tail flicking as I swooped lower. The remaining outliers came toward me, and one grabbed hold of my right wing.

Darian's song filled my ears, but his magic wasn't directed at me. The music was just audible over the sound of the wind, but the outlier that held my wing didn't release me.

"My power isn't working!" my siren shouted in alarm, and he leapt for the outlier, his sword in hand.

The beast snapped its head at him, but he maneuvered his body out of the way of its jaws, and his sword sliced through the creature's neck.

My teeth closed around the body of another outlier on my left, and I tossed its lifeless form away before letting my fire free and incinerating the last outliers. But when I turned my head back, Darian was gone.

Fuck.

My heart pounded as I angled my head toward the ground, pulling my wings in as I shot after my siren.

My mate.

Down.

Down.

Down, we fell.

Darian's tiny form drew closer to the ground, and the battle rose up beneath us, the monsters still killing each other and crying out as they spilled blood.

Down.

I passed Darian and spread my wings, leveling out as he landed on my back, his thighs gripping my neck. Smoke trailed from my nostrils as I screeched, relief coursing through me, but my relief was short-lived when I noticed Asher, Locke, and monsters from the houses of Thorem and Axeran battling a sea of outliers.

Flying toward them, I opened my maw and burned away a section of the outliers. Asher lifted his fist into the air, but he didn't stop running. I looked at where he was headed. Across the battlefield, Warrick still watched from the safety of his beast, and I growled as I eyed the vampire.

"You can't go closer to him, lovely," Darian shouted in warning, pointing to where the sirens of the House of Saceris and the other monsters allied to Warrick were waiting in formation. Veering away from them, I let my fire burn away more outliers.

I circled around Kade and the wolves, and sections of the rebel army, only burning away outliers when I was sure my fire wouldn't harm the rebels.

Vasken, Lyr and her mates, Garan and the gargoyles, Losak, Quinn and the shifters, they all fought divided. In his shifted form, Losak's basilisk head rose up, his teeth sinking into a huge outlier that walked on legs the size of tree trunks. The beast swung one of its meaty arms sending Losak flying, and Quinn's fox ran beneath the outlier's legs distracting the creature. Cassar's boar grunted and barreled into the outlier from the side, causing the creature to stumble a step.

Curving around, I incinerated the outlier's head, my blue flames licking down its body. The creature toppled, crushing outliers as it fell. The rebels cheered, lifting their weapons into the air as they screamed at me, and I roared, flying higher once again as I avoided the spears and magic of the fae.

With my help, the rebels were managing to hold out, but across the battlefield, outliers seemed to come from nowhere, attacking the fae army from behind.

The back lines of the fae turned and began fighting against the creatures, but the silver horses reared up in fright. King Chalir fell from his saddle, landing hard, and a cloaked figure ran to his side. The king was on his feet in an instant, and fae soldiers surrounded him as they fought against the monsters. Fae lifted their hands, sending outliers flying with wind magic, while others created a wall of dirt that slowed the creatures down.

But it wasn't enough.

As I circled around, an outlier the size of a house smashed against the wall of dirt, breaking through and gnashing its jaws at the king.

"Without King Chalir, the fae army will fall," Darian noted grimly. "Their forces are already weakening."

I eyed King Chalir as he and his soldiers faced off the monster. The king was shouting as the fae battered the creature with magic, and King Chalir lifted his arms, yellow fire shooting out and engulfing the creature. The outlier toppled, but the smaller outliers rushed forward, the demon dogs leaping through the hole in the dirt wall and charging at the fae.

If the fae army falls, what hope do the rebels have?

I stared at the soldiers. I was part fae, and I couldn't watch them be slaughtered. I veered closer toward them, snorting smoke as I flew.

"Are you sure about this?" Darian yelled, and I roared in response.

Some of the fae soldiers turned their attention to me as I drew close, but I banked left and right dodging their fire and wind magic. As we neared the ground, Darian jumped from my back, landing on an outlier as he joined the fight. Another massive creature crashed through the dirt wall, and I swooped down, flapping my wings to slow my descent as I grabbed the outlier with my talons and closed my teeth around its neck. When the beast was down, I let out my fire, incinerating rows of advancing outliers.

Seeing what I was doing, the fae stopped attacking me, but they watched me warily as they focused their power on the other outliers. Darian and I continued to fight, and soon the fae were shouting and battling beside us. When the last outlier at the back of the army fell, I shifted back into my human form. *Please, please don't let this be a bad decision.* I grabbed two discarded fae swords from the ground and held the blades up in front of me.

All right, Raine. Now what?

King Chalir lay bleeding from deep wounds to his leg and chest, but a cloaked figure bent over him, and I watched in surprise as the king's wounds closed, healing over. The cloaked figure stood and walked toward a wounded soldier close by, and I frowned at the way their jaw sparkled as they moved.

I watched as the cloaked figure started to heal the soldier, but at the king's command, the fae soldiers circled, closing in on us.

Yep, definitely didn't think this through. Darian stood tall beside me, his blades in his hands. He opened his mouth, preparing himself to sing.

"Wait," I whispered.

My siren closed his mouth, not questioning me.

King Chalir studied us thoughtfully. "And we meet again. The monsters who tried to assassinate my son," he said, but his words didn't hold the venom they had during our last meeting.

I didn't miss the way he said, "tried to". *Does that mean Prince Azaren is alive?* I would have smiled if the fae weren't looking at me like I was one of the outliers they'd just killed.

"The monsters who just saved your lives," I countered.

King Chalir frowned. "Monsters none-the-less." Yellow fire lit up his arms, the flames licking at the air.

Scales started to automatically ripple over my skin, but I stopped myself from shifting. I could handle the heat, but Darian was a different matter. Still, I had to try and talk to him.

"That's right, we're monsters," I replied as the fae closed in around us. "*And* we're fae."

"You abominations are *nothing* like the fae," King Chalir spat.

"You're wrong," I said, lifting my chin. "Queen Izla created the curse using a part of herself. A part of her fae magic. And that magic is now in us. It's in all monsters."

King Chalir laughed, and his top lip curled. "Turning into grotesque beings isn't a sign of being fae. Whatever magic my sister used, it was an ancient dark magic that has long since been forbidden in the fae realm. I loved her dearly, but my sister's curse was a betrayal to her own kind."

As we spoke, the cloaked figure behind the king healed a soldier before walking over to another grievously wounded fae.

My brows slammed down. "You don't get it. We're on the same side. The only real monsters are Warrick and King Adrien, and the outlier creatures who have no control over their new forms. The only way we will all survive this is if the Katakin rebels and your fae army combine forces."

"Combine forces?" King Chalir looked offended. "We're still thousands strong."

"If you don't listen, you'll die," Darian added.

"Agree to peace," I said. "Let us fight together to get rid of Warrick and the outliers. Then we'll have time to squabble over the terms of a treaty."

The fae soldiers crept closer, their swords pointing our way.

King Chalir sneered. "You think I should listen to you simply because your monster is the biggest? Because you helped defeat some of the monsters your kind created?"

"Let me sing, lovely," Darian whispered, his body tense as he eyed the approaching soldiers.

"No," I said to the king with a soft smile. "You should listen to me, because I'm the one trying to help you." I paused, feeling the weight of the fae gazes on me. "And because I'm Queen Izla's descendent, and a member of your royal bloodline." The words that tumbled from my mouth felt so strange. I mean, I still hardly believed them, but at the same time, I could feel the truth settle inside me.

King Chalir's face reddened. "Ridiculous! My sister had no offspring. Your words are heresy." The flames rose higher on his arms. "There's no limit to the lies your kind will spill."

The cloaked figure who'd been healing the wounded twisted their cloaked head toward me. A word escaped from their mouth, but I didn't hear it.

I focused on my power, searching for that spark inside myself. The spark that I hadn't been able to touch since I'd turned into a monster. If I could show him my magic, maybe he'd believe me. *Come on, Raine.* But even when I found the spark, it was buried so deep I could hardly grasp hold of it with my mind.

"No, you were a threat as humans, and now you're dangerous as monsters. You cannot be allowed to live," King Chalir spat, his flames beginning to crackle.

"Stop!" The cloaked figure shouted, scrambling to their feet and rushing toward the king.

Darian sucked in a breath, his mouth opening as fire burst from King Chalir, spearing toward us. Before Darian could utter a note, answering blue fire exploded from me, engulfing my body and racing up the fae swords I held in my hands. Power hummed through me, and I stepped in front of Darian, my swords crossed in front of my chest as I blocked the king's fire.

The force of his magic pushed me back, but I dug my heels into the dirt and braced. Focusing my power, I sent out another blast of energy. My fire swallowed King Chalir's flames and raced forward, propelling the king backward until he landed a few feet away.

As the king's flames extinguished, the cloaked figure rushed forward, stepping between me and the king. "Stop!" the figure cried, their voice oddly familiar as they held up their arms.

King Chalir lifted to his feet, and I glared at the stubborn male.

"You need to stop!" the cloaked figure shouted again.

"Fae, at the ready!" King Chalir commanded.

"She's telling the truth!" The cloaked figure yelled as she moved closer to Darian and me. Spreading her arms, she turned to King Chalir as if to shield us from him.

What the hell?

The figure pulled down her hood, her gaze locking onto mine. With her pointed ears and long, colored hair it was obvious we'd never met before, but... *Those eyes...*

The fae female gave me a small smile before turning back to King Chalir. "I know she's telling the truth, because she's my sister, and I'm a descendent of Queen Izla as well."

The world quieted, the air squeezing from my lungs. My legs wobbled as I stared at the fae with colorful gems glittering on her face. I only had one sister.

The fae female's brow creased with concentration, and before my eyes her form shimmered and changed, her pointed ears shrinking and the tops becoming rounded, her hair turning to a mousy brown, and her face changing shape. The gems remained over her face, but when she smiled...

No, not a fae, she is...

"Cara?" my voice cracked as the name slipped from my lips.

My sister smiled, and I could have sworn the gems on her face lit up like little stars.

"What is the meaning of this?" King Chalir bellowed. "What have you done to my jewel!" He stepped forward, his face twisted with anger as he went for Cara, but blue fire burst from me, creating a wall and stopping him from taking another step.

And then I was running toward her, barely aware of the ground moving beneath my feet. My arms wrapped around my sister, and she hugged me back, tears streaking down her face.

"How?" I wheezed, but she turned to the fae around us.

More outliers had circled around the fae army, and they were climbing the dirt wall the fae had mended.

"We *are* fae, and you must listen," Cara said loudly, projecting her voice. "We fight with the rebels, or we die. I can't heal you all, and as you speak, your kin are dying."

The generals looked to King Chalir, but he only stood speechless, his mouth opening and closing like he couldn't get the words out.

Three outliers dropped from the top of the wall and charged toward us, and Darian squeezed my shoulder. "Protect your sister."

I watched him run toward the outliers in horror, torn between joining him and staying with Cara. "You need to get away from here," I whispered to her. It didn't take much to understand why she was there. The king was using her to heal him, but while healing was an amazing power, it wouldn't help her much against Warrick's creatures.

"I won't leave you," she replied, her gaze moving between the outliers.

I let more fire shoot out. The flames engulfed a few of the outliers and the creatures fell to the ground. "Then you'd better stay behind me," I said.

Before she could respond, I stepped back a few paces and my body was shifting and changing until I was a dragon again. I flicked my tail, lifting her onto my back.

"Well, what are you waiting for?" Cara yelled at the fae. "Do you want to die tonight, or do you want to live?"

The generals looked over the dead fae on the battlefield and the remaining soldiers waiting for their command. When King Chalir still looked uncertain, one of the generals lifted his sword, and shouted, "I say, we fight to live! Let's fight with the rebels!"

CHAPTER 33

Across the battlefield, my mate fought the outliers that attacked the back of the fae army. I howled as she took down another of the giant beasts, and my pack howled with me.

Garan and the gargoyles, and Lyr and her mates fought beside us, along with a large portion of the rebel army. Lyr lifted her arm, pointing to where Asher and the Houses of Thorem and Axeran were fighting to get to Warrick.

Something had changed with the fae army, and they were turning away from us, starting to solely focus their magic and weaponry on the outliers. I could only guess Darian and Raine had managed to sway the king.

"We must get to Warrick!" Lyr yelled, black blood trailing down her chin as she stood in her human form.

I peered at the wolves. Their fur was thick with blood, their tongues lolling from their mouths as they panted.

Kasey and Tristan padded up beside me, and when I changed direction, leading them to where I could see Asher and Locke battling creatures twice their size, the wolves all followed.

· · • • • • • • • • · ·

~ Locke ~

I stayed with Asher, the pair of us fighting beside Kenric and the other monsters as we headed for Warrick. The cowardly vampire still hadn't advanced on his beast. No, he watched with a cold calculation that was all too familiar.

My entire life he had studied me. And once again we were all in one giant experiment. The Katakin monsters under his control stood still, their red eyes glowing as they watched us. Perene remained with the other members of the Taratun council, but I felt no sympathy for my mother. They'd been Warrick's puppets long before he'd infected them, they just hadn't realized it.

I couldn't say exactly when the battle shifted, but soon the rebels were rushing up behind us. Kade and his wolves sprinted ahead, combining with our ranks, and then came Garan and the gargoyles, and Lyr and her mates. Vasken tore outliers apart in his chimera form, his snake tail hissing and striking the creatures that tried to attack him from behind. The rest of the rebels formed up, flanking us.

And then came the fae. They pushed through the outliers, their magic forcing the beasts back. Raine and Darian fought at the back of the fae army, Raine's dragon tearing down the larger outliers like the majestic monster she was. If anyone could have convinced the fae, it was her.

Darian jumped onto her back, sitting behind a female I didn't recognize, and Raine launched into the air, her massive body skimming over the fae army until she was flapping above us. Opening her maw, she burned the outliers blocking our path, and the stench of burning flesh filled my nose as the creatures turned to ash.

Raine dropped down behind me, the rebels making way to accommodate her large body, and Darian jumped from her back, holding the strange female in his arms.

"Who the fuck is that?" I shouted as Darian propped the female on her feet. Her ears were rounded and if it weren't for the gems, I would have thought she was human.

Raine snorted smoke at me, and Darian's lips curled upward.

"This would be Raine's dear sister, Cara," Darian explained as the female eyed me warily. "It's in our best interest to keep her alive."

"Her sister?" My brows rose as my swords cut through an outlier that leaped over its dead comrade and lunged for me.

The beast fell hard, and Darian shrugged. "Seems Raine's entire family is full of surprises."

I shook my head in disbelief.

An outlier leaped over our heads, heading for Raine, and I flapped my wings, lifting into the air as I severed the creature's head.

Raine let out more fire, and another section of outliers turned to ash. There was still over a thousand of the beasts, but with the fae and rebels working together, it finally felt like we had a chance.

Warrick sat up straighter, his black eyes bulging with fury as he watched us draw closer. He turned to the sirens beside him, and they opened their mouths as one.

"Raine, take out the sirens!" I yelled in warning, but she hesitated as she eyed the Katakin monsters.

We were close enough to them now that as their song filled the air, we all heard it. The sirens sang in unison, their sweet notes melding together and becoming a warmth that wrapped around me. My movements slowed, my limbs feeling sluggish as though I was wading through deep water. Desire coursed through me, but as quickly as it came it was gone.

I blinked, and it took me a moment to register Darian stood beside me, his feet braced, and his brow furrowed with strain. My siren brother sang loudly, his tenor voice mixing perfectly with that of the other sirens. As their chorus of voices rang out, their power crackling in the air,

Darian's power redirected their magic, making it twist and turn, and miss us entirely.

The sirens of the House of Saceris sang louder, but Darian's notes didn't fail. Sweat dripped down his temple and dampened his silver hair.

"He won't be able to hold them for long!" Asher barked. "The sirens had their chance to join us. Raine, you need to do this now!"

This time my mate didn't hesitate. Raine lifted her head and opened her maw, letting the fire pour from her, but as the flames speared across the battlefield, King Adrien stepped in front of the sirens. Raine's fire pushed him back, but he leaned forward, bracing against the impact until the fire stopped. Smoke filled the air, but the stone king remained standing.

"Her fire didn't hurt him," Kenric shouted as the smoke cleared. "How are we supposed to kill that thing?"

"We do it quickly," I replied. Darian's head was bowed as he sang, his veins bulging at the side of his neck.

Asher cried out as he surged forward, striding over the ashen remains of outliers, and I followed along with the rebels and the fae. Two armies, two enemies, converged, and Warrick let loose the other Katakin monsters under his control.

The wraiths from the House of Faren disappeared from Warrick's side and appeared beside us as we ran, attacking us with their blades, their movements jerky like undead warriors returned from the afterlife. They weren't as strong under Warrick's control, but they were still formidable. I jumped over the sword that swiped at my legs and drove my blade toward the wraith's face only to find they had disappeared again.

Members of the Taratun council and House of Nesarin joined the fight, along with the monsters from the lower houses under Warrick's control. I turned my head to see Ferene punch her fist through the chest of a fae, her black claws dripping with blood. The other vampires tore through throats, but I didn't stop running. Vasken, Lyr and her mates went for King Adrien, Vasken and Lyr sprinting in their shifted forms and eating up the distance between them and the giant. The stone king lashed out with his large arms, but his movements were slow, and they darted around his legs.

Dean shot out his hand, vines springing from the ground and wrapping around the king's ankles, and fae joined him, using their earth magic to create more vines. The king tripped, falling to the ground, and the vines crawled over him like snakes, wrapping around his arms and torso. With a bellow, the king broke his arms free, but the vines speared into his open mouth, coming out of his ears. The king continued to cry out and thrash, but Raine flapped her massive wings, landing on top of him and prying his mouth open with her taloned feet. With a roar, fire burst from her, pouring down King Adrien's throat until he fell silent.

The sirens from the House of Saceris continued to sing, their song becoming louder as Darian strained to hold them back, and a group of water fae lifted their arms. The ground trembled, pebbles bouncing up off the dirt, and water exploded from the earth. The huge wave crashed into the sirens, washing them away and sweeping them hundreds of yards back.

Asher yanked his ax from the body of an outlier as we ran.

Warrick remained on his beast, and the outlier snorted and stomped at the soldiers on the ground.

Raine moved forward, and Kade and his wolves ran beside her, howling and growling. I took to the sky, flying near her head, and Garan and the gargoyles joined me.

"You will not take this from me!" Warrick screamed as Raine clashed with Warrick's outlier, the two beasts biting and clawing at each other. The gargoyles aimed their arrows, targeting the outlier's two heads and aiming for its eyes, and the wolves attacked the beast's legs. One of the outlier's heads stretched up and its jaws closed over Garan's body. *Fuck!* The beast flicked its head, throwing Garan to the ground a moment before my swords severed the beast's head and Asher's axes cut into its side. I peered at where Garan remained unmoving amongst the other fallen soldiers. The outlier stomped and screeched, and

Raine's teeth closed over its neck, tearing off its remaining head.

As the outlier fell, Warrick took to the sky, his eyes crazed as he watched the defeat of his army. "Years of work!" he raged. "I'm doing this for Katakin, and you're all so blind you side with the fae!"

"You were doing this for yourself!" I shouted, taking aim and spearing my sword through the air. It sliced through Warrick's right wing, and he cried out as he fell from the sky.

Dropping to the ground we stalked closer, surrounding Warrick as a group. I stepped forward and Asher and Darian joined me. Raine and Kade shifted back to their human forms and strode beside us. Leaning down, my mate grabbed a blade from a fallen soldier, and the tightness in my chest eased at her close proximity. Despite being in her human form, thick scales covered her naked body like armor.

Warrick shrunk back, scrambling away from us.

"You killed her," Asher spat as he hefted his axes, his thick arms coated with sweat and blood. "All these years, it had been you."

Warrick smiled cruelly at the demon, like hearing Asher's words gave him a sense of satisfaction. "Ah, so you finally figured it out."

"What's he talking about?" Raine asked, her expression filled with concern.

"Why don't you tell them?" Asher replied, a murderous gleam in his eyes.

Warrick shrugged nonchalantly. "Asher's mother was an incredible empath even before the curse, and once she turned into a demon that sense was amplified. I was only trying to help."

"Help?" Asher clenched his jaw. "You tried to turn her. She never lost her mind."

Warrick sighed heavily. "Yes, it was all going well if I do say so. Her mind was easy to manipulate, but I hadn't managed to perfect my serum yet. She kept fighting me, and I could only seem to control her for short bursts." Warrick frowned. "And after her, I couldn't get anything to work on any other monsters, so I decided to *create* monsters who would be perfectly primed to accept the serum and succumb to my will."

"That's barbaric," Raine said in horror.

"It was brilliant," Warrick countered, "but I have to thank you most of all, *newblood*. Combining your mixed blood to that of Asher's mother allowed me to finally create a serum that would overpower the minds of the Katakin monsters. It wasn't quite right when I tested it on the House of Silat, but as you can see, my experiment was a success."

"No," Raine whispered, her face paling.

"It doesn't matter how you managed to do it," I said, hating that look on Raine's face. Guilt softened her eyes, but she had nothing to do with the fact that my father was the only true monster left in Katakin. "Your outliers are defeated, and without you, the infected Katakin monsters will be freed."

"Freed?" Warrick scoffed. "The Katakin monsters don't want freedom. They merely want the illusion of control, of power. They need me."

"The only thing they need is a new perspective," Darian countered. "And a new treaty with the fae."

At the mention of the fae, a few fae soldiers joined the circle, and Warrick hissed. The vampire shot forward, but I wouldn't let him hurt anyone else. For too long he'd been allowed to get away with whatever the fuck he wanted. And he deserved to bleed for it all.

Before he could reach them, my brothers and I were moving. My blades went through Warrick's chest at the same moment that Asher's ax sliced his head clean off. My chest heaved as his head thudded to the ground, his black eyes changing to a pale gray.

Around the battlefield, the Katakin monsters who had been fighting the rebels blinked, their eyes clearing. They stared around in surprise, the weapons falling from their hands as they took in the scene of death around them.

I stood with Raine and my brothers staring down at the slain vampire who'd tried to end us all.

CHAPTER 34

With the battle over, I walked among the wounded fae and rebel monsters, healing those I could. Silver moonlight bathed the battlefield, illuminating the destruction, and a cold numbness settled inside me.

I'd been too late. My sister was a monster. She was cursed, all because I hadn't found my way back to her. And all the bloodshed...

When I came to King Chalir's crumpled body, I slumped to my knees. For so long, I'd been tasked with keeping the king alive and tending to his every wound, and now seeing him broken and motionless left something hollow inside of me. Fae soldiers started to crowd around us, like they were expecting me to bring him back, but I couldn't heal the dead. I couldn't even tell how he'd died.

A groan sounded, and I moved to where a rebel monster had fallen. The male had stone-colored skin, a strong jawline, and deep-set pale eyes. I'd seen the vampire's giant beast clamp its teeth onto him and send him flying. The rebel monster's stony chest was crushed, his wings bent at odd angles, and black blood oozed from his mouth.

He stared up at me, his expressive eyes taking in the gems on my face.

"Did we win?" he rasped.

I nodded slowly, though it didn't feel right. No one won the battle. We were simply the ones who'd survived.

It was enough for the male. He calmed, his frown slipping away, softening his handsome features as he closed his eyes.

I wasn't sure why his calm unsettled me. Usually, when I went to the sides of the grievously wounded, they cried and begged, terrified at what awaited them after death, but this male was silent. Peaceful.

In a sudden movement, his eyes flared open, startling me. "Move," he barked, and I jerked back in shock as he lifted the sword at his side. A small creature ran at me, but the rebel monster's blade sliced it into two before its fangs reached my neck.

The beast fell beside him, and I gaped at it, my heart pounding. When I couldn't see any other creatures, I rushed back to the rebel monster's side.

The sword fell from his hand, and he closed his eyes again like that last burst of energy was all he had. Without thinking, I pulled my gloves off and pressed my palms against his bare arm.

Pain zapped up my hands, my veins burning like liquid fire, but I didn't let go. His life force was becoming weaker with every passing second, the blood continuing to spill from his wounds, but I wasn't about to let him die. My power flowed into him, and slowly his wounds knitted together, his ribs repairing, and life returning to his body.

When I was done, I hung my head, my eyes heavy with exhaustion, but when I looked down the male was staring at me. His glowing eyes watched me with fascination, like he thought I was one of Mother Falia's angels sent from her haven.

"What did you do to me?" he asked, his voice a low rasp that made my belly tighten.

He reached up like he intended to brush his fingers against my cheek, but he dropped his hand again a moment later.

I couldn't explain the disappointment that went through me. I hadn't wanted any male since Xander, but as I stared at the monster I wanted to climb into his arms, to feel his skin against mine, and surrender to his pale lips. *Goddess, Cara, the male almost died.* My cheeks flushed as I internally chastised myself, and I subconsciously touched the gem that had formed on my neck when I'd healed him.

The male tracked the movement of my fingers, his brows furrowing when he spotted the sparkling crystal.

"Uh, so you should be able to get up again," I said, quickly moving my hand away from my neck.

He lifted to his feet and flexed his wings, marveling as he stretched them out and flapped them slowly. "You saved my life," he said, those penetrating pale eyes finding me again. "I'm Garan."

I squirmed under his intense gaze, but before I could brush off his comment, an achingly familiar voice had me spinning around.

"Cara!" Raine rushed over to me, almost making me fall over as her arms wrapped around me in a vice grip. I hugged her back just as tightly, laughter falling from my lips as my eyes watered with tears.

"You're so big now," I commented. "You're even taller than I am!"

She laughed, pulling back to stare at me. Her gaze traveled over my face, and her eyes tightened.

"It's all right," I told her, running my fingers over the new gem on my neck again. "They remind me of the times when I've been able to help."

She smiled and hugged me again.

"Fuck, I thought you were dead," said a male with dark hair and black wings as he moved closer to Garan.

Garan's gaze found me again, and I tried to ignore the way his attention made heat flare inside me. "So did I," he replied.

I turned my attention to the monsters standing around Raine, hovering like lethal guardians. I'd seen the way they stayed close to my sister on the battlefield, and I raised my brow at her. "Four?"

"Makes life more interesting," she said with a wide grin.

I smiled, glad to see true happiness in her amber eyes.

The monster with silver hair peered over at where King Chalir was being collected by a group of fae soldiers. "Well, that is a complication."

CHAPTER 35

King Chalir was dead. I can't say I felt sorry for the male considering he'd tried to execute us for a crime we didn't commit, but I was sad for the fae. Without their king, they turned to their remaining generals, gathering their wounded, and eyeing the monsters warily. I turned my attention back to my sister. She'd been with the fae and knew about our link to Queen Izla. *How?*

"I still can't believe you're here," I told her, a thousand questions going through my mind. "Have you been with the fae this whole time?" I'd searched for my sister for so long, and now that she was in front of me, I didn't know what to say.

She tucked a loose strand of hair behind her ear. "When the monsters took me through the portal on our island, somehow I ended up in the fae realm instead. The rest is, well, a long story."

I thought of when I'd been selected on my island and taken through the portal with Kade and the others. I could still remember Locke's grip on me as we went through.

Before I could ask her more, shouts came from across the battlefield. Close to where Warrick had been slain, blue flames formed making a distinct ring. *What the hell?*

Holding onto Cara, I pulled her with me as we sprinted toward the portal. My mates and Garan ran with us, pulling out their weapons as we went.

"Did the fae plan reinforcements?" I asked Cara, my heart beginning to race.

"I-I don't think so," she stuttered, stumbling a step before I yanked her forward again.

Fae streamed out of the portal, but unlike the silver armor of King Chalir's soldiers, these warriors wore leather armor that was strapped to their limbs. Twenty fae emerged in quick succession, the warriors forming a circle that surrounded three males.

"Fuck, is that Prince Azaren?" Asher asked, his tail flicking as he ran.

My eyes widened as I stared at the fae prince standing in the middle of the circle with a blade pressed to his throat. The soldier on his left side stood holding the dagger, his hardened gaze taking in the battle scene. On the prince's other side, a dark-haired male held a large book open in his hands, and dread formed in the pit of my stomach.

"Xander, no," Cara breathed, gripping my hand tighter.

Xander? I assumed she had to be talking about the dark-haired fae who looked like he was speaking to himself as he stared at the pages of the open book. *No...not speaking, chanting.*

"Az!" Cara cried out as we neared the ring of fae warriors.

Prince Azaren looked up, a surprised expression on his face as he stared at Cara and then to me and my mates. "Cara, is that you?"

Xander snapped his gaze toward my sister, his eyes softening ever so slightly, but he kept chanting, words spilling from his lips.

I couldn't be sure what the fae was doing, but from the hatred in his eyes, I knew it had to be something bad. I didn't want to harm Prince Azaren, but I had to protect my family and all the other monsters in Katakin. Sucking in a breath, I prepared myself to shoot out fire, but before I could, Xander lifted his hand and black fire rushed out, spearing in all directions. Instinctively, blue fire burst from me as I tried to stop the racing flames, but like a targeted weapon the black fire twisted and swirled, dodging my power like it was a living being. It went straight for the Katakin monsters, and I watched in horror as black flames licked up Asher's legs, ignited Locke's wings, and engulfed Kade and Darian. With a grunt, they fell to the ground, their faces scrunched with agony. Every Katakin monster fell. Lyr. Jade. Vasken. Every one, except me.

"NO!" I cried, releasing Cara's hand to rush over to Asher and the others.

"Keep back," Kade growled as my fingers neared the flames, and I stumbled back a step as an unnatural heat burned my fingertips.

"What are you doing to them?" I shouted, clenching my fists as I turned to the dark-haired fae. I started to shift, ready to tear this new fae apart, but he shook his head at me.

"Uh uh," he said with a cruel smile. "If you kill me now, it'll only make the curse move faster. The magic is coming from me, and if I'm gone, it'll be released at a faster rate."

With a growl, I stopped the change, my limbs returning to their human form.

Xander's gaze locked onto Cara. "I see you removed the glamor."

"I was tired of living a lie," she replied.

He narrowed his eyes as he studied her. "That's a shame."

She glared at him. "What curse is this, Xander?"

"I told you these books would give us the means to finally free Zalei," he said coldly like he was schooling a young child. "This is retribution. King Chalir should have known better than to leave Zalei so defenseless. The Forgotten Fae nymphs found some very interesting books in the forest and brought them to me. After that, everything else fell into place. All we needed was the remaining texts and someone who could decipher them. Luckily for me, the Forgotten Fae succeeded in framing the monsters for the attempted assassination of Prince Azaren. It was just what we needed to convince King Chalir to leave the kingdom and allow us to finally get our hands on our greatest weapon."

"The Forgotten Fae formed because you all opposed the needless deaths of the fae soldiers during the battle two centuries ago!" Cara cried, indicating to the bodies strewn around us. "You're supposed to be fighting for the fae who had been forgotten by the king. Why would you want this?"

"King Chalir always wanted this war!" Xander spat. "We tried reasoning with him the peaceful way, but all he understood was violence. He never cared about making change in Zalei and never would. Without him, we can appoint a new leader. Once I end this, the fae can have a new beginning."

A howl ripped from Kade, and I turned to see his bones crack. He wasn't turning into the beautiful wolf I loved, but something else entirely. Locke's wings twisted and folded unnaturally, and Asher's back curved, his spine protruding as spikes speared from his skin.

"You need to stop this!" I shouted, my voice deepening as I fought against the urge to shift. My dragon couldn't help this time.

"The magic—" Prince Azaren started, but the fae beside him pressed the blade harder against his neck, silencing him.

Xander finally turned his attention to me again, like he was reluctant to take his gaze from Cara. "Izla got it wrong, you see," he replied calmly. "She changed the ancient curse so that the humans of Katakin kept some of their humanity. I'm guessing she hoped King Adrien would see the error in his ways." His lip curled with disgust. "She always had a soft spot for the humans. If our dear Azaren here is to be believed, she did it because deep down she wanted the human king to learn from his mistakes." He laughed cruelly. "But she was wrong, and now I'm simply fixing the curse that she twisted. Anyone without fae blood will become a monster with no conscience, humanity, and a thirst for violence. They will destroy each other and the fae soldiers still in favor of the monarchy. Without the monsters and those allied to the royals, Zalei will finally be free."

"You can't," Cara rasped, her voice cracking as the Katakin monsters let out cries of pain.

"Oh, I can, and I have," Xander cackled. "You could have been by my side, but instead, I'll leave you here to finally witness the destruction of this world."

Xander's gaze went to me, and his lips twitched. "At least, it looks like you found what you were searching for."

The Katakin monsters' cries changed, becoming more animalistic, and Xander turned toward the portal. Claws peeked from my fingertips. If we were all going to die, I sure as hell wasn't letting the asshole leave Katakin alive. Just as I was about to shift into my dragon form, Prince Azaren elbowed his fae captor in the ribs and grabbed the blade.

"Raine, remember what I told you!" Prince Azaren yelled, his blue gaze fixed on me and Cara pointedly. "I won't be able to hold them for long." His brow furrowed with concentration, and Xander and the Forgotten Fae bent over, grasping their heads. I could only guess he'd entered their minds.

"What is he talking about?" Cara cried, her panicked words filling my ears. I scoured my mind, rushing to get the words out.

"The secret to ending the curse," I blurted. "The book said:

One of fae, blood so blue,
One who's cursed, but bold and true,
Forgive the past, pay the price,
Surrender to the sacrifice."

I shook my head. "But there aren't any fae who would be willing to sacrifice themselves for the monsters. We've thought about this."

Prince Azaren stumbled past the Forgotten Fae toward me and Cara. "You're wrong. Because I will," he said as he reached us.

"What? You can't do that," Cara protested. "King Chalir is dead, and the fae need you."

Prince Azaren stared out at the monsters and the fae watching from across the battlefield, their faces streaked with blood as they stood among the dead. "If I don't do this, we'll all die here today. A good leader protects, and that's what my father had forgotten. At least if I do this, the fae might have a future. And so will those in Katakin."

"But what about the other thing?" Cara questioned, gripping his arms. "One who's cursed, but bold and true. Who is—" her words trailed off as Prince Azaren's gaze fixed on me.

I blinked in surprise. "That can't be right. I mean, I'm bold maybe, but I'm not—"

His gaze was apologetic. "I've been in your mind, Raine. And I've seen what's in your heart. You are both bold and true to everything your heart believes. But no one can make you do this if you don't want to."

I stared, unblinking, hardly registering that my mates had begun screaming at me in the background. The final line from the book echoed through my head: *Surrender to the sacrifice*. We'd never thought there would be a pureblood fae willing to sacrifice themselves to break the curse, so we hadn't even contemplated which of the cursed might do the same.

But if what the prince was saying was true, then we had a chance to end this all now. *I can save my mates, my monsters, and my sister.*

"Raine, no," Cara pleaded, letting go of Prince Azaren to grab me instead. "H-how do I become cursed? Let me do it instead."

"It's too late for that," Prince Azaren replied softly. "If we're going to do this, we need to do it now."

"Raaaiiinnne!!" The garbled cry broke through the ringing in my head, coming from Locke as his body continued to twist, his limbs moving in odd directions as his skin bulged. "Don't you dare do this! We're not worth it! None of us are!"

I finally turned to look again at my mates. At the rebels who I'd fought beside. Lyr and her mates, Vasken, Garan, Jade, Kenric, and Kasey. At the fae who watched on fearfully, preparing themselves to fight monsters once again, and then at my sister. My throat grew so sore, even as certainty settled in my aching chest.

"We're of Queen Izla's bloodline," Prince Azaren said. "It's our responsibility to fix this."

I nodded, not bothering to deny it again. Somehow knowing that he was right. I wouldn't walk away from this.

Tears fell from Cara's eyes, and I hugged her tightly. "All I wanted was to find you," I said softly, my voice cracking as tears blurred my vision. "I always promised myself I would save you. And if this is what it takes, I will gladly be the sacrifice," I whispered.

She sobbed harder at my words, her hands cupping my cheeks. "You were never meant to save me," she said. "I was always the one who was meant to find my way back to you."

"RAINEEE!!" Kade's howl was an anguished cry, and I almost shifted on instinct, my dragon desperate to return his call. My mate marks burned against my skin, reminding me of the ones I loved.

"Forget us, lovely," Darian said, his eyes no longer a crystal blue, but black like a night sky. "Live for us instead."

Asher's face was tight as his tail cracked, his violet horns aflame, but somehow, he still gave me that lopsided smile of his. Like he knew that no matter what happened this was the last time we would see each other, and he wanted me to remember him with a smile on his face. "It's been fun, sweetheart. Just remember, we love ya."

"I love you, too," I whispered back, tears spilling down my face as I stared at my mates one last time. I would do this, for my sister and my mates. For the fae, and the Katakin monsters.

Turning back to Prince Azaren, I said, "I need you to remove the protection curse from me first."

"No, Mahareeee," Kade's weakening voice turned to a howl as his body changed, a wrinkled black snout protruding from his face that was so different to that of his usual form.

Prince Azaren didn't hesitate. He whispered words under his breath and lifted his hands, letting his magic flow into me, and I felt the bond dissolve, the protective spell that bound me to my mates, tying my life to theirs, disappearing as if it had never been there. But even as that link was broken, my mate marks tingled, reminding me that they were still linked to me, just in a different way. And nothing could take that from us.

Prince Azaren watched me, and when I nodded, he lowered his arms and sliced the blade deep across his wrists, blue blood spilling onto the ground at an alarming rate.

Giving Cara one last weak smile, I took the dagger from the prince and cut my own wrists, my numb body blocking out the pain. Prince Azaren caught me before I could fall, and we gripped each other tight as the prince began to chant words that I couldn't understand.

A burst of magic came from me, my fire enveloping us, energy swirling around our forms like a windswept inferno. Prince Azaren's magic mixed with mine and reached out, connecting with the minds of those around Katakin, and I screamed in agony as thousands of voices filled my head at once. I heard their cries and soft fearful whispers, their hopes and dreams, and their pain. *So much pain.* I heard the voices of Prince Azaren, of my sister, and of my mates, their weakening anguished cries reaching out for me.

And then all I felt was…peace. Like I was right where I needed to be. Even as the cold started up my fingers, as my warmth began to leech away, my fire extinguishing. Even as my inner dragon curled up ready for sleep, my exhaustion dragging me down into darkness. I felt Prince Azaren sag, his long fingers loosening his grip on me, and we slid to our knees. My eyes grew too heavy to open, and Prince Azaren whispered the words in my ear:

"One of fae, blood so blue,
One who's cursed, but bold and true,
Forgive the past, pay the price,
Surrender to the sacrifice."

Forgive. The word repeated in my mind. It was the final piece. I thought of how the monsters had taken women from my island. Of the trials they'd put the newbloods through. Of the death on the battlefield around us. All of it had stemmed from the hate King Adrien had ignited. But then I thought of the hardships my mates had endured because of the curse Queen Izla had created. Asher and his mother, and the countless other monsters who'd suffered. I thought of Warrick and his outliers. Both the king and queen had caused this, though I couldn't believe Queen Izla had wanted it to end this way. She'd tried to twist the curse, but it had still gone horribly wrong. Either way, it didn't matter. The only way it would all end was if the fae and the monsters learned to forgive one another. It wasn't just about Azaren and me.

Holding onto that thought, I projected the word, *Forgive,* in my mind as images filled my head. Images of Queen Izla creating the curse, and of King Adrien's hate-filled eyes. And then I thought of the beauty of Katakin and Zalei, and all the surprisingly wonderful things I'd encountered. Prince Azaren understood my meaning. Still linked to the fae and monsters around Katakin, he sent out my message to everyone. The curse had never been about death or becoming a monster. It had always been about acceptance and forgiveness.

I felt one last surge of Azaren's magic, and then I was falling. I hardly noticed the ground rush up at me, or the scent of ash that reminded me so much of my vampire. All I knew was the frigid cold, and the darkness that wanted to pull me under.

But as the last breath squeezed from my lungs, a hand slammed over my heart. Power crackled through me, like lightning was zapping through my body, lighting my every nerve on fire.

I gasped, my chest heaving as my fire reignited, warmth racing through my body and chasing away the cold. My eyes burst open, and Cara was above me, one hand on me while the other rested on Prince Azaren. Twin red gems adorned both of her hands, and she sobbed at the sight of me. "Thank the goddess."

She wobbled, but I lifted, holding her in my arms.

Prince Azaren lifted onto his elbows, his pink lips forming a smile.

"You saved us," I whispered in disbelief. I stared down at my smooth wrists that had not a single mark on them.

"No, *you* saved us," she answered with a smile. "And once I felt the curse change, I knew it wasn't too late for me to save you in return."

She gestured with her head to where I'd last seen my monsters, and I followed her gaze to see they were no longer being afflicted by black flames and the magic Xander had unleashed. My mates scrambled to get to me, and when Prince Azaren laughed, Cara and I laughed with him, feeling lighter than we'd ever felt.

"Raine," Locke croaked as my mates fell to the ground around me. And then their lips were on me, their kisses on my skin, and their noses burying into my hair as they held me tight.

"Never again," Kade rasped, his voice deep with emotion.

"Never again," I agreed. Asher's tail curled possessively around my waist, and Locke's wings flared, covering our group like he was determined to keep me there. Darian pressed his forehead against mine, and he let out a long breath, like for a moment there he thought he might never be able to breathe again.

My monsters were whole. And alive. But...

I frowned at Cara and Prince Azaren who were still laughing and holding each other as they watched us. "We're still monsters," I said in surprise. I could feel my inner dragon, preening at all of the attention she was getting from her mates. My eyes met Cara's.

Prince Azaren answered casually, "The magic in this land is a part of Katakin now, the curse couldn't be taken away."

I stared at my mates. The monsters who had captured my heart just the way they were.

"But we changed the curse," Prince Azaren continued to explain. "We removed the magic Xander had unleashed, and instead of those in Katakin being tied to the curse, the curse is only tied to the land."

"So, what you're saying is..." Darian began, his blue eyes sparkling.

"You all now have a choice. Instead of dying when you're away from Katakin and the magic for too long, you can leave Katakin indefinitely if you wish," Prince Azaren responded. "And if you do, you'll become human again while you're away. You're not cursed. Only this land is. Or you could say it's blessed, depending on how you want to look at it. You won't die after you've been away from the magic for a long while. You'll merely become mortal."

"Human?" Locke said softly, folding his wings back behind him.

Around us, the monsters and fae were all getting to their feet, staring at each other uncertainly, but with less hatred and wariness than they had before.

The Forgotten Fae watched on. Xander still held the book in his hands, but his expression was empty, defeated. My mates lifted to their feet, still protectively shielding me as they watched him carefully. Like nothing and no one could ever try to take me from them again.

Prince Azaren lifted from the ground and rose to his full height as he strode over to the Forgotten Fae. Soldiers from the fae army jogged over to stand with him.

The Forgotten Fae warriors lowered their weapons as he approached and bowed their heads in respect.

Xander stood awkwardly, his expression lost. He'd seen it all. *Felt* it all. Just as we all had.

Prince Azaren spoke loudly, "There are many things my father did that I don't agree with. If you're willing, I propose to work together with the Forgotten Fae to mend the rift amongst our kind. Maybe then we can all get the peace we desire."

Xander was silent for a long moment, the weight of over a thousand gazes upon him. The soldiers around Prince Azaren tensed like they were preparing to defend him, but slowly, Xander closed the book. His gaze went to Cara before finding the prince again. "It won't be easy..." he responded as he passed the book to Prince Azaren.

The prince gripped the leather-bound tome and tucked it against his chest. "I never said it would be."

At that moment, the sun began to peek over the horizon, a beautiful display of yellow, and orange staining the sky. Darian smiled as he took my hand and lifted me to my feet. And as the first rays of sunlight washed over us, my siren began to sing, his powerful notes ringing out over the battlefield. Cordelia and the sirens from the House of Saceris crested over a hill, and as they moved forward, they joined the sacred song. They were still battered and wet, but *alive,* and their melodic voices weaved together in a perfect harmony sending magic humming through the air.

I began singing as well, something I hadn't done since Cara had been taken. My first notes were shaky and probably out of key, but I didn't care. Darian's eyes glowed so bright as he sang, like he'd been waiting for me to join him. Locke, Kade, and Asher crowded around us, each adding their voices to ours, and Cara began to sing as well. Soon all of the Katakin monsters and fae were joining in. Some sang, some clapped, some let out roars and howls, and a few drummed their feet on the ground. The monsters and fae laughed and cheered, their weapons long forgotten, and despite the bloodshed, hope spread across the battlefield. Because we knew our worlds would never be the same.

CHAPTER 36

~ **Raine** ~

One week later

When I emerged from the portal, Locke offered me his arm, and I let him lead me from the cave.

"You ready, sweetheart?" Asher asked from my other side, and for a moment I couldn't answer. I wasn't. Not really. Excitement and nerves made my stomach clench, and I wasn't sure whether I wanted to laugh or cry.

"Yes," I lied, letting out a long exhale.

Asher nudged my arm. "Any time you want to leave, just say the word and I'll happily sling you over my shoulder and start runnin'."

I almost snorted as I pictured him doing just that in front of Chief Shaasi, the village leader. "Better not," I replied with a grin. "You'll give someone a heart attack."

Cara had visited our island days earlier with Azaren and an escort of fae. After a little initial hostility, the fae managed to explain our history and the situation between the fae and the monsters. After some searching, the fae had found another hidden cave that had been glamored by fae magic. The crafted diaries in Queen Izla's handwriting and paintings on the walls were enough to convince the islanders the fae were telling the truth. Still, after over a century of offerings to the monsters, I doubted the islanders had yet truly accepted their new reality.

Kade and Darian came up behind us, and we stepped from the cavemouth out into the light. As we entered the clearing, tingles rushed over my body, and I felt the moment my dragon disappeared, her fire leaving me. I paused, unsettled by the strange silence inside me, and peered at my mates. Their features changed in the morning light, the glow leaving their eyes. Locke's wings disappeared, and Asher lost his horns and tail. Kade's expression hardened, and I knew he was feeling just as empty without his wolf as I felt without my dragon.

"We're human," I said softly, forcing a smile and reaching up to brush my fingers down Locke's cheek. His skin was no longer cold and pale, but warm with a pink flush. I knew how badly Locke had wanted to be human again, and I expected him to smile, but he only kept staring at me, his serious gaze fixed on my face.

"I don't care what I am, as long as you're with me, Raine," he replied, and my throat bobbed as he traced a finger along the black mark that still remained on my neck. I thought then of our protective bond that had been severed. None of us had spoken about it, but I could tell my mates missed it as much as I did. Like the curse over Katakin that turned us into monsters, that magical bond between us had become a part of who we were.

A long moment passed, but the sound of chatter in the cave had us moving further into the clearing. A constant stream of monsters and fae exited the portal and made their way through the forest, passing by us.

"Damn," Asher said, twisting his head to try and stare at where his tail had been. "I know Azaren said this would happen, but it's still fuckin' weird."

Darian's lips curled into a devilish smirk. "At least, unlike in the fae realm, this time you have another pair of pants."

Asher grinned and began changing into the spare pair of pants he'd brought. "Now I know how shifters feel," he murmured.

I smiled, admiring him as much as he appreciated me when I was naked.

Noticing the attention, he winked at me and made an extra effort to tense his muscles as he pulled his pants up.

Kade shook his head, but I laughed.

When he was dressed, Asher stalked over to me and stole a kiss that made my lips swollen. When our lips parted, he continued to hold me, and I stared up at my mate. Heat flared low in my belly, but slowly I pulled away from him. "We can't be late," I commented, smoothing my dress and fighting against the temptation to coax my mates further into the forest.

Turning back to the clearing, I breathed in deep, taking in the island air. The area looked different during the day than it had when I'd been in the line up on the Night of the Offering. It was...smaller somehow.

I remembered glimpsing my monsters for the first time. It felt like an age had passed since then, but now, instead of standing there with my makeshift dagger, I had the blade Asher had gifted me strapped to my inner thigh. I thought of the other newbloods reuniting with their families. Many had already voiced their intentions to remain in Katakin, but at least this time the choice was theirs.

Kade pushed my hair away from the side of my face. "You sure you don't want us to come with you?" he asked, his voice still rough and scratchy, even though he no longer had his wolf.

"If I turn up with four guys behind me, it might be too much for him to handle," I replied, smiling despite the way my heart was hammering.

Asher's lips stretched into a boyish grin, his eyes filling with mischief.

"Don't even think about it," I warned him.

"What?" he replied innocently.

I stared pleadingly at the others.

"We'll make sure he behaves," Locke commented, though he was smiling as well, and the expression was so casual, so relaxed, that before I knew it we were all laughing.

"There you are!" a familiar voice came from the forest, and I turned as Cara emerged from between the trees.

For a brief moment, the image of her being taking by the monsters ten years ago flashed across my mind, but then she was in front of me, pulling me away from my mates. "We'd better hurry if we want to catch him before the ceremony," Cara chirped, leading me further into the forest. "We won't be long!" she called over her shoulder, and I gave the others one last nervous look before they disappeared from sight.

As we walked toward our old cottage, Cara and I rambled, filling each other in on what our lives had been like for the past ten years. In the days after the battle, Cara had already told me about the Forgotten Fae, and the king who'd used her, but so much time had passed and there was always something new for us to say. When the twisted palm that marked the beginning of the path to our cottage came into view, I paused, my heart beginning to race faster.

Cara tugged on my arm. "What's wrong?"

Using my free hand, I fidgeted with the side of my dress. "What if he doesn't want to see me?" I said uncertainly. "You don't know what it was like. He wasn't the same after you were taken. What if he still blames me?"

Cara's eyes softened with understanding, but she didn't let go of my arm. "We're doing this together," she said firmly. "I wanted to wait for you before I visited. We need this. All three of us."

I nodded slowly. I knew she was right, but it didn't make it any easier. Reluctantly, we started forward again, walking up the wooden steps. Cara knocked on the door, and I bit the inside of my cheek.

When there was no answer, Cara twisted the knob and pushed the door open. I braced myself, not entirely sure what we'd see. I could still picture how our father was the last time I'd seen him, sitting at our wooden table, staring at his cup of wine with a vacant expression. I was suddenly overcome by the intense fear that we'd find him like that. A skeleton of the man who'd once cared for us.

But as I followed Cara inside, the cottage was full of light that streamed through the windows. The space was small, but clean, and a pot of water bubbled on the stove.

"Father?" Cara called out tentatively, and the sound of shuffling came from our father's bedroom, followed by a bang and a muffled curse.

I held my breath, my heart pounding so loud in my ears that I hardly heard the bedroom door creak as it opened.

But then he was there. Striding through the doorway, our father was dressed in his finest suit, the one he'd worn when he'd married our mother. His hair was neatly slicked back, and his jaw was clean-shaven. His eyes widened as he took in Cara and me, and I could hardly look at him.

"I know it was my fault she was taken," I blurted before he could utter a word. "But I promised I'd bring her back, and here we are. She's alive, and—" My words were cut off as he rushed forward, crushing Cara and me into a hug that was so tight I was sure if he pressed slightly harder, I'd break a rib.

"Thank the goddess," he breathed, kissing our hair, and then he started laughing. I flinched, surprised by the abrasive noise that I hadn't heard since our mother had died when I was little. "I heard about the talks with the fae and there were whispers of Cara's name being mentioned, and I hoped," he said. "Goddess, I knew if you came home, I had to be ready, but I couldn't let myself believe it. But here you are." He pulled back, his brown eyes filled with tears as he smiled at us. "My girls."

"If I hadn't gone into the forest that night—" I started, but my father shook his head, silencing me again.

"It was never your fault," he croaked, his thin arms still gripping us tightly. "You were only a young girl. I was the one who failed you both. Your mother told me about the fae before she died. She told me her bloodline was special, and that I had to protect you from the monsters. She was terribly sick at this point, and I'd thought it was the disease causing her to become confused, but I'd still vowed to keep you safe. Then when Cara was taken, I knew I'd failed her. I let my grief control me, and then you, Raine." His gaze fell onto my face, and I couldn't stop my own tears. "When these fae folk began arriving on the island, I knew your mother had been telling the truth, and I prayed. If only I could see you both again and apologize." A tear slid down his wrinkled cheek. "I'd hoped for a miracle, and here you are."

I hugged him back, my heart feeling a little less broken at his words. "Wait, mother knew we were part fae?" I asked, trying to remember the woman who'd sung me lullabies at bedtime.

"She said the stories were passed down from her ancients," Father replied, his face filled with regret.

I sat up straighter. "Did she leave any notes or say anything else?"

Father shook his head. "I don't think so."

My hope deflated as I wondered at the secrets that had been lost, but I guessed it didn't really matter in the end. The fae had the diaries Queen Izla had left, and hopefully that would be enough to find out how the queen had died.

We stayed together for what felt like a long time, sobbing and laughing and apologizing until I sniffed and said, "We'd better get to the ceremony. Chief Shaasi might have agreed to let the fae hold the memorial, but I'd rather make sure we're there to make sure everyone behaves."

Cara gave me a teasing grin. "You mean, you just hate being away from your men for too long."

Father's brow furrowed as he stared at me in confusion. "What men?"

My cheeks flushed. "Come on," I said, pulling them both to their feet. "You'll have time for more questions later."

CHAPTER 37

The cool wind teased my hair and tugged at my gauzy white dress, and I breathed in deep, enjoying the scent of the ocean on the air. I stood beside Cara and Father at the top of Mount Traie, the tallest mountain on our island, and my mates crowded behind us.

Twice I caught my father giving my mates the side eye, but he didn't say anything as they remained protectively close to me, close to *us*. Because we were all family now.

"Did you ever think we'd see this day?" Darian commented from close by, strands of his long silver hair blowing across his face.

I smiled, staring over the mountaintop to where the thousands of islanders, fae from Zalei, and the humans of Katakin stood together, a sea of white as we all stared up at the giant stone positioned at the point of the mountain.

The Stone of Shetan. More names had been added since I'd last seen the stone, including my own which my father had added. The rock was filled with so many that almost every part had been covered, but it didn't matter if there wasn't any space left. We wouldn't need it now.

"She knew we'd get here," I said quietly, staring at where I'd marked Queen Izla's name at the top of the stone. The fae would spend the next few days researching the texts she'd left and scouring the island for any further information about what happened to the fae queen, but for now, she was remembered.

King Azaren stood with Chief Shaasi and Lyr in front of the stone. After the battle, Azaren succeeded the throne and was coronated as the new fae king, and Lyr had been nominated as a leader to handle matters on behalf of Katakin. At least until a new council was formed, that was. According to some of the monsters, being the descendants of Queen Izla, Cara and I held claim to Katakin, but I'm not sure if either of us really wanted that. And with the curse no longer keeping the Katakin residents tied to the land, many decided to leave. Some had chosen to live on the island, while others planned to travel further inland from Katakin. Some of the older texts spoke of lands and cities beyond Katakin's borders, and they were eager to see what was out there. Most of the wolves from the House of Worzel had chosen this path for themselves. Kasey had hoped Kade might go with them, and she extended an offer to me, Locke, Darian, and Asher, to also join, but Kade was quick to refuse on our behalf. I was sure a part of him would miss the wolves, but he seemed certain that they no longer needed an alpha, and that we'd see them again one day.

A few select monsters took up King Azaren's offer to explore the fae realm and see if they'd like to reside there. There was still unrest in Zalei with the Forgotten Fae, but it sounded like things were headed in the right direction.

When the treaty was signed, King Azaren held up the parchment, and all around the mountain, fae and humans alike applauded, cheering and laughing.

"Whether the peace will last is another matter," Kade commented, his scratchy voice making me shiver.

Asher scratched his neck. "Let's fuckin' hope so."

Father twisted his head like he was about to chastise Asher for cursing, but he promptly closed his mouth, like he only just realized how tall Asher was and that he had no clue how the male would react.

Darian nudged Asher in the side with his elbow.

"What the fuck was that for?" Asher griped, and I grinned as Darian gave me an apologetic look.

When the ceremony was over, the fae and humans took turns placing flowers at the foot of the Stone of Shetan, the petals fluttering in the breeze.

I watched as Vasken lingered, his fingers trailing over where I'd etched Queen Izla's name. I still hadn't spoken to him to find out if I was right, and Cara and I were his descendants, but I was going to have to get around to it.

When the crowd began to disperse, everyone making their way back down the mountain to join the celebration in the village, King Azaren came over to us.

· · · · ●·●·● · · ·

~ Cara ~

King Azaren turned to me, his fine robes flapping in the wind, and his crown nestled in his azure-colored hair. "Well, I think that went rather well, don't you?"

I returned his smile but noted the exhaustion clinging to his eyes. "You make a fine king," I replied. I meant it, too. The kind-hearted prince was exactly what the fae needed to heal.

"Are you staying for the celebration?" Raine asked, no doubt noting Azaren's weary expression like I had.

"Wouldn't miss it," King Azaren said with a broad smile, but his eyes softened a moment later. "Though I can only remain for a few hours. Then I must get back." There was a beat of silence before he added, "You know you're all welcome in Zalei. As members of the royal bloodline, you're Queen Izla's rightful heirs and all of her remaining assets belong to you. You will also always have a place in my court."

"As tempting as that sounds, we promised Lyr we'd stay in Katakin for a while to help rebuild," Raine replied.

"My sister and I still have more catching up to do," I said when King Azaren's gaze fell on me. "But I should be in Zalei by the end of the week."

At that, he dipped his head, his eyes sparkling. I wasn't ready to separate from Raine just yet, but the fae needed me. Xander might have agreed to stand down during the battle, but until the negotiations were over, the risk of more violence was still there.

"And what about your new...friend?" King Azaren said, gesturing with his head to where Garan stood a short distance away, watching us with a stoic expression.

I smiled softly. Raine had explained what had happened between the gargoyle and me on the battlefield. Whatever protective spell Queen Izla had placed on our bloodline, it only activated when we visited Katakin. As Raine told it, likely the first four monsters I touched with my bare hands would be bound to me. I fidgeted with my gloved fingers. One monster was enough. I wasn't going to be taking the gloves off anytime soon.

"My offer to break the bond is still there," King Azaren added.

I blushed. "Actually, Garan doesn't want us to break it just yet. He believes he owes me a debt because I saved his life, and he thinks there's a practical side to the bond. It's silly, because he saved my life first, but he insists."

Raine and her mates grinned stupidly as they looked at Garan and then me, and my cheeks warmed even more. Not that I could blame them for thinking we were like that. Ever since we left the battlefield, Garan had been staying close to my side. He was mostly quiet, but lately, he'd started speaking more, and at times he'd accidentally projected images in my mind. Some of them being a little more...detailed, than I expected. It was strange having the monster around, but it was surprisingly nice to know someone was there.

Many of his gargoyles had been lost during the battle, and most of those that remained had chosen to stay on the island or explore the surrounding lands. So, I think he liked having me as a distraction. In any case, King Azaren had pointed out that since Captain Pezar was also killed during the battle, he was in need of another Captain. I told Azaren not to get his hopes up.

Feeling my stare, Garan peered over, his gray gaze locking with mine. I tried not to think about how having the attention of the handsome man made my stomach twist.

"Though, I guess I can understand you keeping it," King Azaren said his gaze softening as he stared at Raine and her mates.

The five of them shifted uncomfortably, and I didn't miss the way Raine's mates were all touching her in some way. Like talking about the bond they'd lost made them more vulnerable.

"We're simply glad we survived the war," Raine commented with a sad smile.

King Azaren stared at Raine for a long moment, and just when I realized his lips were moving almost imperceptibly as he whispered something under his breath, he smiled abruptly.

"Aren't we all," he chirped, way too upbeat for the current conversation. His blue eyes gleamed as he straightened his collar. "Anyway, I'd best not be late for the celebration. Especially not when I intend to leave early." Striding forward, he made his way toward the mountain path, six royal guards following after him. Before he reached the gravel road, he stopped and turned around, peering at Raine and her mates. "Oh, I forgot to mention, I've left you five a gift," he called back.

My sister narrowed her eyes. "What kind of a gift?"

King Azaren grinned mischievously. "You shall see. It'll be waiting for you back in Katakin."

Raine frowned in confusion, but the king turned from us and started walking again before she could continue to question him.

Father stood awkwardly, but I took his arm, pulling him along with me to follow after King Azaren.

"Do any of you know about this gift?" Raine asked her mates, but they shook their heads.

"Let's focus on the party for now, shall we? I hope it's better than the last one we went to," Darian commented as he took Raine's hand.

"I don't care what's there as long as there are none of those damned mushrooms from the fae realm," Asher responded seriously, making a disgusted face.

Raine chuckled. "None of those, but I hope you like coconut."

Asher leaned down, brushing his nose against her hair as he breathed in. "I *love* coconut."

EPILOGUE

~ **Raine** ~

Weeks later

Morning light streamed through the high stained-glass windows, reflecting patterns on the books lining the walls of the dome structure. Crafted by the goblins, the windows told the story of the curse, the outliers, and the war with the fae and Warrick. I stared at the arched glass pane which showed an image of Azaren and me embracing as we sacrificed ourselves. In the background, my mates were trapped in fire, their faces contorted as they cried out to me. Only a month had passed since the battle, and my throat tightened at the memories that were still too raw.

"Trust the goblins to pick the scene when we're gettin' our asses kicked," Asher commented, coming up behind me and resting his chin on my head as he wrapped his thick arms around my waist. His tail curled around my leg, high up on my thigh, and my attention quickly went from the battle scene.

The bond between us sparked, and I smiled as my body warmed. *A gift, huh?* It was lucky I came through the portal with my mates, because the moment we stepped into Katakin and I touched my monsters, energy crackled through us. Somehow the mischievous fae king had restored the protective bond Izla had created, and I hated to think what would have happened if I'd touched four different monsters first. Either way, I was going to have to thank the fae when I saw him next. My mates and I didn't need the bonds between us to be happy, but that magic had become a part of us, and it felt right for my life to be linked to theirs again.

"Hmm, somehow I don't think we're the main focus of this piece, brother," Darian replied with a wry grin as he came up beside us.

Asher chuckled and moved his head to press a kiss to my hair. "You ready to go, sweetheart?"

I peered over at where Kade and Locke were lounging on armchairs, a pile of books strewn about between them. "Yeah, I don't think I'm the one you need to convince," I replied with a smile.

Asher released me, and I walked over to them. "Ash is getting hungry."

Locke's black gaze lifted from the text he was reading. In the weeks after the ceremony on my island, we'd been helping the monsters rebuild the city. It had been Locke's idea to restore the ancient library that had been locked after Katakin was cursed. According to Kade, my vampire had already read all the texts we had, but King Azaren had gifted us some translated fae fairytales from Zalei to add to the collection. These ones weren't written by Sharou Zanae, and I was enjoying devouring them just as much as my monsters were.

Locke raised a brow. "...Just Asher?" he asked inquisitively, and my body heated at his intense stare, my possessive inner dragon enjoying the attention of my mate.

"Well, I never said that," I replied, my voice coming out more breathy than I'd intended.

In a swift movement, Locke was before me. He ran his thumb along my lower lip, and I had to stop myself from biting it, but my thoughts sobered as I noticed the window behind him. The glass showed the last scene from the battle, when the monsters and fae all cheered, finally united. I frowned, distracted. "When we've finished helping to rebuild Katakin, you can be human again," I said slowly to Locke, though the idea of losing my dragon side made my stomach tie in knots. "We could go anywhere."

My mates crowded around me, their scents making my mouth water.

Locke stared into my eyes. "I told you, it doesn't matter where we are. As long as we're with you. Our beautiful mate."

THE END

Thank you for reading The Wars of Monsters!
If you enjoyed the story, it would mean the world to me if you could leave a review on Amazon, Bookbub, or Goodreads. Reviews help other readers decide whether a series is worth their time, and it helps out indies so much. Thank you!

GAME OF PSYCHOS

Look out for Mia Hartson's next series!

I'm a demon without her horns, and a princess without her fated mates.

Dear old Dad, the demon king, raised me to be ruthless, cunning, and if I'm honest, a little psycho. Being feared is kind of a necessity when you're the daughter of the most powerful king to rule a land of deranged demons. Unfortunately, being a half-angel and half-demon means I'm not truly accepted by either race. It also means I don't have a tail or horns, two main, glaringly obvious things demons look for when they want to get some lovin'. Sucks to be me, right?

Well, it's not all bad. Despite my mixed blood I'm next in line to rule over this place, but when Dad learns he's dying, our realm turns to chaos. Without my fated mates, I can't unlock all my power, and the demon clan leaders are circling for the throne like vultures honing in on their next meal. If one of them rules it'll be certain war, and I'm pretty keen to stay alive and not let all Dad's hard work go up in flames.

So, hoping to secure my succession and find my mates, Dad announces a royal competition with me as the prize, as well as a rare treasure. Whoever turns out to be my fated will rule by my side, but the invitation has been sent to five realms, and it's not only demons fighting for my attention. Now I also have angels, wraiths, giants, and beast shifters after me, and some of them would rather me dead.

All I know is, if I can survive this my mates will have to prove themselves...or die trying.

Deranged Demons is the first in a new paranormal fantasy series and features lethal, possessive monsters, a fierce, sarcastic heroine, and all the twists and humor to keep you turning the pages.

THANK YOU

First and foremost, thank you to my readers. Words cannot express how thankful I am that you found my books and continued to read until the end of the series! Your support, enthusiasm, and love of Raine and her monsters has fueled my creative spirit and helped me to believe I might be able to make a living following my dream and writing the books I love.

To my husband, Chris. Thank you for the brainstorming sessions, for reading all my books and picking out niggling plot holes, and for being so supportive of me taking this time to follow my dreams. And my girls, Blair and Kiara. Thank you for understanding when mommy needs quiet time to write. I promise, one day when you're *much* older I'll let you read my books.

To my sister, Clare, who has read all my books, including the one I started as a teenager and that will likely never see the light of day. Your feedback always helps to make my stories better. And to my sisters, Michelle and Dahlena, for always being so supportive. I'm so lucky to have you all.

To my parents, for showing me how to dream and letting me believe I can do anything if I want to. Believing is half the battle. Thank you for your support. Though, Dad, you're still not allowed to read any more of my books ;).

To Jessica, thank you for reading my books and picking out those pesky typos. It's been so fun to have someone I can obsessively talk about my characters with without worrying you'll think I'm a weirdo.

To my ARC readers who took the time to read my books and post reviews. You're amazing and so appreciated!

And lastly, to my fourth-grade teacher who always had time for my stories and encouraged me to pursue storytelling. You'll probably never read this, but if you do, know that your words of support helped me to become the writer I am today.

ABOUT THE AUTHOR

Mia Hartson is an Australian fantasy and paranormal romance author who enjoys writing stories about badass heroines who have multiple partners. (Because the only thing better than one mate is four, right?) Mia enjoys writing stories with a heavy dose of fantasy, adventure, and spice that keeps you up at night. When she's not writing, Mia's going on adventures with her husband and two girls, binging the latest fantasy TV series, singing her heart out, or devouring another book.

For more information about Mia Hartson, her books, and upcoming releases, sign up to her newsletter by visiting her website www.miahartson.com. You can also find information on her Facebook page, Facebook group, Goodreads page or Bookbub.